PRC

MW00928109

16 years earlier

"Take them! Mary take them! You have to go!"

Mary stared down at the two blond children that had been thrust into her arms. Her son was staring at her with wide blue eyes that were startlingly wise, and more than a little unnerving, for a one year old. His small hands curled around his blanket as he watched his mother silently. The other baby was just as quiet, her eyes wide and a shocking violet blue that also appeared far to knowing for her age. Though Mary had never said anything, the age within the children's eyes had always slightly unnerved her.

Now it *terrified* her.

She blinked in startled surprise at the man before her, the man that had just handed her the children, John. He was her husband, but now, when it was too late, she realized that she didn't know him at all. That she had never known him. The thought sent a fresh wave of cold terror down her spine. Goose pimples broke out on her flesh; she could barely breathe through the anxiety clutching at her chest.

"Mary, you must get them to safety."

She began to shake, clinging tighter to the children who had yet to make a sound. "Take them! Take them where?" she cried, battling against the tears that filled her eyes and clogged her throat.

Jessie, the girl's mother, pushed John slightly out of the way as she stepped forward. Her dark blue, almost violet eyes were wide and fearful; her golden hair was wild around her face. "To my mother in Florida, she'll know what to do. She'll keep you safe."

"Safe from what?" Mary inquired, hating the hysterical

note in her voice, but her body hummed with panic and confusion.

"She will fill you in," Derek, Jessie's husband informed her. "You must go Mary." Unlike Jessie and John, Derek was relatively calm. To calm considering the fact that he was telling her to take his daughter and flee to Florida. Flee from what, Mary didn't know, but they seemed adamant that she go. "If you stay, you will die. *They* will die. Now go!"

Mary gaped at him, her heart hammering, and her body cold with fear. "I don't understand," she cried. "I don't understand any of this!"

"I am sorry for that honey, but you must listen to us. You must get yourself, and the children, to safety," John insisted.

"What about you? Why don't you come with me?" she demanded. She wanted to grab hold of his arm, to cling to him, to shake some answers out of him, but the children within her grasp stopped her from doing so.

"We can't, they will only follow us. We will meet you later," Jessie informed her, though Mary realized with heart wrenching certainty that Jessie was lying. They would not be meeting her later. In fact, Mary was beginning to realize that she would never see any of them again.

"The police, we must go to the police," she whispered.

"Are useless," Brent said sharply. Mary's gaze darted to the man that had been silent until that moment. Mary didn't know Brent well, he had never seemed to like her, or approve of her much, for some reason. However, he had been friends with Jessie, Derek, and John for years, even though he was a good twenty years older than them. Mary had never understood their strange relationship, but they were extremely close, and often kept her in the dark as they whispered and spoke quietly with each other. She had always resented their relationship, and her exclusion from it, but she had kept her bitterness hidden, unwilling to hurt or anger her husband. "If you involve them you will only get them hurt, and yourself killed."

"They're coming," John said softly, his body tensed, his face twisted with anger. "Go!" he hissed, dropping a kiss quickly on her head before shoving her toward the door. "Go now, before it's too late!"

Mary stumbled as he shoved at her, pushing her out the back door to the waiting car. A car that she had not started, but it was running expectantly, and appeared to have bags shoved into the back. "Wait!" Mary froze as Jessie snagged hold of her arm; fear and misery were evident in her intense gaze. "Take care of my daughter. Please Mary I am begging you to keep Cassie alive!"

Mary stared back at the frantic woman she had considered her best friend. Mary had never been more wrong about someone; Jessie was a stranger to her. Mary managed a small nod; her mouth was dry with terror. "I will," she vowed.

Jessie released her; she took a step back as tears rolled down her cheeks. Mary had no idea what was happening, but their terror spurred her into action. Fleeing down the back stairs, she hastily strapped the children into their car seats. The children continued to watch her in eerie silence as she jumped behind the wheel. Her hands were shaking as she shifted the car into reverse and pulled out of the drive as calmly as her thumping heart would allow.

She glanced back at the house, the home she had shared with her husband and his friends. People she now realized she knew nothing about. Nor, she realized with bone shaking certainty, did she know her own son. She glanced at the eerily silent children in the rearview mirror. The girl was usually fussy in the car seat; she was immobile now and did not fight against the straps. Her son was usually fast asleep the minute he hit the car, he was staring intently at her. With their blond hair, and wide unblinking eyes, Mary was suddenly reminded of the Children of The Corn.

A chill ran down her back as she gasped and choked on the tears that burned her eyes.

Shrill screams pierced the night. Mary jumped in surprise, her eyes flew wildly back to the house as the sound of splintering wood shattered the air. For a moment Mary could not move as more shouts, and the sounds of an ensuing battle, rent the silent night.

Then, her survival instincts, for herself and the children, kicked into gear. Shifting into drive, she stomped on the gas. The tires spun on the asphalt, squealing loudly, before finally grabbing hold. The car lurched forward; the smell of burning rubber followed her as she sped down the road. She headed toward the highway, and Florida. It was almost a ten hour drive, but she had a feeling she would make it there in record time, as long as she didn't get pulled over first.

She never looked back; she knew she would see nothing but death behind her. There would be nothing left of her life, or her loved ones. In fact, she was certain that they were already dead, and that whatever had killed them would be coming for *her* next. But the fact that she had lost her loved ones was not nearly as unnerving as the fact that though she squealed through turns, raced through red lights, and people blared their horns at her, the children remained quiet, and knowing.

***

Twelve years later

Sorting through the change in her hand, Cassie hastily picked out the nickels and dimes, absently shoving aside the pennies. Sighing in aggravation, she glanced at the unattainable Coke machine before digging into the pocket of her cutoffs once more. All she wanted was a cold soda, was that too much to ask? Apparently as all she pulled out were a few pieces of lint, a gum wrapper, and dirt.

Cassie fought the fierce urge to kick the machine in frustration; it was not its fault that the price of soda had gone up fifteen cents. It was the stupid, greedy, owner of the store. Glancing past the machine, she peered into the dingy windows of the Five and Dime. Mr. Lester was watching her intently, waiting to make sure that she didn't do exactly what she longed to do most. She wanted to stick her tongue out at the man, but then she would be banned from the store, and he did have the best selection of baseball cards, candy, and comic books in town.

Glancing longingly back at the bright red machine, Cassie heaved a sigh of regret, shoved her change back into her pocket and turned away. She would just have to drink from the water fountain during baseball practice, instead of having the nice, cold, wonderful can of Coke that she *really* wanted. She scrunched her nose slightly, already dreading the taste of the metallic water fountain.

Grabbing her mitt from the store windowsill, she turned back to the main thoroughfare. She didn't make it one step before she was brought to an abrupt halt by a tall, thin man, with a pair of glasses perched at the end of his hawkish nose. His light gray eyes ran quickly over her as he studied her intently. Cassie's hand tightened on her glove as she took a small, instinctive step back. She was not some five year-old who would wander away with a stranger, but she didn't know what the odd man's intentions were.

Glancing briefly over her shoulder she was relieved to find Mr. Lester still watching intently, his eyes slightly narrowed as he observed the man. Though he liked to squeeze as much money as possible out of the kids, he wouldn't allow anything bad to happen to her. She turned slowly back to the strange man. His eyes were still fixed upon her, but she saw no ill will in his steady gaze. Instead, there was an odd sense of relief in his eyes.

A slender girl stepped beside him, her hand slipped into his as she squeezed it gently. Cassie's tension eased at the sight of the black haired girl who was so trusting of the strange man. The girl studied Cassie from exotically slanted eyes; they were as dark and shiny as a gleaming onyx. Those eyes pierced Cassie, pinning her to the spot as they seemed to see straight into Cassie's soul.

Slightly unnerved by the girl's intense gaze and scrutiny, Cassie turned her attention back to the man. Though he seemed to be in his late thirties, maybe forties, old enough to be the girl's father, they looked nothing alike. His hair was a light brown, going gray at the temples. His eyes were far from dark in color, and unlike the girls smooth olive complexion, he was very fair.

"Are you Cassandra Fairmont?" he inquired, the faint hint of an English accent in his tone.

Cassie frowned at him, not understanding how this man knew who she was, let alone her full name. Her grip tightened on her glove, her stance shifted slightly as she prepared to bolt into the Five and Dime at a moment's notice. "Do I know you?" She was proud of the fact that her voice didn't waver.

"No, but I may have known your parents."

Cassie's heart leapt into her throat, her arm dropped limply to her side. Her fingers eased their tight grip on her glove to the point that she nearly dropped it. Other than her grandmother, and Chris's mother, Cassie knew no one that had ever met her parents. Though Cassie often asked questions about her parents, her grandmother rarely spoke of them. Once in awhile, she would share stories of Cassie's mother when she was a little girl, and her father, as her grandmother had also known him as a child.

However, Chris's mother never spoke of them; she hated any mention of Cassie's parents, or Chris's father. She used the mere mention of them as an excuse to retreat deeper into her drunken stupor, or to hit the bars in search of a new conquest. It was a fact that had once bothered Chris, but lately he had taken to ignoring his mother as easily as she ignored him.

Now, this strange man was standing before her telling her that he may have known her parents, and quite possibly, Chris's father. It was a lifeline, a level of hope that she had never experienced before. This man, this *stranger*, could be their one chance to get to know their parents better.

"My parents?" she managed to choke out.

The man's eyes were gentle as he nodded slowly. "Yes, if they were Derek and Jessie Fairmont?"

The man blurred as Cassie's eyes filled with water. She rarely heard their names spoken, rarely had the chance to acknowledge that they had ever even lived. It was as if everything about them had ceased to exist when they were killed in the car accident. Not just their bodies, but their memories, history, their entire *lives* had been buried forever.

Now, they were being openly acknowledged, openly conversed about, and it was by a total stranger. Cassie glanced at the slender girl, surprised by the wealth of caring and understanding that filled her warm onyx eyes. Swallowing heavily, Cassie rapidly blinked back her tears, trying hard not to completely fall apart in front of the strange pair.

Taking a deep breath to steady her pounding heart, and raw nerves, she turned slowly back to the man. "Yes," she said softly. "Those were my parents."

Relief filled him; his shoulders slumped as he broke into a brilliant grin. The girl squeezed his hand harder, doing an odd little jump step as she beamed happily. "I told you," she said excitedly.

The man shook his head at her, but there was no censure in the gesture as he continued to smile brightly. He thrust his hand out to Cassie. "My name is Luther Long; I've been looking for you for a very long time Cassandra."

Cassie stared silently at his extended hand as confusion swirled through her. Though she sensed no ill will from them, they still scared her a little. But then again, the strange man did seem to know her parents, and best of all, he seemed to actually want to speak about them. The temptation was more than she could withstand.

Thrusting her hand out, she grasped hold of Luther's warm, well calloused one. His grin widened as he shook her hand briskly.

In that moment, when he found her, when their hands joined, her life was irrevocably changed. The course of her destiny forever altered. Over the years that followed, Cassie often wondered if she would have run screaming from him, and the changes that he would bring to her life.

Though, she eventually came to realize that there was no outrunning destiny. It was very much like the Reaper in that way, as there was no escape. And like The Reaper, destiny could be cruel, unfair, and indiscriminate. Though these were things that Cassie later learned, she was still ill prepared for her life to be forever changed, her innocence to be shattered that day.

Nor was she prepared for the day when *he* walked into her life four years later, forever altering it, and her, once again.

CHAPTER 1

Cassie ducked low, spinning as she threw a swift roundhouse kick. Her foot connected solidly with the twisted creature, catching it beneath its chin and knocking it back a good five feet. The startled grunt of surprise and pain it issued was music to her ears. The man/monster got caught up on a headstone and flipped over top of it; it sprawled out on its back in the thick grass, its legs momentarily caught up over top of the headstone. Cassie sprang gracefully to her feet, slipping the stake easily from her belt loop. The creature's eyes widened upon her, he had expected an easy kill. Its eyes turned a fierce red as his face twisted into an animalistic snarl of fury.

The rage that blasted from him pounded against her but did not slow Cassie down. She had grown accustomed to the hatred over the few past years. However, she didn't know if she would ever become accustomed to the bloodlust that poured from the monsters in nearly suffocating waves. It was daunting to know that something wanted to rip out her throat and drain the blood, and life, from her.

Though it was slightly overwhelming, it did not slow her down, and did not cause her to hesitate. There was no room for hesitation here. The smallest distraction could get her, and her friends, killed. No, her entire focus had to be upon the creature, and destroying it. She could not allow human emotions to slip in here; there was no place for them now. Here, there could only be the fight.

And the death of someone. Preferably not her.

Though she had the creature down, she was not fooled into thinking that she had him beat. Bracing herself, she leaned slightly back on her left foot as he threw his hands behind his head and thrust himself elegantly to his feet. Cassie eyed him with wary amusement; he was predictable.

With a fierce snarl, he lunged at her, racing across the ground with the grace inherent to his kind. Cassie did not kick out at him again, did not throw another punch. She simply ducked low, spinning around as he raced past her. Thrusting the stake out, his forward momentum was enough to drive it deep into his chest cavity and pierce his deadened heart. He looked at her in shock and horror, his face contorted in pain as she twisted the stake deeper.

He fell back, his body convulsing as he clawed at the stake. Though he tried to rip it free, it was more than obvious that the damage had been done. There was no reversing *this* death. Cassie waited until he stopped struggling, and his eyes clouded over, before she ripped her lucky stake free. In life, he had only been a year or two older than her, barely a man yet. Though Cassie felt a twinge of regret about killing him, she quickly buried it.

There could be no regret in her life; there could *never* be any regret. It would only eat her alive, and she hadn't been the one to originally end his life. She could not question the where's and why's of her life. It was simply her duty, her birthright. Though she didn't always enjoy it, and often resented it, she was good at killing, and she helped to keep people safe and protected by doing it. Even if people didn't know that she was helping them.

She turned her attention back to Chris and Melissa. Chris was struggling back to his feet as he had been knocked flat. The vampire they were fighting rushed past Chris, focusing on what he apparently (and wrongly) thought was the weaker female. Melissa grinned back at the creature in amusement, her stance widened as she braced herself for his attack. Her dark eyes twinkled brightly in the moonlight.

In their lives it was just another night in paradise, Cassie thought with a sigh.

Shaking her head, Cassie moved slowly toward them. Unlike herself, Chris and Melissa relished in the fight, the hunt, and the kill. They both loved what they were, and eagerly embraced their heritage. Then again, Melissa had been raised with the knowledge of what she was. And Chris was a teenage boy; anything he could beat up, punch, kick, and maim was fun for him. However, Cassie was not a boy, and she had been oblivious to what she was until Luther and Melissa had walked into her life at thirteen. She had never relished in the fighting, or the killing.

Well, that was not entirely true. There were times when she loved the thrill of the fight, times when she loved the fact that she was making the world safer one murderous vampire at a time. She did *not* like the fact that this life had been forced upon her by birth, or that her life expectancy had been drastically lowered by a flip of the cosmic switch. She chafed against the bonds that had confined her to a life she had never even *imagined* could exist, and had never wanted.

But what choice did she really have? She could not turn her back on what she was. Innocent people would die if she did. She may hate her role in life, but she could not live with herself if people were killed because she wasn't there to protect them. She could not live with the fact that Chris or Melissa might be hurt, or killed, because she was too selfish, and too scared to accept her birth right, her destiny.

Destiny, she had learned, was a cold bed fellow. One that left her chilled to the bone, and hollow inside. Destiny had left her vulnerable to the more brutal side of life, and it would likely destroy her before she ever saw her twenty-fifth birthday.

A loud grunt shifted her attention back to the battle Melissa was still waging. Chris had regained his feet, but Melissa was wearing the trademark grin she displayed when she already knew the outcome of a fight. Cassie sighed softly; she wiped her hands on her jeans as she joined Chris.

"I don't see how it can be any fun when you already know what's going to happen," he complained.

"Just think about how much fun it will be if she ever foresees a battle she loses," Cassie retorted dryly.

Chris shrugged and nodded slowly. Shoving a strand of sandy blond hair off his forehead, he sighed wearily as he shoved his hands in his pockets. "Yeah, that would suck."

Melissa lunged suddenly, shoving the stake forward in a killing blow. With a satisfied grin she ripped her stake free, flipped it in the air, and caught it lightly before shoving it into her belt. "It will never happen though; I'm never going to lose!" she announced proudly, smiling brightly.

Cassie bit back her retort. There was no need to remind them that that was probably what every Hunter had believed, until the Grim Reaper had called for them far too early.

Sighing in aggravation Cassie wrapped her arms around herself, not understanding the strange melancholy enshrouding her lately. But try as she might, she could not shake the misery that clung to her like a second skin. Her funk was not a good place to be; becoming worn down by her life would only get her killed sooner.

"Of course not," Chris agreed.

"Yeah," Cassie mumbled absently.

Melissa's onyx eyes focused intently on Cassie, her pretty face scrunched slightly as she studied her. Cassie prickled under the scrutiny, but she had grown accustomed to Melissa's fixed stares. It was a look Melissa often wore when she was trying to decipher the future paths a person might take. Cassie never asked about her future, she didn't want to know, but she was certain that Melissa had already glimpsed some of it. Although, Melissa never let onto whether it was good or bad, and that was the way that Cassie liked it.

Cassie broke the stare first, becoming slightly unnerved as Melissa's gaze went on longer than normal. Shaking her head, Melissa broke into a beautiful grin that showed off her perfect white teeth. "Let's dispose of these guys."

Between the three of them it did not take long to drag the bodies into the woods and hide them within the shadowed interior. Cassie didn't worry that the bodies would be discovered. Once day broke the bodies would burn away, all evidence of their existence would disappear into a pile of ash. The animals would not come for these bodies either, there was nothing but evil for them here.

"I'm hungry," Melissa announced wiping the dirt from her hands.

"Yeah, me too," Chris agreed, patting his flat stomach.

"What else is new?" Cassie inquired lightly.

His handsome face lit up as he threw his arms casually around both their shoulders. "B's and S's," he suggested.

"Ugh you're going to become a giant puddle of grease if you keep eating at that place," Melissa groaned.

Chris shrugged as they began to make their way through the darkened cemetery. "What can I say? I love my grease." He smiled brightly, pulling them tighter against his side. "I'm a growing boy."

"You're arteries are growing closed!" Melissa retorted.

Chris rolled his eyes and leaned closer to Cassie. "Please rescue me from the vegetarian Nazi."

Cassie chuckled softly and shook her head at him. "You're on your own with this one."

Cassie tried to keep her gaze focused straight ahead, but despite her best intentions not to, she glanced back to the edge of the dark cemetery, and the thick woods. Though it was quiet now, it was from there that the two vampires had emerged tonight. She didn't know why, but for some reason vampires were attracted to the cemetery. She thought it might be because they had never had a proper burial of their own, but she had no way to know what the monsters thought, or why they acted like they did.

She spent far too many of her nights with Chris and Melissa, stalking out the cemetery and waiting to see what might pop out of the woods. She also spent far too many nights hanging out around restaurants, and busy places, trying to keep people safe from the monsters that lurked in the night. By reading the papers and keeping an eye on the news, they were usually able to discern when a vampire was hunting in the area.

When reports of strange disappearances, or wild animal attacks started to surface, they all knew they were going to be in for long nights, and long weeks, until the things causing the disappearances and deaths were caught and destroyed. "Wild animal" was often the term used to describe anything that the authorities couldn't fully explain, or understand, in the area. To the three of them, it usually meant vampire, as there were few dangerous wild animals on Cape Cod. Cassie didn't know what the authorities told themselves in order to go to sleep after these attacks, and their poor explanation about the deaths. Nor did she particularly care.

She sometimes envied them their blissful, deep rooted denial though. She could never experience it again. When she read about the "wild animal" attacks, there was no peaceful denial for her to slip into. There was only hunting, stalking, skulking, and death.

A momentary flash of guilt shot through her, shaking her slightly with its ferocity. She was not the one that had killed these monsters first, she reminded herself forcefully. That had been some other monster, not *her*. The lives of the vampires they hunted had been forfeit long before the three of them ever came along. If the men they had killed tonight had not been stopped, they would have caused even more death and destruction. More innocent lives would have been lost; they *had* done the right thing here. Though she kept telling herself this, it did not ease the knot of guilt that encircled her.

Cassie's gaze darted over the darkened headstones. The night was quiet, but she couldn't help the chill that crept down her spine. She spent half of her nights in this cemetery, but she never got used to the coldness that enveloped it, the pain that suffused it. Loss and anguish permeated the air, lingering remnants from the living that had been left behind to mourn their lost loved ones.

Making their way slowly out of the wrought iron gate, Cassie allowed them to lead her down the quiet street toward the center of town. The sidewalk was dark; streetlights had not been placed this far away from the center of town. Cassie glanced toward the woods surrounding them, her eyes narrowed as she studied the darkened recesses. An owl hooted, fluttering from the branches of an oak to a maple. The leaves of the trees were a bright green against the dark night. Nothing else stirred, not even a mouse emerged. It seemed that even the animals sensed the gloom in the air and did not want to come out.

Reaching the end of the road, they made a right toward the large rotary marking the center of town. From the giant rotary five roads branched off, leading toward back streets and residential homes. But the first fifty to a hundred feet of each road was packed with stores, restaurants, and bars.

They finally reached the streetlights that lit the sidewalks and roads. A few cars were driving around the rotary, their headlights bounced across the pavement, music filtered from their open windows. People wandered the streets, enjoying the places still open at this time of night.

Though it was almost nine, there was still a large crowd gathered around B's and S's. The front of the burger place was bright against the dark night. An old wooden sign hung from the side of the building, the name Burger's and Shake's was spelled out in bright red lettering. Burger's and Shake's wasn't a very original name, but it was the two things the restaurant did best. It was also the two things that most people stuck to, as the rest of the menu was a little iffy at times. That was the main reason why B's and S's had been designated the teen hang out for the past twenty years, as people over the age of twenty one rarely ate there again.

"What do you guys want?" Chris asked, removing his arms from their shoulders.

"Strawberry shake and fries," Cassie answered.

"Garden salad, but make sure that it is freshly washed, and no dressing," Melissa told him.

Chris and Cassie rolled their eyes. Chris was still shaking his head as he wound his way swiftly through the crowd gathered around the outdoor picnic tables. It wouldn't be long before the tables were taken in, and the outdoor area was closed for the winter. Until then, everyone was enjoying the last bit of good weather that September had to offer.

Cassie and Melissa made their way to one of the few empty tables in the back. Eager greetings followed their every step as people turned toward them. They returned them politely, but neither of them stopped to talk. Cassie barely got her butt on the seat before Marcy Hodgins, the class president, was standing beside her.

"Hey Cassie, I was wondering if you had started planning for the homecoming dance."

Cassie fought the urge to groan and roll her eyes. She had been head of the dance committee since freshman year, but every year it became harder and harder to find the time to dedicate to planning the dances. And this year she simply didn't feel like doing it at all. She had not planned on running for the dance committee again, but earlier this year she had been automatically voted in.

"Homecoming isn't for another two months Marcy," she gently reminded the girl.

Marcy fidgeted slightly, her hands clasped and unclasped before her as Cassie's answer obviously irked her. "Yes, but it will need a theme, decorations, fliers."

Cassie sighed heavily. "Maybe you should just find someone else this year…"

"But you're the best!" Marcy interrupted loudly. "You did a great job last year, and now that we're seniors don't you think we deserve the best memories possible!"

Cassie shot Melissa, a just shoot me now, look. Melissa smiled brightly, annoyingly, in return. "Of course I do Marcy, but I'm really busy this year…"

"I'll get you more help!"

Cassie didn't know if she wanted to scream in frustration, rip her hair out, or throttle the obtuse girl. Instead, she shoved all of her irritation aside, and forced a bright smile. "I'll work on it Marcy."

"Let me know if you need anything, anything at all."

"I will."

"Also, I do have a few ideas for themes that I would love to run by you. Maybe we can get together after school tomorrow to discuss them."

Cassie's hands clenched as she tried hard to keep a tight hold on her patience. Marcy meant well, but sometimes her OCD was enough to drive a saint to murder, and Cassie was far from a saint. She glanced at Melissa again, silently pleading for some sort of reprieve, but it came in the form of Chris as he dumped their food on the table.

"Hey Marcy," he muttered absently, his mind on the food he was rapidly dolling out.

Marcy's pretty face flooded with color as she ducked her head shyly. Cassie lifted an eyebrow, she turned to Melissa who grinned brightly back at her. "Well… I uh… I have to go, but I'll talk to you tomorrow, ok Cass?" Marcy stammered out.

"Of course," Cassie replied happily, glad to be free of the girl and amused by her obvious crush on Chris.

Marcy made a hasty retreat back to the table of girls she had been sitting with. Cassie turned eagerly back to Chris. He looked as if he was trying to solve the problems of the world, his eyebrows drawn tightly together in concentration. His attention was focused upon the shakes as he lifted the lid on one before plopping it down in front of her.

"I think someone has a crush on you," she teased lightly.

"Huh, what?" He glanced up, a handful of fries, *her* fries, already halfway to his mouth. Before he could eat them all, Cassie surreptitiously slid her plate away from him as he scanned the dwindling crowd. "Who?" he demanded.

"Marcy." Chris's frown deepened as he looked toward the girl who was determinedly not looking their way again. "Short brunette just speaking to me," Cassie reminded him.

Chris snapped out of his food trance as he grinned down at her. "No way, Marcy's to prim and proper, likes the more refined guys."

"Well you are definitely not refined, but she does have a crush on you," Melissa insisted.

"Why, did you see something in my future?" he asked eagerly.

Melissa rolled her eyes as she shook her head. "I am not your crystal ball Chris."

He rolled his eyes at her as he propped his leg on the bench. Striking a pose, he rested his arm on his leg, and gazed intent at Marcy. "Very sexy with the mouthful of fries," Cassie teased.

"You know it." He flashed a bright grin as he popped more fries in his mouth and sucked noisily on his shake.

"Don't you think she's a little much?"

His blue eyes twinkled merrily as he shook back his disheveled hair. "I'm a teenage boy Cassandra, there is no such thing as a little much to me. All girls are acceptable."

"Ugh!" Melissa and Cassie both groaned as Cassie threw a fry at him.

He dodged it easily, catching it before it hit the ground and popping it into his mouth. "You're gross," she told him laughingly.

"But you love me."

She couldn't argue with that. Turning away from him, she focused her attention on her greasy fries, and delicious shake. Cassie glanced across the table; Melissa had a distant look on her face as she poked absently at a cucumber. To any passersby it simply appeared as if Melissa wasn't hungry, but Cassie knew that Melissa's concentration was actually fixed upon something that *no* one else could see.

This was not one of her fleeting glimpses of the future either, but a full premonition of something to come. It was one of the premonitions that took Melissa over, and held her hostage until it was done. A chill ran down Cassie's spine, she hated these moments. They always left Melissa drained, and with an old, knowing look in her eyes that went far past her seventeen years.

Chris leaned slightly forward, his handful of french-fries forgotten as he studied Melissa intently, worry etched his brow. Melissa shook her head, she broke free of the claws hooked into her as her onyx eyes snapped into focus again. She did not seem as beat down by this vision as she was by many of the others, but a secret look lingered in her dark eyes.

"Did you see my death?" Chris inquired like he always did when one of these premonitions seized hold of her in his presence.

She smiled at him, shaking back her black hair as she popped a cucumber in her mouth. "Not this time."

Chris shrugged as he ran a hand through his shaggy hair. "Just remember, if you ever do see it, you had better tell me."

"You wouldn't want to know," Cassie and Melissa replied simultaneously.

They grinned at each other across the table. "You owe me a Coke," Melissa quipped.

"You don't drink Coke."

"You owe me something then."

Melissa chewed on her cucumber before grabbing a tomato. Cassie studied her questioningly, wondering what Melissa had seen, but she didn't really want to know. The thought of knowing scared her. Besides, Melissa would not tell them, not unless their lives were on the line. And even then, Cassie didn't want to know what Melissa saw, not unless there was a way to stop it.

And most of the time, there wasn't.

It was very rare that Melissa ever saw anything she wanted to, but she had no choice as her "gift" overtook her whenever it wanted.

Although, to be fair, Cassie had to admit she was a little disappointed she hadn't inherited a "gift" like Chris and Melissa had. Apparently they ran rampant through The Hunter line, but for some reason Cassie had come up short. She definitely would not want the ability to see the future, like Melissa, for she didn't want to bare that cross, and she wasn't sure that she could handle it. But she wouldn't have minded Chris's talent of being able to read people, to know what they were feeling, and to know who and what they were, good or bad, upon meeting them. And unlike Melissa, Chris was able to keep people blocked out, and control his ability if he wanted to.

But then, any ability would have been better than the nothing she had been given. Well, unless she counted her ability to fight, and fight well, as a gift. And she was a good fighter, she was even better than Chris and Melissa. But, to her, that was not a gift. She didn't care if the people she killed were no longer human, it bothered her to kill at all, and it bothered her even more that she was outstanding at it.

It was a fact that wore at her every day, slowly eating at her spirit. She sometimes wondered if that was where the growing hole inside of her had come from; if that was the reason she had been feeling less and less like herself lately.

Maybe all of the death and murder that surrounded her had started to take away bits of her soul. Whatever it was that was missing, or off in her, she desperately needed to find it, and fix it.

She could not keep living like this. She could not keep going on without knowing why she was so lost, and why she couldn't shake her misery. She needed to drown out the feverish need for something more that had encompassed her. She needed something to ease the pain that suffused her. She had been living with the emptiness for the last few months, but over the past two weeks it had gotten worse. The hole had become a chasm within her soul, ripping her open, leaving her raw and exposed.

She was greatly afraid that if she didn't mend it soon, it would swallow her whole.

Cassie shoved aside her morose thoughts, sick of them. Sick of herself even. Wallowing in her misery, and loneliness, was not going to ease it.

"Are you going to tell us what you saw?" Chris demanded, leaning forward on his knee.

Melissa shook her head as she sat back in her seat, shoving the remains of her salad aside. "Nope, it doesn't involve you so there's no need for you to know about it."

Chris groaned in disappointment, but his frustration did not affect his appetite as he took a big bite of his bacon cheeseburger. Grease dropped onto his paper plate but he paid it little mind as his attention focused on Marcy again. "She is cute."

Cassie glanced over at Marcy, tilting her head as she studied the petite brunette. Despite her over exuberance, she was a pretty girl. "Does it matter?"

Chris grinned down at her as he shook back his mop of blond hair. "Not at all."

Cassie couldn't help but laugh at him, loving the bright sparkle in his sapphire eyes, and the cocky grin that flashed across his handsome face. She leaned against his leg, relishing in the easy comfort, strength, and reassurance he gave her. He had been her best friend, her rock, since she was born. Though many people thought they were a couple, or soon would be, there had never been anything other than sibling-like feelings between them.

Chris patted her back for a brief moment before turning his attention back to his cheeseburger, and Marcy. The hair on the back of Cassie's neck suddenly stood up, a tingle swept down her spine that was neither pleasant nor unpleasant. With sudden certainty she knew that someone was staring at her, watching her. Straightening away from Chris, she frowned as her gaze rapidly scanned the forest, but she could see nothing, and no one, within its dark depths.

Turning slowly, Cassie was surprised to realize that her throat had gone dry, and her heart was trip hammering with excitement. She didn't know what was causing the strange reaction inside her body, but she couldn't stop it either. She was certain that there was something out there, and that it was waiting for her.

She froze, her gaze latched onto a man standing at the edge of the building closest to the road. He was highlighted by the splash of light pouring out of B's and S's, his features indiscernible in the shadows that played over him. He was completely still, his hands shoved into the pockets of his leather jacket. Even though the shadows kept him half hidden, she could see the startling, brilliant, emerald green of his eyes. Those eyes were oddly alight in the dark surrounding him, a dark that caressed his hard, unmoving body.

To Cassie's utter amazement, the world around her suddenly ground to an abrupt halt. Everything around her fell away, the crowd disappeared; Chris and Melissa no longer existed as *he* became the central point of her world. All she could see, all she could *feel*, was him. He was inside of her, flowing through her veins, burning into her extremities, filling her. His presence eased the painful hole she had been living with. Though it made no sense to her, and she certainly couldn't explain it, he somehow helped to heal everything that had been hurting, and broken, and *wrong* within her.

Unknowingly, tears sprang to her eyes. She would be ok; everything would be ok as long as *he* was here. The thought blazed into her mind, seared through her heart, and though it seemed crazy she knew that it was completely right. She didn't understand how he made everything right, but he did. She *needed* him, the realization slammed into her with the force of a sledge hammer. It was a terrifying thought, confusing and unsettling. However, she knew that the thought was completely true. She knew it with the same certainty that she knew she needed air to survive.

"It's about time," Melissa said softly.

With those three words the world snapped back into frightening, lurching focus. The force of it left Cassie stunned and breathless. Her hand trembled as she wiped away the single tear that had unknowingly slid down her cheek. She was completely shaken by the bizarre encounter, unnerved, and yet completely exhilarated. Though she tried, she could not break eye contact with the stranger. If she looked away it would only reopen the giant hole within her. He didn't seem to want to look away either, as his eyes never left hers. His piercing gaze kept her pinned to the spot.

Though she had no special gifts, no abilities like Chris and Melissa, she knew instantly that her life would never be the same again. She *knew* that the presence of this strange man marked a significant change in her life.

Complete and utter panic tore through her.

CHAPTER 2

"Bout time for what?" Chris asked, sucking fiercely at his chocolate shake as he lifted a dark blond eyebrow quizzically at Melissa.

"Oh, uh, it's about time to go," Melissa answered absently. She neatly wiped her hands before tossing her napkin aside.

Cassie spun wildly in her seat, desperately needing to flee, needing to run. She had to get as far away from here, and *him*, as possible. "Yes it is," she eagerly agreed.

Leaping to her feet, she ignored the surprised looks that both Melissa and Chris shot her. She hastily grabbed her tray and tossed the plates haphazardly onto it. "Hey!" Chris cried as she grabbed his few remaining fries and threw them onto the heap.

"It's late, we have to go," she said urgently, her voice trembling slightly. To her utter surprise, and horror, so were her hands.

What was the matter with her? She didn't know this man; she didn't *know* that he meant anything to her. She simply knew that he affected her on a physical level, so why was she acting like a loony? Why was she so certain that he was going to drastically change her life?

She had no way of knowing for sure, but something inside of her, something instinctual and primal was screaming at her that he would. And that was something that she did not want to happen. It was something she could not *allow* to happen.

Her life had already been turned upside down once; she couldn't go through it again, she didn't think she was strong enough to survive it. Just four short years ago she had been a perfectly happy thirteen year old girl. Now she was a Hunter, spending far too much time in cemeteries, and killing vampires. *Vampires* for crying out loud! They were something she had thought of as a myth, something made up for movies and books in order to entertain people, or scare them. They certainly weren't anything she had ever considered real. Neither had she ever entertained the notion that she would be expected to kill them, all the while knowing that she would inevitably lose the fight one day.

No, she absolutely did not want her life to change drastically again. She had just gotten it straightened out, just gotten it to the point where she could accept her heritage, even if she didn't like it. And she knew that this man could completely change her life. She had wanted a change, something different, but not this, not this big, and not *him*. And she knew that his presence would be a big change.

"Cassie..."

"I'm tired," she interrupted Melissa sharply. "I want to go home."

Melissa's questioning onyx eyes gleamed in the light, but she bit lightly into her lower lip as she refrained from saying anything more. Cassie's heart beat fiercely as she hurried to the trashcan. "My fries," Chris mourned morosely.

"I'll buy you two batches next time!" she snapped, immediately feeling guilty for her angry retort. Chris's eyes widened slightly but he didn't say anything more. Apparently he had decided that sacrificing his fries was far better than arguing with her further. It was a good decision as she felt half crazed at the moment.

Though Cassie tried to ignore it, she could feel the stranger's eyes burning into her with every step she took. Her hands were shaking; her heart pounded loudly in her ears, and her throat was so dry that she could hardly swallow.

She could not deal with this, not right now. The strange sensations pounding through her were causing her composure to unravel. Something was going to happen, and *he* was going to be the cause of it. She didn't know if that something was going to be good or bad though, could not sort through it, not with the emotions careening wildly through her. She could not handle losing everything that she had ever known, ever thought, felt, and believed all over again. Yet, deep in the very marrow of her bones she *knew* that this strange man could do all of those things, and more, if she allowed him to.

She was not about to let him though.

"What put you in a pissy mood all of a sudden?" Chris mumbled.

Cassie shot him a dark look as she started to push him in the opposite direction of the man. She didn't trust herself to look back and see if he was still standing there. She was afraid that she would stand, frozen like a deer in the headlights, if she looked at him again. She was afraid she would be lost to the startling force of the stranger's magnetic gaze once more. "I just want to go home."

"Well, you're going in the wrong direction!" Chris protested, trying to twist away from her shoving hands.

Cassie looked helplessly at Melissa, needing some assistance from somewhere, but Melissa was not looking at her. In fact, her attention was riveted upon the spot where Cassie had last seen the man. Melissa glanced sharply back at Cassie, her eyes narrowed slightly as she took in Cassie's frantic expression.

Chris pulled away from her, shaking his head in disgust. "Women," he muttered. "I'll never understand them."

Cassie stared after him as he stalked a few feet away, heading toward the man still half hidden in the shadows of the building. Chris turned back to them, tapping his foot impatiently as he folded his arms over his broad chest. "Are you coming or not?" he demanded irritably, obviously still aggravated with her for being snippy, and throwing away his fries.

Cassie glanced pleadingly at Melissa but her attention was still focused upon the strange man. Cassie wanted to reach out to her, to hide behind her, to seek protection from her, but she found herself unable to move. She could still feel his gaze upon her, pinning her to the spot, burning into her soul. Melissa turned slowly back to her; a half smile curved her full mouth.

"Come on Cassie, it's getting late," she said, her voice irritatingly bright.

Cassie stared helplessly at her. She wished she could understand what was going on, why this man made her feel so strange and excited and frenzied. She desperately wished that she could go back in time, wished that she had never come to B's and S's tonight. She wished for many, *many* things, but none of them were going to come true within the next minute. And even if they did come true, she had the unsettling feeling that he still would have found her. That he *still* would have walked into her life.

That realization did nothing to ease the tight knot of anxiety crushing her chest.

No matter how much she didn't want to, she had to face this. Whatever *this* was. She had never run from anything before, no matter how much she wanted to, and she was not about to start now. No, she was not a coward, but she was shaking like a leaf.

Taking a deep breath, she straightened her shoulders, and faked a bravery she did not feel as she fell into step beside Melissa. Melissa's gaze was steady upon her, but she didn't ask any questions. Chris moved beside them, a dark look in his eyes as he continued to shoot Cassie disgruntled looks. For someone that was so good at reading people, he was frustratingly oblivious to her emotions right now. Clenching her hands tight, her nails dug into her palms as they moved swiftly toward the corner of the building.

Though she tried hard to fight it, her gaze was drawn back to the stranger as surely as a magnet was drawn to metal. He stood silently amongst the shadows, but the light from B's and S's was enough to highlight his perfect, hard features. The world seemed to slow again, fading away, blending into nothingness as his presence filled her universe.

Like a black hole, she could not resist falling into him, becoming lost to him as she was sucked in. He was the moon, and she wanted to gravitate toward him as she became trapped within his fierce, compelling pull. And like the moon with the earth, she needed him to survive. And she *wanted* him! Slowly the hollowness inside her began to mend itself again, she became whole once more. It was right, *she* was right in a way that she hadn't been in so long. He healed all of the hurt and loss and confusion that had been enshrouding her, choking her.

Suddenly she couldn't recall why she would even want to fight against the strong draw he had over her. Couldn't recall why she shouldn't just throw herself at him right now. No matter how pathetic and crazy it would be. For some strange reason she was certain that he would not deny her, that in fact he would eagerly accept her in his arms.

He was magnificent, his face hard and beautiful all at once. His strong jaw and firm mouth were clenched together, a muscle twitched in his cheek as his emerald eyes blazed into hers. His wavy black hair was wind tossed and disheveled as it fell around his chiseled face. The boyishness of his tussled hair added an almost vulnerable air to him that she was sure he did not possess.

Shifting slightly, his lithe muscles flexed and flowed fluidly beneath his jacket and the tight black t-shirt he wore. He reminded her of a dark panther, lurking within the shadows, hunting its prey. For that brief moment she truly enjoyed the fact that she seemed to be his prey. It became difficult to breathe through the anticipatory constriction in her chest; her skin tingled with the fierce urge to touch him.

"Hey," Chris greeted, nodding to the stranger. Chris slowed slightly, his head tilted to the side as he studied the man curiously, apparently trying to get a read on him.

The man nodded back, but his gaze didn't leave hers. Cassie could not stop herself from slowing her pace, her body tensed as she moved past. She had to force herself not to stop, not to reach out and touch him, not to run her fingers through that thick, tempting hair. Her body was alive with electricity; her nerves sparked and fired, thrumming with her fierce desire to feel him.

For a moment she thought that he was going to touch her as he moved subtly again, his body coming within centimeters of hers. Every molecule inside her screamed for his touch, she *needed* his touch. Though the two of them did not make contact, she could still feel the warmth of his skin against hers. Instinctively, she knew that to touch him would be the most exquisite thing she would ever experience.

She had never imagined that she would feel like this about someone. She had never thought it was possible to be this lost, and found, all at once. And she had been found. *He* had found her, and he was not going to let her go. The thought was frightening, as was the certainty that immediately followed it.

"Cassie! Cassie!"

The call of her name was like a bucket of ice thrown onto her. It slammed her harshly back to reality. The strange spell shattered around her, snapping her head around as her gaze focused upon Marcy. For the first time, Cassie was actually thankful for Marcy's obsessive, overeager ways. She needed a reprieve from the stranger in order to gather her wits again, and calm the racing of her fiercely pounding heart.

Marcy thrust a piece of paper at her as she came to an abrupt halt in front of Cassie. Her leaf green eyes were bright and enthusiastic as she grinned up at Cassie, her pretty face aglow in the light coming from the restaurant. "My cell number, call me later so that we can go over some ideas."

Cassie stared at the paper, unable to fully form a coherent response. She managed a brief nod as she shoved it into her pocket. "Hey Marcy," Chris greeted, nodding to her as he grinned brightly.

Marcy turned five shades of red, a bashful smile spread across her lips as she ducked her head. Chris's grin grew even wider; he folded his arms over his chest and rocked back slightly on his heels. Melissa rolled her eyes, shoving at him as she pushed him forward a step. "You can flirt some other time," she muttered, soft enough so that Marcy couldn't hear.

"Tomorrow," Marcy said quickly before hurrying away.

Cassie glanced briefly back at the man, not surprised to find his gaze still focused intently upon her. She thought that she should be unnerved, or even a little frightened by his intense scrutiny of her, she wasn't. In fact, she was still thoroughly excited and entranced by it. She found herself unable, and unwilling to move for a moment, but Chris tugged her sharply forward, his displeasure with her still apparent. The man quirked a dark eyebrow at her, but other than that he remained completely still.

She allowed herself to be pulled away, not because she wanted to leave, or flee from this stranger anymore. No, she allowed herself to be pulled forward simply because she didn't know what else to do. And no matter how much she wanted to, she could not stand there gaping at the stranger like a complete idiot. Which is exactly what she looked like.

Cassie shook her head, tearing her gaze away from the man. The odd sense of loss encompassed her once more, but it was not as suffocating this time. She chanced a quick glance back at him, not surprised to find that he had turned to watch them leave. There was a hungry gleam in his emerald eyes that sent a shiver of fear and desire down her spine. He looked like he wanted to devour her, and she found that she didn't mind that thought at all. In fact, she thought she might like being devoured by him.

That fact just confused and flustered her even more. She shouldn't want this, but she did.

***

Cassie slid the window open and leaned on the sill as she met Chris's twinkling gaze. "Why don't you just use the door?"

He shrugged as he heaved himself through the window. As big and muscular as he was, he was surprisingly agile and graceful. It was why he was the star of the football team. Well that, and his enhanced speed and strength gave him an advantage. "The window's more fun."

Cassie shook her head as she closed the window again, leaving it slightly cracked to allow the cool September air to flow through. Chris moved swiftly around the room, he plopped down on her bed and crossed his long legs before him. Resting his elbow on his knee, he snatched the remote up and turned on the TV. Though he flipped idly through the channels, his easy demeanor was belied by the fierce tension she sensed running through him.

Sighing softly, she walked over to sit beside him. She didn't have to ask what was wrong she knew it was his mother again. If he wished to talk about it, he would. If not, they would sit silently until he was ready to go to sleep on the air mattress tucked under the bed for him.

"Is your grandma home?" he inquired softly.

His gaze was focused on the TV, but most of his attention was on her. "No, she went to the church social tonight. There's left over lasagna in the fridge for you if you want some."

He shrugged, setting the remote down as he found the Red Sox game. "Someone did take my fries," he muttered.

Cassie couldn't help but grin as she shoved lightly on his arm. "There were only a few left."

"The last ones are always the best."

Laughing softly, she pushed him again. "Do you want me to heat some for you?" she inquired though she knew that was exactly what he was trying to guilt her into doing.

He turned to her, smiling softly as he nodded. "Think you owe me."

Cassie climbed to her feet, shaking her head at him. "You're lucky I love you."

He flashed his bright grin with the easy charm that most girls couldn't resist. "You'd better!"

Cassie was still shaking her head as she made her way downstairs. She may have been born an only child, but she still had an annoying, two week older brother. Finding her way easily through the darkened halls she entered the kitchen. She didn't bother with the lights, she could see almost as well with the lights off as she could with them on. She pulled the door of the fridge open and removed the hefty piece of lasagna her grandmother had set aside for Chris. Un-wrapping it, she tossed it into the microwave and hit the buttons.

Leaning against the sink, she stared out at the dark night, her mind not on the street before her, but on the strange man from earlier. She had done nothing but think about him since arriving home. He preoccupied her every thought, her every moment. She could not get him out of her head, could not rid her skin of the strange electricity he had created in her.

Her body hummed with a fierce need to see him again, to touch him, and to finally ease the tension knotted through her. Instinctively she knew that if she could just see him again, just touch him, than things would be better. She could not shake the feeling of rightness that had filled her from the moment she laid eyes upon him. It was as if she knew him, as if her very *soul* knew his.

The thought filled her with excitement, but also with a level of fear that she couldn't shake. She shouldn't feel this way about someone she didn't know. It made no sense to feel this intense of a connection with a complete stranger. Though she tried to remain logical, she could not shake the certainty that what she felt was right and good.

She hated it when Chris came to her house lost and angry, however she was grateful for the distraction he now offered from her strange thoughts and emotions. But now that she was alone again, the stranger was back on her mind, back in her system. She was truly afraid that she would never feel normal again until she touched him, and knew exactly how he felt. Though she already knew he would feel exquisite.

If she saw him again. The thought of never seeing him again sent her heart racing in fear.

Cassie shook her head fiercely, desperately trying to rid herself of her strange, irrational thoughts. She was acting crazy, she was *feeling* crazy. Maybe everything that had happened to her over the past four years had finally caused her to lose her mind. 'How many people could actually know of the existence of vampire's, and fight them, and not go a little crazy?' she wondered absently.

Not many.

Something moved amongst the shadows, drawing her gaze sharply back to the street. The shadows shifted again, moving slightly before settling down once more. Cassie focused intently upon them, but they didn't move again, and nothing emerged from the copse of trees at the edge of the yard.

The sudden beep of the microwave caused her to jump in surprise, spinning her toward the machine. She shook her head, aggravated with herself for allowing someone to affect her this much. And a stranger no less. She didn't know him, what she felt for him could not be real, and he should not be affecting her this way. Hell, she didn't even know his name.

Grabbing the lasagna from the microwave, she cast another glance out the window. Nothing moved amongst the shadows, but Chris's mom had come onto her porch. She held a beer bottle in one hand, a cigarette in the other, as she stared into space. A man emerged behind her; he wrapped his arm tightly around her waist. Cassie had never seen him before, but then, she rarely saw any of Mary's men twice in a row.

The man explained why Chris was here tonight.

Shaking her head, she hurried back upstairs, eager to get the food to Chris. She was also eager to help ease some of the hurt that clung to him, eager to try and bury some of her own swirling emotions. She swung into her room, not at all surprised to find the air mattress already set up. "Thanks," he muttered as he took the plate from her.

Cassie nodded and plopped herself onto the bed beside him. This was going to be one of the nights that Chris didn't want to speak; one of the nights when he had no words to convey his unhappiness. That was just fine by her, she wasn't much in the mood for talking either, but there was one thing that she had to know.

"Chris?"

"Hmm," he murmured around a mouthful of lasagna.

Swallowing nervously, Cassie's hands knotted in her lap. "Do you remember that man from earlier?" When he shot her a confused look, she elaborated. "The one standing next to B's and S's?"

He nodded as he took another large bite of lasagna. "What about him?" he inquired when he swallowed.

"Did you um, well did you feel anything from him?" she hedged.

Chris's eyes narrowed on her. She never asked him these questions, never wanted to know anything about what he or

Melissa knew. But she could not stop herself from asking. She had to know why she could not get the stranger out of her thoughts, and Chris might be able to help her with that. "No, not really," he answered slowly. "Why?"

She turned her attention back to the game, hoping that Chris wouldn't notice or pick up on the anxiety, excitement, and fear wracking through her. "Just wondering, haven't seen him around before."

It was not a lie, she tried to reassure herself. But she didn't think Chris bought it. Fortunately, he knew her well enough to know not to push her anymore. Sitting silently, she gained some sense of comfort from his steady, reassuring presence. Without Chris in her life, she had no idea what would have become of her. He kept her sane in a world of madness and confusion.

Sighing softly, she dropped her head to his shoulder. For the first time all night, she finally began to feel normal again.

CHAPTER 3

Cassie slid her sunglasses onto the top of her head; she surveyed the crowded school parking lot as she stepped away from Chris's beat up Mustang. Though the car looked like junk now, Chris planned to restore it to its former nineteen sixty four prestige. Cassie had no doubt that he could do it, the only thing she doubted was that he would ever get the time he needed to devote to it. Just as he hadn't had time for his job once school had started again. Not with hunting vampires, thrown in with some school work and football practice.

Melissa slid out of the car beside her; her black hair was pulled into a sleek French braid that hung almost to her waist. "Freaking death trap," she muttered.

"I heard that!" Chris shouted from inside as he fiddled with the only thing he had updated in the car, the stereo. Disturbed blasted loudly from the large speakers stuffed in the trunk moments before Chris popped his head above the roof. "I'll have you know that this car is a classic."

"More like an antique," Melissa retorted.

He shrugged, dropping his hands on the roof as he leaned forward. "And one day it's going to be awesome."

"Well, until that day, it *is* a death trap," Melissa retorted sharply.

Chris made a face at her before ducking away again and turning the music up more. Cassie rolled her eyes; she heaved a large sigh as she grabbed her backpack and slung it over her shoulder. Cars were lined up and down the senior parking lot, music blared from most of them as students tried to outdo the stereos surrounding them. Puffs of smoke floated from some cars, drifting into the air in slow tendrils that marked the vehicles.

Students milled everywhere, calling greetings to their friends as they moved swiftly through the cramped spaces. Some juniors had wandered over from the lot below, but most stayed by their own cars, trying hard to make their systems heard over the rising cacophony. Cassie usually enjoyed the noise and confusion of the mornings, it helped to wake her up. But today she found herself wishing that everyone would keep their music at a normal level, and their voices pitched below screaming. She had gotten very little sleep, and the dull throbbing in her temples was a constant reminder of that fact.

"I'm going in," she muttered to Melissa.

Melissa frowned at her. "Are you ok?"

Cassie frowned as she nodded and pulled her glasses back over her tired, aching eyes. "I didn't sleep well, and that sun is awfully bright."

"Yeah, it tends to be."

Cassie didn't have the energy to come up with a witty retort as she tightened her grip on the straps of her bag and made her way into the crowd. People called out loud greetings to her that she returned with a forced smile, and a cheery demeanor she didn't feel. Her skin was still oddly electrified to the point that she wanted to rip it off, her mind still focused upon one clinging thought. *Him*. Being bright, cheery, and happy was not in her today, but she did a good job of faking it.

Swiftly climbing the steps, she was grateful when she reached the cool interior of the dimly lit foyer. The shade felt much nicer against her skin and eyes than the hot, bright sun. On days when she was run down, the sun was oddly draining, and painful to her. It stung her eyes more, and made her skin feel tight and itchy. She had never understood it, but that was the way it was. It was easier to avoid sunlight when she was overtired. And she was most certainly tired today.

A sophomore boy held the door open for her, making a grand, sweeping gesture that brought the first true smile to her face. With few students in the halls, it was far easier to move as she gathered her things from her locker and strolled to homeroom.

***

Devon stood silently in the shadows, leaning against the cool wall as he watched her move slowly down the hall. Her head was bent forward; her golden hair cascaded in thick waves to the small of her back. Though he couldn't see her face, the utter perfection of her beautiful, delicate features had been burned into his memory last night. Cassie, he recalled the small girl from last night calling her.

Sighing softly, he stepped away from the wall as she disappeared into one of the near empty classrooms. He didn't know what he was doing here, he had never stepped foot in a high school before. He had never had *any* intention of ever doing so. But for some reason, somehow, he found himself standing amongst the stark, foreign halls.

Well, he knew the reason, and it was *her*.

Ever since he had first laid eyes on her, first *smelled* her, he had been inexplicably drawn in. He had been passing through town, heading for the woods in search of food, when he had caught her scent. The blood flowing through her veins was strong, its fragrance deliciously alluring. It had reeled him in like a fish on a hook, snagging hold of him and refusing to let go. She had been a bright beacon against the dark night encompassing her.

Though he hadn't fed off a human in a very long time, he had been unable to resist the appeal of her enticing aroma. He was so ensnared by it that he hadn't been able to wander far from her since he had first seen her. Somehow, strangely, she was a shining light against the darkness residing in him, and he had to get closer to her. Though he had not wanted to come here, he'd had to see her again in order to try and figure out the strange hold she had over him, or to see if he had just imagined it. He had neither figured it out, nor had he been imagining it. In fact, her pull over him felt even stronger today. Hence, why he was here, and why he had stood outside of her house last night for a bit.

There was a wealth of sadness in her, a longing and need that called to him. It touched something in him, sparked to life something that he had thought cold and dead centuries ago. Hell, she touched something that he hadn't even known he possessed. It had taken him awhile to name the strange emotion building inside him, and it had shocked him when he finally recognized it as hope. Seeing her again now, he felt the strange hope once more, and a strange spark of life that kept him rooted in place. She made it damn near impossible to even think as he struggled with the astonishing feelings threatening to consume him.

He had not felt like this since Annabelle. Had not felt this pull, and need, and… obsession? Yes, it was definitely obsession he felt for this girl, but it was different from what he had felt for Annabelle. This felt good, it felt *right*. This girl affected him in such a different way than Annabelle had. He had simply had to have Annabelle, had to possess her, had to break her, but this girl…

This girl he wanted to protect and hold and cherish for some unknown reason. This girl made him feel oddly alive again, almost normal, almost *human* even. He didn't understand her hold over him, but he could not fight the sensations pulling at him. No, this girl was completely different than Annabelle. With Annabelle it had been a game, one that had changed him forever.

But last night, when this girl had turned to him, his heart had leapt in his chest, or at least it had felt like it for a moment. He had not thought of his heart or the missing beat of it in centuries, because he had not felt anything in the region of his heart in years. However, he swore he could hear it beating now, could almost feel it pulsing blood through his deadened veins once more.

This girl was beautiful, spectacular, perfect, but it was not her looks that captivated him. It was the splendor of her wounded, bright spirit. Though she radiated loss and loneliness, he also sensed a steel rod of strength and pride running through her.

Looking upon her, seeing her, he instantly felt as if he were complete, as if he had found his home. Somehow, in her, he had found the one person that could make everything all right. He knew with absolute certainty that she could ease the aching loneliness that had eaten at his soul for centuries. That had nearly destroyed him time and time again. He did not understand his strange reaction to her. In all his many years, he had never felt anything like what he suddenly felt for her. After all of his time on earth, he had never expected to be shocked or thrown off balance again. He had thought that he had seen it all, that he knew it all.

He had been wrong.

He was completely thrown off balance now. He was unsettled and enchanted by this girl, a *teenage* girl no less. He needed to know more about her, see more of her. He needed to understand the strange effect she had upon him. He needed her to ease the ache that filled his deadened spirit, and he knew that she could do it.

He watched silently as the halls began to fill up, the chatter and laughter grew louder as students milled about. Lockers opened and slammed as they prepared for the day. He found himself oddly captivated by the simplicity of their lives, amazed by the easy flow of their days. It was something that he had never witnessed before as he tended to stay away from humans, and the allure of their warm blood, and pumping hearts.

Though he had control over his baser, more murderous instincts, he felt it best to avoid temptation as much as possible. And humans were a great temptation, no matter how much control he had now. Even after all of these years, he could still clearly recall the taste of their warm blood, recall the thrill of the hunt, and remember the surge of power that their deaths had brought to him. However, no matter how much of a temptation their blood was, he had been drawn here by her, and he was loath to leave her now.

Slipping from the shadows, he ignored the startled looks his sudden emergence caused the students closest to him. He sensed the fear, curiosity, and lust that followed his movements. Ignoring them all, he became intent upon his goal as he made his way toward the offices he had seen at the front of the building.

If he was going to stay close to her, and get to know her better, than there was only one thing he could do. He glanced around the crowded hallways, ignoring the fluttering beat of the hearts surrounding him as he took in the people that he would be spending the rest of the day with.

CHAPTER 4

Cassie played idly with the pages of her notebook as the principal droned on about the daily announcements. She honestly didn't know if she was going to make it through this day. She was wound tight as a spring and about ready to snap. Closing her eyes, she folded her arms and dropped her head on the desk, stifling a yawn. Chris shot her a questioning look, but she ignored it as she allowed her eyes to drift shut.

The morning announcements finally came to an end and attendance began. Cassie shot her hand up, not bothering to lift her head when her name was called. Chatter started up the minute that attendance was over. Homework was discussed; plans for the weekend were made in the few minutes left before the day started.

"You ok?"

Cassie opened her eyes, her lids felt like lead as she met Chris's worried gaze. "Fine, just a little tired," she assured him.

The class suddenly quieted, a strange silence settled over everyone. Cassie frowned at the startled look that came over Chris's face. He froze where he was, his hand tightened upon her desk as his eyes became riveted upon the front of the class.

A feeling of foreboding stole through her. The strange tingling sensation once again raced down her spine. Her already frayed nerve endings leapt to blazing life, seeming to sizzle and crack with electricity. She remained frozen, unable to lift her head to see what had captivated everyone's attention; she was certain she already knew.

She just wasn't certain how she was going to deal with it. Swallowing heavily, she tried hard to rid her throat of the fierce lump that had lodged itself there. Taking a deep breath, she gathered all of her courage, and whatever strength she had left, to lift her head. Her eyes instantly found him at the front of the classroom. Her heart leapt like a trapped bird in her ribcage at the sight of his powerful body that seemed so out of place in the classroom.

Her classroom!

It took her a moment to truly comprehend that he was really there, that she had not fallen asleep, and that she was not dreaming about him. She had to be awake though, for she could never dream anything so wonderful, or so frightening. She also never would have dreamed that he was a high school student. He seemed far older than her, or any of her other classmates. He exuded a raw power and confidence that none of them possessed. Yet he was standing there as if he truly belonged; standing there as if he didn't look as out of place as a platypus would.

Even Mrs. Mann looked slightly flabbergasted as he spoke softly with her, and extended a slip of paper to her. Cassie stared at the paper as she struggled to get her wildly spinning mind focused upon something other than the snapping of her body, and his startling presence in her normally calm day.

With a bolt of certainty she knew that she was never going to have another calm day again.

He turned slowly away from Mrs. Mann, his bright emerald eyes instantly latching upon her. Cassie inhaled sharply, tears once again flooding her eyes as a sense of peace and rightness stole through her. She wanted to cry, wanted to sob with the joy that suffused her entire being. She wanted nothing more than to go to him and bury herself within his embrace.

His gaze did not leave hers; his eyes were bright and fierce. He did not look at anyone else in the class as Mrs. Mann cleared her throat to get everyone's attention. But everyone's interest was focused upon the stranger in their midst. Few new students ever moved to their small town, let alone one that was as strangely fascinating, and magnificent, as he was. He would be the center of attention for the rest of the year.

"Class, I would like to introduce you to Devon Knight."

Something flickered in his eyes; a small smile curved his full mouth as he finally turned his gaze to the rest of the students. That strange sense of loss suffused her again as his gaze left hers, but she found herself finally able to inhale once more. With the connection broken, panic set in as a crushing sense of being trapped descended upon her. She could not be stuck here with him; she could not be forced into a destiny that she did not want again.

And she *did not* want this, whatever it was, she told herself fiercely. Even though she secretly feared that she did.

"You are lucky Devon; we have plenty of people in this class who would be more than happy to show you around." Cassie slid further down in her desk, trying hard to become invisible as Mrs. Mann's gaze scanned the classroom. The last thing she wanted was to be chosen for this task. "Melissa, would you be willing to show Devon around?"

Relief and disappointment crashed through Cassie in fierce waves that left her shaken and unsettled. Melissa stiffened slightly, her shoulders tightened in front of Cassie. "Of course," she replied pleasantly.

The bell rang, but nobody leapt to their feet as they all remained focused upon him. "Have a good day everyone," Mrs. Mann announced loudly.

The enrapt trance seemed to snap as everyone moved into action. Melissa turned to Cassie, a strange gleam in her onyx eyes. "Would you like to join us?"

Cassie opened her mouth to answer, but no words would come out. She snapped it closed, and shook her head fiercely. She lurched to her feet, knocking her chair back. Both Chris and Melissa studied her in surprise as she scooped up her bag, and flung it over her shoulder. "Cassie…"

"I have to go, I'll see you later," she interrupted abruptly.

Her gaze darted back to the front of the class, where he was standing patiently, his eyes still focused on her. Cassie bent her head, afraid to stare at him much longer in case she got sucked in by him again. If she did, she knew she would never escape. Keeping her head down, she joined the crush of students pushing into the crowded hallway.

She hurried down the hall, barely acknowledging the greetings she received. Pushing her way into the bathroom she ignored the girls huddled by the window smoking cigarettes. They didn't acknowledge her presence either. Turning the faucet on, Cassie eagerly splashed her face with cold water. She was trying hard not to spill the tears that burned fiercely against the backs of her eyes.

She would not cry, she could *not* cry. If she did she knew she would never stop. Turning the water off, she placed her hands on the edge of the sink, gasping in air as she struggled to keep control of her wildly swaying emotions. She wanted to sob over the events that kept throwing her life into a fierce tailspin. That kept knocking her off balance and taking things from her. She wanted to sob for the joy and electricity that still sizzled through her, making her feel whole and alive in a way that she never had before. She wanted to sob in order to purify her spirit of the turmoil that plagued it.

She did not know what was going on, but she wanted it to stop. She wanted it to end and for him to go away so that she could feel normal again. "Are you ok?"

She glanced up at one of the smoking girls now hovering by her elbow, worry marred her delicate forehead. Her hazel eyes were flecked with streaks of gold, and surprisingly caring for a stranger. "I'm fine," Cassie answered shakily.

The girl gave her a worried frown as she handed her a wad of paper towels. "Are you sure?"

Cassie's hands shook as she took the towels from the younger girl, slightly ashamed to realize that she didn't know her name. "Yes. I'm Cassie."

"I know." The girl smiled as she nodded swiftly. Her short brown hair, streaked with shades of green, bobbed around her shoulders. "Danielle, but my friends call me Dani."

Smiling tremulously, Cassie's hands tightened briefly around the crumpled towels. "Nice to meet you Dani, thank you."

A small smile flitted across the girl's pretty face before she retreated back to her hazy corner. Drying her face slowly, Cassie glanced only briefly at her reflection. She already knew that she was a mess, but her frantic, bloodshot eyes were a bit of a shock. She looked half crazed, and it was not a good look on her. There was nothing she could do about her eyes though, she had no eye drops, and she wasn't even sure they would help right now. She didn't think anything could help her now.

Taking a deep breath, she retrieved the backpack she had dumped hastily on the floor. The hall was almost deserted when she poked her head out of the bathroom. She was still shaky and distraught, but at least she didn't feel like she was on the brink of tears anymore. Making her way slowly down the hall, she slipped quietly into her history class. People shot her questioning looks as she made her way to her desk, but thankfully no one stopped her.

Sitting at her desk, Cassie dropped her head in her hands. She forced herself to remain seated and not to get up and leave class, and school. Though it was a tempting thought, she knew she could not run forever, and apparently he was going to be in her life from now on. Or at least in her school. She would have to find another way to deal with the situation other than running.

She felt that avoidance would be best.

***

Devon searched the cafeteria as he made his way swiftly through the thick crowd, Melissa led the way. "No matter what, bring your own lunch on Thursdays, the spaghetti is awful," she was telling him in between the vast amount of hello's she received, and returned. "I just bring my own lunch anyway as they have nothing healthy here, except for apples."

He turned his attention back to her as she stopped before him, her dark eyes searching his face. She was a nice girl, but the intense way she studied him was more than a little unsettling. He had the strange feeling that she saw more of him than he wanted her to. Her head tilted, her exotically slanted eyes narrowed as a small smile flitted over her full mouth.

"Thanks for the warning."

She grinned as she shrugged a dainty shoulder, and made her way back through the crowd. "The seniors sit in the back of the cafeteria, when it's not nice enough to sit outside."

Devon hardly paid attention to her as his eyes returned to the mob of students. He could sense *her* somewhere amongst the crowd; smell the wonderful aroma she emitted. He had not seen Cassie since this morning, when she had fled the classroom in an obvious panic. It was not the reaction he had hoped for from her, but at least he knew that she was feeling something too. He just wasn't sure what.

The crowd suddenly parted, opening to reveal her. She was sitting at a table, an apple held casually in her hand as she stared up at the boy standing at her side. The boy was tall and muscular, his brown hair curled at the collar of his shirt as he leaned forward, resting his hands on the table. She shook her head at him, placing the apple down as her face hardened slightly. Devon did not like the aggravation that emanated from her; it was more than apparent that she was annoyed by the boy.

"Who is that with your friend?" Devon inquired, trying to sound as casual as possible.

Melissa glanced toward the table, her eyes narrowed. "Mark Young. He's been chasing Cassie since middle school; unfortunately he doesn't take a hint."

Devon stiffened, his eyes narrowed as Cassie shook her head more fiercely at Mark. He already had enough competition in the form of Cassie's boyfriend for her attention; he did not need, or want, anymore. "And her boyfriend doesn't do anything about it?" Though he tried, he was unable to keep the aggravation from his voice.

Melissa frowned at him; her dark eyebrows drew tightly together over her petite nose. "Cassie doesn't have a boyfriend."

Devon's eyes widened in surprise, his gaze darted back to the table as the tall blond he had seen with her last night appeared. He nodded briefly to Mark before sliding into the seat next to Cassie. Leaning toward her, he grabbed a handful of fries from her plate. Devon would have sworn the two of them were together. Hell, the boy had crawled through her bedroom window last night. And he had not come back out.

A surprising jolt of anger and jealousy twisted his gut. He had never experienced jealousy before. It was an emotion that had been utterly foreign to him, until now. For most of his existence he had always taken what he wanted, when he wanted it. He did not like the feeling of helplessness that filled him, and anger was an emotion that he could not allow himself to experience. It was an emotion that he had learned to keep tightly under wraps. Anger made him volatile, and when he was unstable, innocent people were hurt.

Devon took a deep breath as he tried to steady the pendulum of emotions that swung through him. He was beginning to realize that this was a giant mistake. He never should have come here; he should not have placed himself in closer proximity to her. She helped to salve the ache and hurt in his soul, but she also served to unhinge all of the hard work he had done to keep himself under tight restraint.

Being around Cassie unbalanced him. He could not allow that to happen, he could not risk losing control of himself and hurting someone, possibly even her. Shockingly, that thought was completely intolerable to him. He would rather destroy himself than see her hurt in anyway, least of all by his own hand.

Though he knew that he should leave, he could not bring himself to move. He was completely captivated by her as a small smile spread over her full lips and she shoved playfully against the blond sitting beside her. Their ease, and obvious affection for each other, made it hard to believe they weren't together.

"Then who is that boy beside her?" he asked quietly, his voice tight with the tension that pulsed through him.

Melissa glanced toward the table; a bright smile lit her exotic face. "Oh, that's just Chris." He glanced at her in confusion. "They've been best friends since they were born, more like siblings actually."

An immense, startling sense of relief flooded him as he glanced back at the table. Their blond heads were bent close together as they talked. Mark, completely forgotten, shook his head and turned away. "Come on, let's get you some lunch."

He glanced back at Melissa, not surprised to see her shrewd eyes narrowed upon him. He shook his head, not at all interested in the mounds of human food. He only had one interest, only one thing that he wanted to taste in this cafeteria. "I'm not hungry."

She nodded and led him over to the table. Chris looked up at him first, his sapphire colored eyes widened slightly as he stopped speaking. Cassie's shoulders stiffened, her back straightened as she seemed to brace herself. Very slowly, she turned toward him, her eyes clashing with his.

The full force of her gaze rattled him, shaking him to the very marrow of his bones as he once again felt an odd little skip in the deadened area of his heart. She had the most beautiful eyes he had ever seen. They were a bright azure blue with flecks of pure, deep purple speckled throughout. The most pure amethyst could not match the beautiful purple streaks that highlighted her irises. In all of his many years, he had never seen eyes the like.

"Cassie, Chris, this is Devon."

"We were in homeroom too Melissa," Chris reminded her gently. "Nice to meet you."

Devon had to force himself to tear his gaze away from Cassie as Chris thrust his hand out. He took hold of it, noting the thick calluses on Chris's palm as they shook firmly. Chris's eyes darkened slightly, his hand tightened around Devon's as his gaze became sharper, more intense. His face hardened for a moment, the smile slipped swiftly away. Melissa stiffened beside him; she took a small step forward as she reached out to grasp Chris's shoulder.

Chris shook his head; his eyes darted away from Devon to Melissa. Pulling his hand away from Devon's, Chris turned toward Cassie with a small, worried frown. Devon stared at them in bewildered confusion, unable to understand what had just happened. For a moment, he could have sworn that Chris had looked inside him, had seen something there, and it appeared that he had not liked it.

Chris slid back in his seat, still frowning as he stared at his tray of food. Devon shook his crazy thoughts off, he didn't care what Chris thought of him. *She* was the only one that mattered. Cassie was still staring at him, her head tilted slightly to the side as she watched him from slightly wary eyes. She did not extend a hand, did not move as he slid into the seat across from her. Well, he thought wryly, at least she wasn't bolting like a rabbit again. Melissa dropped her lunch on the table; she dug into the cotton bag as she hummed cheerfully to herself. She seemed happily oblivious to the tension thrumming through them all.

"Are you going to eat that?"

Cassie blinked in surprise, looking away from Devon as Chris leaned over her to point at her brownie. She shook her head, her gaze focused upon the table as she pushed her tray toward him. Devon watched her for a few moments more, oddly fascinated by the way the light played over her delicate features.

She was stunningly beautiful, but it was not desire for her that drew him to her like a moth to a flame. No, it was simply just her. Though he did want her, he wanted even more to be *near* her, and make sure that she was safe. These protective, tender emotions were new to him, and slightly disconcerting, but he found that he liked them. He wanted them.

More students wandered over to them, they dropped their trays down as their chairs squeaked over the linoleum floors. "Man did you see that game last night?" one of the newer boys asked Chris.

"Yeah," he mumbled. "Jason, this is Devon."

Jason was well built, his letterman's jacket stretched tight over his broad shoulders. Hazel eyes glanced inquisitively at Devon as he gave a brief nod. "Hey," he greeted absently.

"Hi."

"And this is Kara, Susan, Billy, and David," Melissa continued, pointing out the four other new people that had joined them.

The boys nodded to him, the girls stared with open admiration. He could hear the increase of the girl's heartbeats; sense the excitement that enshrouded them as their blood pulsed more rapidly through their veins. His hunger perked slightly, but drawing on his tight self control, he was able to bury it once more. Though he wasn't sure how much longer he would be able to keep doing that. Eventually the hunger would take over, and he would need to feed. He hoped he would be able to make it through the rest of this tiring, draining day first.

"Where are you from?" Susan asked eagerly, crossing her hands before her as she leaned forward. Her brown hair had been highlighted with streaks of light blond and twisted into a lose knot. Her light brown eyes were inquisitive and keen.

Devon lifted an eyebrow, fighting a smile. He was from everywhere, but he was sure that they would not appreciate that answer. "New York," he lied easily.

"Oh really, you don't have an accent. You must *hate* having to move to this small, nowhere town after such a big place!"

Melissa and Cassie both sighed heavily, drawing his attention briefly back to them. Cassie's gaze was still focused on her tray, but he could sense her disquiet. "I was from upstate New York, a town smaller than this one, so it's actually an improvement."

"Why did you move here?"

Devon shrugged, he didn't like to lie, but most of his existence was based on one giant lie. "I needed a change of scenery."

"I hope you're not a Yankee's fan," Jason muttered.

"I don't really follow sports."

Cassie glanced up at him, a small smile curved her full mouth and her eyes twinkled with amusement. He found himself lost to her, unable to think straight as her eyes took him hostage. "That's great. Maybe I could show you around tonight or something. You know, show you where all the hotspots are," Susan continued eagerly.

"What hotspots?" Billy retorted irritably.

Susan rolled her eyes at him. "There are a few."

"B's and S's?"

"The Lookout and Standish beach," Susan retorted impatiently.

"Whoopee."

Susan glared at Billy briefly before focusing her attention back on Devon. "Anyway, if you would like, I'll take you around and show you everything."

Billy and David shook their heads in disgust; they turned their attention away from Susan as they started talking about football. "Thank you, but I think I'm all set."

Susan's pretty face fell in disappointment. "Well, if you change your mind let me know."

He gave her a brisk nod before focusing on Cassie once more. She was watching him silently, her eyes steady and calm as he met her gaze. His heart seemed to lurch again, for a moment he felt it beating fiercely in his chest, and then it was dead once more. Whatever the strange connection between him and this girl was, he didn't think he would ever get used to it, or understand it.

He couldn't take his eyes away from her as she lowered her lids slowly, once again focusing on the table as she dropped her half eaten apple on the tray. The loud ringing of the bell caused everyone to lurch to their feet like Pavlov's dogs. Devon raised an eyebrow at the sign of automatic obedience, but he found himself following suit.

Her eyes met his again, her hands clenched tighter upon her tray. There was a sad acceptance in her gaze that he didn't understand, a look of resignation that touched something deep inside him. He longed to reach out and touch her, longed to ease the aching loneliness he sensed radiating from her.

Melissa was before him again, her dark eyes twinkled brightly, amusement radiated from her as she smiled. Melissa glanced briefly at Cassie, her knowing smile widened. "What's your next class?" He tore his attention away from Cassie, slipping the well used schedule from his pocket as he handed it to Melissa. "Oh good, Cassie and I have American history now too."

Cassie inhaled sharply, a look of utter panic descended over her face once more. He was becoming accustomed to that look, he didn't like it, but he was adjusting to it. For a moment it seemed she was going to bolt from the room again as her eyes darted frantically around. Then, her focus came back to him; a steely resolve descended over her as she nodded briskly, turned sharply on her heel, and hurried to the nearest trash can.

She dumped her mostly untouched lunch.

CHAPTER 5

Cassie shifted uncomfortably, her whole body hurt. She had taken quite the pounding in training today, pushing herself extra hard in the hopes that the exertion would help to bury the memory of the strange man that had walked into her life. It had not worked.

Cassie rolled her shoulders, trying to work the tension out of them. The hot water of her shower had helped to ease some of the tightness in them, but it had not relaxed them completely. She dressed slowly, listening to the TV as she ran the brush through her tangled hair. She winced as it got caught on a snarl but pulled it swiftly through.

Limping slightly, she pulled the door open. Chris was sitting Indian style on her bed, his hands folded before as he leaned toward the TV. The Red Sox were in the race for the playoffs and he was riveted. Cassie shook her head as he groaned loudly, pounding his fist onto the bed. "Damn, these guys are killing me!"

Cassie laughed softly as she settled onto the bed beside him. "Is it over?"

"Might as well be," he muttered.

Cassie patted his knee gently. "Are you going to stay here tonight?"

Chris shook his head before rising slowly to his feet. "No, it's pretty quiet over there and I suppose I should go home once in awhile."

"I guess," she muttered.

"Are you going to miss me?" he asked teasingly.

"Always." Though it was true, Cassie didn't tell him that she didn't wish to be alone tonight. If she was alone then she would think, and if she thought, she knew that her thoughts would be centered upon *him*.

Cassie shuddered; she wrapped her arms tightly around herself. She didn't want to think about Devon, she wanted to forget his existence entirely, but she knew that was going to be impossible, especially if Chris went home. Unfortunately she couldn't bring herself to ask Chris to stay. He would know something was wrong if she did, and she didn't want anyone to know just how much Devon affected her.

Swallowing her anxiety, she drew on her pride as Chris swung a leg out her window to take his normal exit from her house. "I'll see you in the morning."

Cassie nodded as he leapt onto the tree branch, swinging for a brief moment before scurrying down the limb hand over hand. His legs wrapped around the trunk as he swiftly used the other branches to climb to the ground. She watched as he loped across the street, disappearing through his front door.

Sighing softly, Cassie closed the window most of the way. Turning off her lights, she slipped into bed, knowing that she would not be able to sleep. Staring blankly at the flickering TV she tried hard to shut her mind off of Devon, tried hard not to think about him, but the harder she tried the more she found herself fixated on him.

Tossing and turning, Cassie finally managed to slip into a restless sleep at almost two in the morning. And the moment that she slept, she dreamed.

Of him.

***

Cassie squinted against the bright light of the morning, wishing that she had darker and stronger sunglasses. Her eyes were killing her; she was exhausted, twitchy, and extremely agitated. Her skin felt two sizes to small as she tried hard not to scratch at it with the strange urge to rip it off. The sun seemed to be burning it and she tingled with pain and discomfort.

It was going to be a miserable day and she hadn't even made it into the school yet. Rubbing the back of her neck, she eased further into the shadows of the giant oak overhanging Chris's Mustang. "Are you ok?" She glanced over at Melissa, nodding slowly as she hugged her books tighter to her chest. "Cassie…"

Melissa's voice trailed off as a strange quiet settled over the student body. The tingling sensation of her skin increased tenfold, the hair on the back of her neck stood on end. She turned slowly, her eyes instantly latching onto the sleek black Challenger that moved slowly past. Her heart turned over, her mouth went dry. She knew instantly who was behind the wheel, even though the tinted windows were to dark to get a glimpse of the driver.

"Wow," Chris breathed his eyes so wide Cassie was certain they were about to pop out of his head.

Cassie took a step back, wishing that she could disappear into the oak as she bumped up against it. Memories of her dreams from last night suddenly assaulted her, flooding her body with heat and making her skin crawl even more. Though the dreams had just been bits and pieces of him standing by B's and S's watching her, they had left her longing for more. The searing look in his eyes as he had stared at her still left her shaken and trembling with a strange sense of unfulfilled desire and need. She had never experienced anything like these feelings before. Although they left her confused, she could not deny that the excitement tearing through her was a wonderfully alive sensation, and something she had not felt in a very long time.

She watched breathlessly, her heart hammering loudly in her chest as the car slid into a parking spot and Devon climbed out. Though he wore dark sunglasses, she knew the moment when his gaze locked onto hers. Her legs went weak, her body turned to rubber as she felt his gaze burning into her. Trembling, Cassie hugged her books tighter to her chest, unable to move as she stared back at him. She felt like a fool for being caught staring, no *gaping* at him, but she could not bring herself to care.

His gaze was torn from her as Marcy and Susan hurried eagerly up to him. Cassie slumped against the tree, trying hard to catch her breath, and ease the pounding of her heart. She was shaking, trembling like a leaf as the lingering effects of his gaze coursed through her. Chris was staring at her questioningly, an eyebrow lifted in surprise.

"What's wrong with you?"

Cassie shook her head, trying hard not to completely fall apart. "Nothing."

He continued to stare at her, but thankfully Jason and Kara picked that moment to arrive and distract his attention. The game was discussed, plans were made, but Cassie barely heard any of it. Unwillingly her gaze returned to Devon. He was still standing by the car, but he now had a large group of female admirers surrounding him.

Cassie's heart lurched, jealousy filled her. She shifted uncomfortably, trying hard to deny the emotions suffusing her. There was some strange connection between them (or at least she believed so), but it was more than apparent that he could have his choice of any of the girls, and that none of them were avoiding him as much as Cassie was trying to. Her anger mounted as Marcy touched his arm, grinning brightly as her hand lingered far longer than Cassie would have liked. All she wanted was to know what he felt like, and now Marcy did.

"He is wicked hot," Kara gushed from beside her.

Cassie started in surprise; she had been so focused on Devon that she hadn't realized Kara had moved to stand beside her. "Who?" she managed to croak out, knowing full well who Kara meant.

Kara grinned at her, her light brown eyes sparkling merrily. "The new guy, the one you're staring at."

Cassie shifted uncomfortably. She hadn't realized that

she had been so overt in her ogling. "Um yeah, he's ok," she hedged.

Kara laughed softly as she flung her backpack higher on her shoulder. Melissa moved over to join them, her gaze steady and intense as she watched Cassie. "You want to go over there with me?" Kara inquired.

Panic tore through Cassie as she fervently shook her head. "No."

Kara shrugged. "Suit yourself."

Kara slipped eagerly away to join the growing group of girls surrounding Devon. "You ok?" Melissa asked softly.

Cassie nodded, though she knew it was a lie. "Fine. I'm going to head inside."

"I'll go with you."

Cassie moved slowly away from the tree, wincing as she stepped into the harsh sunlight. She could almost feel her skin burning, her eyes watered as she squinted against the bright light. She left a wide berth around Devon, but she could feel his eyes burning into her as she moved slowly toward the much needed shelter of the school.

It was going to be another very long, very hard day, and she wasn't at all prepared for it.

CHAPTER 6

Devon was growing tired of being avoided. And she was going *well* out of her way to avoid him. Though he sat at her lunch table again, she did not return to it. In fact, she didn't even come into the cafeteria, for three days in a row. He was growing impatient and aggravated with her. Every other girl in the school was throwing themselves at him. It was a fact that he was used to, but he most certainly was not used to women going out of their way to avoid him.

And that was exactly what Cassie was doing. And she happened to be the only girl in the whole school that he even remotely cared about talking to, and getting closer to. And now, finally, she was back in the cafeteria. He watched as she glided deftly through the crowd with an ease and grace that was captivating and amazing.

Her hair was a golden shimmer in the harsh light as she moved toward the lunch line. She was unable to move fast as she was accosted by endless people. Though she spoke with everyone, and smiled brightly, he could sense her impatience. He was just as impatient as she was. He wanted her over here, with him, where he could finally try and talk to her again.

He slid into the chair that had become his, tapping his finger impatiently on the table as he waited for Cassie to reappear. People slid in around him, and though they talked to him, he barely acknowledged them as his gaze remained focused on the wall she had disappeared behind. He still didn't understand why he was so captivated with this girl, but he was. He dreamed of her every night, haunting dreams that left him shaken and unfulfilled in the morning. He wanted more of her, he wanted to know what she felt and tasted like. Wanted to know what she would *really* feel like in his arms, not just what her ghostly dream image felt like.

"Hello," he glanced over at Marcy, nodding briefly as she slid into the seat next to him and leaned annoyingly close.

Devon shifted slightly, wanting to get further away from her. He knew he had a large group of admirers now; there was nothing that he could do about that, but Marcy was by far the most persistent and overt. She moved closer to him, her small hand dropped onto his arm. Cocking an eyebrow he turned slowly toward her, trying hard not to lose his patience with the clingy girl.

She smiled brightly back at him, her leaf green eyes twinkling merrily. She chose to completely ignore the impatience radiating from him. "Are you going to come to B's and S's tonight?"

Devon glanced back at where Cassie had disappeared, but she had not reemerged yet. He had not been back to the restaurant since he had first seen her. She had not returned there either in the past three nights, choosing instead to go to Melissa's house with Chris. He was a little dismayed, and found himself more than a little pathetic for knowing that fact, but he did. For some reason though, he wanted to make sure that she was safe at all times and had to know where she was in order to do so.

He tried to convince himself that this was true, but he knew in his heart that he was bordering on obsessive and stalker. Neither of those were things he had ever thought he could be. It was a brutal realization to know that one girl could make him become something that he could barely recognize. But then again, it had been another girl that had completely changed him in a way he had never expected before.

But Cassie was an exceptional girl, she was a unicorn, he realized with a start as she reemerged from the lunch line. She was a rare, never imagined find, but one that he was never going to release again. She even reminded him of a unicorn with her graceful mannerisms, golden hair, and bright violet flecked eyes.

Her smile was easy and bright as she conversed with the girls by her side. He had only known her for a few days, but he had come to realize that she was *never* alone. There was always someone by her side, demanding her attention. It was an annoying fact, especially when she was so giving of her time with them, while she ignored and avoided the hell out of him.

Mark swiftly approached her, honing in like a missile upon its target. He walked briskly, with a stride that was not to be deterred. Devon's senses went on high alert; he stiffened as he sensed an undercurrent of anger and impatience running through the boy. He arrived at Cassie's side, touching her elbow to grab her attention.

She turned slowly toward him, her eyes widening slightly as she took a small step back. Anger rolled through Devon as Mark moved closer to her. Using his height as an intimidation factor, he bent slightly over her. Cassie's eyes narrowed fiercely, her shoulders straightened as she tilted her chin up proudly. Though Devon was impressed by her show of strength and defiance, he also wished that she would simply back away. He sensed an instability and anxiety within Mark that worried him, and he knew that the boy would snap if pushed too hard. And Cassie seemed intent on pushing him away.

Devon rose to his feet, with every intention of intervening. Her safety was his number one concern, and around Mark, he knew that she was not safe.

Chris appeared at her side suddenly, using his shoulder to push slightly past Mark. Chris smiled brightly at Mark, but there was tension in his solid frame, and no sparkle in his sapphire eyes. He spoke briefly to Mark for a moment while gently nudging Cassie further back. Cassie did not look pleased to be pushed out of the way.

Chris finally managed to disentangle the two of them from Mark, though Mark glared after them as Chris continued to nudge Cassie toward the glass doors at the back of the cafeteria. He suddenly recalled Melissa's words on his first day. The senior's sat outside when it was nice out. Until now, he had not noticed that a fair amount of senior's was missing as his table was packed with girls, and they would not leave his side as long as he remained inside.

And if he moved outside right now, they would only follow. The last thing he wanted was a gaggle of giggling teens following him around while he tried to talk with Cassie. He watched her as she moved stiffly toward the doors, her tray clenched tight in her hands, her head held immobile, and her neck straight. He could feel the stress radiating from her, the struggle that waged throughout.

He also felt the snapping point when she lost the struggle and her head turned slowly toward him. The impact of her gaze was like a lightning bolt as it seared through him, it sizzled through his dried veins and caused his deadened heart to vibrate with pulsing electricity.

She hesitated briefly, her eyes warmed slightly; a wave of heat flooded her porcelain cheeks. Her long dark lashes swept swiftly down, shadowing her startling eyes as she bowed her head. Her golden hair fell forward, hiding her face as she hurried on. She dropped her sunglasses back into place before following Chris outside.

Disappointment filled him as he turned away from her, his anger sparked as he caught sight of Mark. He was staring after Cassie, annoyance and irritation radiating from him. Mark hesitated for a moment longer before turning and slinking over to a table packed with boys just as large and muscular as he was. They were all wearing black and gold jackets with a white horse on the back of them.

Devon had no idea why they were all wearing the same coats, but they seemed to think that the jackets were special as none of the boys were taking them off, even though the cafeteria was hot. Devon shook his head, not understanding human customs at all, and least of all not understanding teenage customs. Staying here for much longer was going to drive him crazy, but he wasn't leaving here without finding out exactly why he was so drawn to Cassie.

And that meant finally getting closer to her.

He turned back to Marcy, deciding to use her clinginess to his advantage for a change. "What do you know about Cassie?"

Marcy was slightly taken aback as she leaned away from him, her eyes widened in surprise before narrowing fiercely. He should have taken a different approach, he realized belatedly, as he recognized her jealousy and anger instantly. "Why?"

Devon shrugged negligently. Leaning closer to Marcy, he placed his hand briefly upon her arm, hoping to soothe her. "I am simply curious; Mark seems to truly like her."

She relaxed slightly, but her eyes still radiated distrust. "He's liked her for awhile, but she just strings him along like she strings Chris, and everyone else along."

Devon quirked an eyebrow, tension and anger radiated from Marcy, along with a strong wave of jealousy. He wondered if it had been Mark, or Chris, that she had liked before he had walked into this school and she had become fixated on him. "I thought she and Chris were just friends."

Marcy shrugged, her eyes darkened as her nose scrunched slightly. "That's what they say, but I doubt it. There is something strange about *that* relationship, neither one of them really date anyone else." Her bitter tone confirmed the fact that it had been Chris she liked.

"Come on Marcy, you know they're just friends," Kara interjected, leaning forward as she rested her chin on her hands.

"He sleeps in her room Kara," Marcy retorted sharply. "You can't tell me that nothing has ever happened between them!"

Kara shook her head as she rolled her eyes. She turned toward Devon, her pretty face softening from irritation to kindness. "They've been friends since they were little.

Cassie's parents, and Chris's dad, were killed in the same car accident when they were only a year old." Devon kept his shock over this revelation hidden as Kara turned narrowed eyes on Marcy. "So yes, I believe that nothing has happened between them."

Marcy rolled her eyes but tried to keep her irritation hidden from Devon. She failed miserably. "Cassie's parents are dead?"

Kara nodded; sadness crept over her delicate features. "Yes, and so are Melissa's."

Devon started in surprise. The three of them either had no parents, or were missing at least one. It was a strange coincidence, but it also explained the strong bond that they seemed to share. Though they were all popular, always surrounded by people, yet they still remained aloof, separate from everyone but each other. And when they were together they were like one unit. A unit that was able to communicate without a word, but with a simple look or a touch.

He had been amazed, impressed, and a little confused by the tightness of their bond. But the fact that they had all experienced the loss of a parent explained the closeness they shared. Unwillingly his gaze went to the windows, but he could not see Cassie amongst the crush of students that had finished eating and moved outside. A whiffle ball and bat had been brought out and a pickup game was starting.

"That's awful," he muttered.

The intense desire to be free of this room, and to see her, suffused him. Though he could not understand, or relate to her pain, he was beginning to get a better understanding of the hurt, loneliness, pride, and strength that surrounded her. A hurt and loneliness that he was determined to help ease, whether she wanted his help or not.

He rose suddenly, ignoring the startled looks that Marcy and Kara shot him. "Excuse me," he mumbled before moving swiftly through the crowd toward the glass double doors.

He stepped outside, the excited sound of laughter and chatter suffused him. He scanned the crowd, but did not spot Cassie amongst the mass. He did spot Melissa though. Winding his way through the students, he made his way steadily toward her. Melissa turned toward him, a dark eyebrow lifted as her mouth quirked in a small smile.

"Hey stranger," she greeted warmly, her onyx eyes gleaming with amusement. He hesitated for a moment, briefly puzzled by the startling amount of knowledge within those dark eyes. He was certain that she knew exactly why he was here, and she was happy about it. "How is everything going?"

"Fine." His gaze darted over the crowd as he searched for Cassie, but he didn't see her, and he couldn't smell the delicious scent that she emitted in waves.

"You seem to be making a lot of friends."

"I suppose."

Her smile widened, her smooth olive complexion shone in the bright light of the sun. She knew why he was here, and she was enjoying every moment of torment she was handing to him. He didn't know if that fact pissed him off, or if he wanted to join in with her obvious amusement.

"Not interested in friends?"

Only one, he wanted to tell her, but he bit back his words. "Of course," he said softly. Though Melissa was enjoying this conversation, he was tired of being toyed with. "Where is your friend Cassie?"

Melissa quirked her head to the side, her exotic eyes slanted as her hair fell forward. "Having most of the female population chasing you around isn't enough for you?"

Though he knew she was trying to be playful, Devon's patience was at a snapping point. He wanted to know where Cassie was, and he wanted to know now. Melissa seemed to sense this as her smile slipped away and a strange sadness crept over her. That dark look passed over her eyes again as they seemed to pierce straight into his soul.

"No," he said simply.

She snorted slightly in surprise, her eyes sparked with amusement once more. "Good." She said flatly. "Cassie went home."

He frowned in surprise as he shoved his hands into his pockets. "Why?"

"Not feeling well."

"She ok?" he demanded, surprised by the wealth of worry and concern that filled him.

"She's fine, just hasn't been sleeping well."

Devon frowned as he recalled the strange dreams plaguing him, dreams that Cassie was always a part of; dreams that haunted him throughout the day. Dreams that he did not want to have, but looked forward to every night.

He hated what Cassie was doing to him, knew that he should leave this town, but he also knew that he wouldn't. Not yet anyway.

***

"Cassie come on! Pay attention!"

Sighing in aggravation, Cassie tossed aside the stake she had been holding and stormed over to the bench. Grabbing a water bottle she squirted it into her mouth, trying to drown the annoyance consuming her. She was exhausted, she could barely function, and she had been completely blowing all of her training for the past week. She was doing awful, and Luther was not about to let her forget it.

"You are so very lucky that things have been quiet this past week!" he barked at her, his gray eyes narrowed angrily. "You wouldn't survive five seconds in the field!" Cassie was struggling to control her temper, he was right after all, but she was just as frustrated as he was with her inability to do anything right. "What is wrong with you?"

Cassie closed her eyes, shuddering as she thought of the many things that were wrong with her lately. And they were all centered on one very disturbing, frightening man. "I'm tired," she mumbled, knowing that although it was the truth it was also a very poor excuse.

"Tired! Tired!?" he demanded sharply.

Cassie hung her head, peeking up at him from under lowered lashes. She deserved whatever she got, but it was still killing her to keep from defending herself. Luther sighed angrily; pulling off his Lennon style glasses he cleaned them briskly on his shirt as he tried to gather his patience. He slid them back on, relatively calmer as he studied her wearily.

"Alright." He tugged on his graying brown hair; he paced briefly away before he turned sharply on his heel and coming back. "Maybe I am working you to hard. Maybe you need a break, you all do. We'll take the rest of tonight off."

Cassie wanted to protest, taking time off wouldn't help her. She knew that. Just as she knew that none of them could afford to lose time practicing their fighting skills. "Luther…"

"No, no." His English accent became slightly heavier the more discombobulated he became. "A night off will do us all some good. But you need to come back refreshed and rested Cassie. You are the best fighter we have, if you don't get your act together than we're all in danger."

Cassie bit on her bottom lip as she struggled to keep hold of the anger and shame threatening to consume her. Tremors rocked her, tears burned her eyes, but she would not allow herself to shed them. She had to get her act together, and she had to do it soon. She was overtired right now, that was her whole problem. She just needed some sleep.

Fighting to keep hold of her wildly swaying emotions, she glanced around the converted garage. It was packed full of weapons, punching bags, and exercise equipment. Luther had added onto the two car garage a couple years ago, making it twice as big as its original size. She had spent a lot of time in this room, poured a lot of sweat, and shed more than a few tears along with some blood.

And she hated it, she hated everything that this room represented and the change it had brought to her life. She kept her hate hidden though, kept it locked away, buried beneath the fear and terror that she didn't allow to show. Turning away from the metal swords and crossbows strapped to the wall, she focused her attention on Luther, Melissa, and Chris.

"It's time to go home," she said softly.

"Yes, yes," Luther agreed. "Rest for the next night and then we'll hit it hard again tomorrow."

Cassie nodded, though the last thing she wanted was to ever have to come back here. However, she didn't have an option. She would have to come back over and over again until they left town, or she died. Both options sucked.

"Will you be ok after tonight?" She nodded in response to Luther's question. His aggravation had been replaced with a deep worry that rattled her. He was the closest thing to a father she had, and right now he looked completely terrified for her. She didn't like it one bit. "Are you sure?"

"Cassie." She turned toward Melissa, hating the knowledge in her onyx eyes. Though Cassie had not mentioned her dreams to anyone, or her bizarre attraction to Devon, Melissa saw far more than Cassie wanted her to. But then, she always did. "Maybe a sleeping pill would help you."

Cassie hid her surprise, nodding briskly as she turned toward Chris. He offered her a wan smile as he held his arm out to her. Though she loved them both dearly, there were times when she wished they didn't know her so well, or possess such probing gifts. Hiding her irritation, she slipped her arm into Chris's, squeezing it briefly as she leaned against his side.

She had always hated taking any medicine, but maybe she should take a pill tonight, she was so damn tired she could barely see straight anymore. And if she didn't get some sleep soon, she was scared that she would break completely.

CHAPTER 7

"Is this a dream?"

Cassie stood across the clearing from him, her golden hair tumbling in a riotous mass about her bared, creamy shoulders. The white dress she wore billowed gently about her bare feet. She was stunning, breathtaking, and he knew that if his heart could still beat it would have stopped at the sight of her. The soft breeze pushed strands of hair around her delicate features. She reached up, pulling it back as it drifted across one of her eyes.

Her eyes drifted away, a small smile played over her mouth as she stared at the pristine lake in the middle of the field. Her toes curled into the thick grass beneath her bare feet as her smile widened. "Beautiful," she breathed.

He completely agreed, but his gaze did not stray from her. She turned slowly back to him, her head tilted to the side as she studied him questioningly. "You're everywhere," she whispered.

He started slightly, his hands fisted at his sides. His own bare feet curled into the springy grass he stood upon. The long blades tickled slightly, but he ignored them as he took a small step toward her. For a moment fear flashed through her eyes, she didn't move away from him though. "Am I?" he inquired softly, his entire body aching to touch her, to hold her, to pull her close to him.

"Yes." Though she looked like she wanted to bolt, she didn't move. "You're in my school and my thoughts, and you haunt my dreams." She turned slowly back toward the lake, her delicate brow furrowed slightly. "But this one is so very real." The words were a bare whisper; the surprise was evident and raw in her voice. "So real. It must be that pill I took."

He stopped moving for a moment. "Pill?" he inquired.

She turned back to him, her eyes somber and distant. "Yes. I needed to sleep. I *had* to sleep before I dropped." She shook her head, causing her hair to cascade around her. "But you make it so very difficult for me to function at all, never mind sleep. I hate taking medication though, and apparently these pills cause some intense dreams. I can feel the grass, *actually feel* it beneath my feet. That is so *odd*!"

"Yes," he agreed, because he could find no other words for her. *He* made it difficult for *her* to function! If she only knew what she did to him on a daily, hourly, secondly basis! And yet he couldn't stop the elation that filled him, this may only be a dream, but there was also something different about it, something very real and solid. Something that made him believe that she was actually standing there with him, that she was actually expressing her true emotions.

"Cassie," he breathed, suddenly needing to touch her with a desperation that bordered on insanity.

Fear trickled across her amazing features, horror widened her eyes, but she did not move as he stepped closer to her. Instead, a resignation seemed to settle over her. The fear faded as need and desire suddenly blazed to fierce life within her. "I don't want to fight my dreams anymore," she whispered.

A single tear trickled down her cheek as he stopped before her. He could almost feel the fierce beat of his heart, almost feel the pulse pounding through his veins as he reached out and gently wiped the single, shimmering tear from her face. Her eyes were wide with awe and wonder as she watched him. Her cheek was silken beneath his thumb as he caressed her.

This was the strangest dream he had ever had, and he didn't give a damn. It was also the best one he'd ever had. "Cassie," he whispered again, leaning closer to her. All he wanted to know was what her mouth would feel like, what her wonderful lips would be like against his. All he wanted to know was how she would taste. All he wanted was to hold her and feel her.

"Devon." Her hand, delicate and small, came up to his. Her fingers wrapped tightly around his, her breath caught in her throat as her eyelids drifted down to shadow her eyes. "I've wanted this for so long," she breathed. "I think I wanted this even before I met you. I think I knew you were out there somewhere. It makes no sense." She shook her head in confusion. "I am so glad this is only a dream. I sound like an idiot."

"Never," he whispered fervently, relishing in every one of her baffled thoughts. He was so very glad to hear that she felt as confused and desperate as he did. "I understand exactly what you mean." And he truly did. Though the feelings made no sense, and he did not understand how they could be so strong when he hardly knew her, they were very real, and very true.

Her eyes sparkled with amusement; the bright amethyst flecks in them were bright in the midmorning sun. She was the most achingly innocent, beautiful woman he had ever met. And she was far too good for him. He should stay away from her; he should flee while he still could. It would be far safer for her if he walked out of her life, he would only bring her heartache and misery, no matter how much he didn't want to.

But he could not bring himself to move. Even though this was only a dream, he knew that whatever happened within this world would change their waking world also. And he fervently wanted for their waking world to change. Fervently wanted to be able to touch her, and feel her, and speak with her for real. His hand trembled on her cheek for a moment, he needed this. He needed *her*.

"Tell me no," he whispered.

Her smile widened. "I don't want to."

His deadened heart seemed to kick start again at her words. Joy and desire tore through him as his hand wrapped around the back of her skull, savoring in her silken hair. He pulled her gently toward him, tilting her head up. Her eyes drifted closed, her lips parted on a soft sigh. Her sweet breath washed over him as he brought his mouth to hers.

Electricity surged through him, for the first time in so many centuries he felt alive again, and so completely whole. She eased the aching loneliness inside of him, made him forget his entire awful existence. She was everything good and right in the world, she was everything that he had been searching for, and she was completely *his*.

Possession and desire tore through him. His hand wrapped around her waist, pulling her tighter against him. He could feel the wild beat of her heart as her chest pressed tight to his. Her pulse pounded through her veins, but yearning for her blood did not seize hold of him. With her, he had complete control of himself. With her, bloodlust did not take over. He did not want to drain her dry as he had done to so very many other people. Maybe just because this was a dream he could keep control of himself, but he felt that even awake he would be able to do anything for her. Even control the monster that always lurked just beneath the surface of his existence.

A gasp of pleasure escaped her as her hands wrapped tightly around his shoulders, and her fingers dug into him. Her mouth parted beneath his demanding quest. A groan escaped him as his desire for more of her seized hold of him. His hands drifted over her bare shoulders, the feel of her silken skin left him shaken as he moved closer to the collar of the dress she wore. She moaned softly, he caught hold of her as her knees went limp and she slumped against him.

His composure swiftly unraveling, he seized hold of her dress, wanting to rip it free of her. This was *his* dream after all, and he could do anything he wanted in it. And he wanted her.

The scent of her tears stopped his rushing, heedless movements. He pulled slightly back from her, horrified that he had hurt her, or that he had frightened her with his urgency. Even if it was just a dream he couldn't bring himself to hurt her. He did not know the extent of her experiences with men, but he sensed that they were not much. And there was no way that she had ever been pawed and molested by a nearly crazed vampire before.

But it made no sense, if this was his dream she shouldn't be crying, she should be throwing herself at him with reckless abandon. If this was his dream, he shouldn't be feeling like he was actually experiencing her emotions. Something niggled at the back of his mind, but he shoved aside any doubts and questions, he didn't want to face them right now.

"Cassie what is wrong? Did I hurt you? Please," he whispered. "Please tell me that I did not hurt you."

She shook her head wildly. He gently pulled back the strands of hair that fell across her damp cheeks. Cupping her chin, he lifted her face to his. Tears slid silently down her cheeks, her eyes were bright and damp with unshed ones. Though he had been frightened that he had hurt her, there was happiness and joy radiating from her.

"Cassie?"

"I'm fine," she breathed, reaching up to cup his hand in hers as she leaned into his touch. "I'm just so happy here. This, this is just the most wonderful thing that I have ever experienced. *You* are the most wonderful thing that I have ever experienced. I can say that here because it isn't real." Her eyes darted away from his for a moment. "But out there…"

She shook her head, closing her eyes as she nestled closer. "Out there what?" he asked softly, knowing that she was talking about the world that existed outside of this dream one.

Her eyes darkened, her face hardened slightly with anger. "Out there everything is hard. Out there, this cannot be."

Confusion filled him as he studied her. She kept her gaze focused on the lake, more tears filled her eyes. But he sensed these were tears of sorrow and loss, not of joy. He did not understand what she was talking about, but it was more than apparent that she was greatly upset about something.

"Cassie look at me." Her attention returned to him, her forehead furrowed. "Why is it hard? Why can't this be?"

Though she smiled wanly, the depth of her sorrow was nearly palpable. "I wish that I could tell you." She shook her head. "You wouldn't believe me anyway."

"I would believe anything you told me."

Her eyes warmed and melted. "You are wonderful," she whispered. "So wonderful. I've never felt like this with anyone before, never even knew it could be possible to feel like this. Even though it's a dream, I feel like you would be like this in the real world, that you would make me feel this good."

"I would," he promised, surprised by the strange turn of events this dream was taking. It was *his* dream after all, she should be in his arms still, she should be happy still. She should not be lost and wounded and talking in riddles that he couldn't unravel. She should tell him what was bothering her, not keep it hidden from him.

What kind of crazy damn dream was this anyway?

Though she kept her face pressed into the palm of his hand she turned her attention back to the lake. "I used to love coming here," she whispered.

Devon started in surprise as he turned toward the pristine lake. The field surrounding it was covered with blue, yellow, and white wild flowers that flowed toward the edge of a thick forest. The blades of grass, and wild flowers, swayed beneath the soft breeze that trickled over them. There was a dock stretching toward the middle of the lake.

A single tree was off to the side, a rope swing was tied to a branch that dipped over the water. He could almost hear children laughing as they swung out over the water and released the rope.

Though it could have been one of a hundred lakes in the world, it was not one that he had ever seen before. "You know this place?" he inquired softly.

She turned back to him, the sorrow momentarily slipping from her as she grinned brightly. "Oh, very well. It's Lake Waldorph. Chris and I used to spend three weeks every summer at the camp just beyond those woods. Those were wonderful summers."

Devon focused on the lake again; horror filled him as he turned from its smooth surface back to her. This was not only his dream, he realized with a start, but also *hers*. Though he was the one that had brought her into the dream, it was her mind that had created the setting. It was why she was not telling him the things he wanted to hear from her. It was why her sorrow and reluctance were real. It was why things were not going the way he wanted them to, because they were also going her way.

His body began to go numb with the shock and disbelief filling it. He knew how their minds had connected, knew *he* had been the one to do it. But he'd had no intention of ever letting such a thing happen. But while asleep, his subconscious must have reached out to hers. It had taken hold of her mind, and drawn it in. He had never had any intention of *ever* seizing hold of her mind, but apparently his subconscious had not felt the same way.

Devon bit back a curse, not wanting to frighten or upset her anymore. There was no reason for her to know what had happened, how this had occurred, or the reason that it felt so real was because there were two minds creating it. It was better for her to continue to consider this just a strange, oddly real dream. She could never know what he was, what he was capable of, what he could do to her. He didn't know her well, but she would run screaming if she knew the truth, and he would not blame her in the least.

The only problem was that no matter what she said, or what she *wanted*, he was afraid that this dream might mean she wouldn't have an option. And he feared that neither did he. They barely knew each other, but his ability had taken them both over, and brought them both here. He had never had such a thing happen before, had never lost control of his ability in such a way. Even when he had been a novice, floundering and uncertain of his powers, he had never lost control of them.

He had a bad feeling that he finally knew what all of this meant. He just didn't want to recognize the truth of it. He still didn't even have a place to stay in town yet and hadn't intended to stay in town for much longer. Now he was fearful that he may not have a choice about staying or going.

Wrapping his fingers through hers, he shut his thoughts off, not wanting to deal with them right now. He knew that it would only result in a tangled mess of confusion that he was not in the mood to sort through. For now, all he wanted was to hold her, talk to her, and make both of their dreams come true.

"Would you like to sit by the lake?"

Her face lit with pleasure, her eyes sparked merrily. He knew in that moment that he would do everything he could to make her smile like that as often as possible. "I would love to."

He led her slowly down to the water, stopping at the edge of the lake. The water lapped gently against his feet. "Just as warm as I remember," Cassie whispered.

"Why did you stop coming to camp here?"

She shrugged, her hand tightened briefly as a tremor of tension raced through her. "There wasn't any time for camp once Luther and Melissa came."

He stared at her in surprise; his eyebrows drew tightly together as he thought over her strange words. "Who is Luther?"

"Melissa's father, adoptive father," she amended.

Devon shook his head in confusion. "I don't understand. What does he have to do with the fact that you could no longer go to camp?"

She turned toward him, holding her hair back as the breeze briefly picked up. For a moment grief enveloped her and that lost look filled her eyes again. But then her gaze cleared, and she smiled brightly at him. She squeezed his hand before standing on tiptoe to kiss him briefly. Devon started in surprise; he enjoyed the playful demeanor that suddenly enveloped her. He was certain that it was not an attitude she had very often.

"This is a dreary topic for such a wonderful dream, and one that I do not want to think about right now. I think about it too often during the day."

Devon was once again confused as to what she was talking about. What did Melissa's adopted dad have to do with anything major in her life, other than taking care of her friend, and maybe driving them to the movies or dances once in awhile? Those things were certainly not something that would occupy her thoughts often during the day, at least not as often as she had just suggested.

Before he could question her further, she tilted her head to the side, looking impish and striking. "I would much rather go swimming."

With that she released his hand and plunged into the water. Her beautiful laughter trailed off as she dove beneath the surface. Devon stood in shocked wonder for a moment before shrugging negligently. It had been a very long time since he had gone swimming, and he could think of no one he would rather do it with.

Cassie burst back to the surface, inhaling deeply. Her skin glimmered in the light of the sun, her dress was tight against her and drops of water clung to her as she smiled beckoningly at him. Excitement spurted through him. She was tantalizing, irresistible, and completely delicious looking. He could not refuse her as he began to wade into the warm water.

He was only feet from her when her head tilted to the side, her eyebrows drew sharply together and irritation flitted over her delicate features. "What is that noise?" she mumbled.

"What noise?"

He could hear nothing except for the gentle lapping of the waves against their skin. "Alarm," she whispered.

And then she was gone. Horror and terror filled Devon as he looked frantically around for her. It took him a few moments to realize that she had simply awakened. She had not disappeared for good. He still couldn't help the disappointment that crashed over him in suffocating waves. He had wanted more time with her, wanted to enjoy her more, hold her more. He had not wanted this to end so soon.

Retreating from the lake he returned to the shore, ignoring the feel of the grass now. It did not matter as much without her here to enjoy it with him. Sighing, he slid to the ground, draping his arms over his knees he stared at the serene lake that Cassie had placed here. He wanted to know more about her. He wanted to know about her days at camp, her childhood, and life experiences both happy and sad. He wanted to know everything that there was to know about her, and he was tired of being avoided all the time.

He did not care about the confusion and doubt that resided inside of him; did not care about her strange talk, or the fact that he had lost control of his ability. There was only one thing that he cared about now. It no longer matter that Cassie fought him every step of the way, he was going to get closer to her in real life. He was going to make their dream come true.

CHAPTER 8

Cassie breezed into the kitchen, humming cheerfully under her breath as she grabbed an apple from a bowl on the center island. Her grandmother looked up at her in surprise, freezing in the act of beating some scrambled eggs. Her eyes widened, her delicate strawberry colored eyebrows drew sharply together as her azure eyes tracked Cassie's every movement. Reaching over her grandma turned down the country song drifting softly from the radio.

"You seem much happier today."

Cassie nodded, stopping to drop a kiss on her grandmother's soft cheek. Though she was in her late fifties, she barely looked a day over thirty. Only soft laugh lines marred the corners of her eyes and mouth. Her shoulder length, strawberry blond hair, was pulled into a lose ponytail that bounced against her neck.

"A little."

"Did you finally get some sleep?"

Cassie nodded, a small smile flitted over her mouth as she recalled the night of sleep she'd had. Though she knew that it had only been a dream, and could only *ever* be a dream, it had still been wonderful. It had still left her feeling warm, and alive, and strangely loved this morning. Her gaze darted to the window as Chris emerged from his house.

"Yes," Cassie answered absently.

Though she had woken up strangely revived and optimistic, the sight of Chris's slumped shoulders reminded her that this was not some strangely realistic dream. This was her life. And in her life, there was no room for hope and optimism. There was no room to have feelings for someone, because in the end they would only both get hurt. Though she reminded herself of these things, she could not stop the excitement and eagerness that filled her at the thought of seeing Devon today. She was playing with fire, and bound to get burned, but at this moment she could not put the matches down.

"Luther is working you all too hard," her grandmother muttered before returning to her eggs.

"We're fine, grandma."

She glanced sharply back up at Cassie. "You haven't been fine for the past week."

Cassie shrugged as she shoved the apple into her bag. She didn't want to meet her grandmother's eyes; she knew how sharp the woman was. She would not see past Cassie's pretense of being fine. "I was just a little stressed over school."

"Hmm," she grunted. "You're too young for such responsibilities."

Cassie sighed softly as she heaved her backpack onto her shoulder. Chris was already parked on the street, waiting for her. He usually came inside in the morning, either to say hi to her grandma, or to steal some food. The fact that he was not coming in led Cassie to believe that he'd had a rough night, and he did not want her grandma to pick up on that fact. Though sitting outside did nothing to keep it hidden.

"You were younger than me when you learned what you were," Cassie reminded her gently. "And you had the same responsibilities."

Her grandmother turned toward her. "I *always* knew what I was Cassie. It was not a shock to me, and at the time we did not fear for our lives as fiercely as we have to now. At the time, we never could have imagined that such a thing as The Slaughter would occur. You should not have had to know either."

"Grandma…"

She waved her hand impatiently. "I know. I know. Luther had to find you; it was part of your destiny after all. I just wish that I could have kept you sheltered from it."

Cassie hurried to her side and hugged her gently. "I know grandma, but there are things in life that we cannot predict, or avoid."

Cassie thought over her words, starting slightly as she realized that they could apply to her situation with Devon. She could not have predicted his arrival, and she was beginning to feel that it would be easier to stop a locomotive than to continue fighting her strong attraction to him. Fear and excitement tore through her; she trembled with anticipation at the same time her mouth went dry with dread. If she did this, there would be no turning back, but she wasn't sure that she wanted to turn back anymore.

"When did you get so smart dear?"

Cassie blinked as she was brought back to the present. "A wise person raised me."

Her grandmother's face lit with her smile, her eyes twinkled with love. "And don't you forget it. Now hurry up, get going, Chris had a rough night."

"Yes," Cassie agreed.

Cassie kissed her cheek again, squeezed her hand, and hurried out of the house. The day was bright and warm, the chill of fall hadn't settled in completely, but the leaves were beginning to change. Cassie glanced up at the clear sky, eagerly inhaling great gulps of fresh air as she tried to steady her tingling nerves and pounding heart. She had a feeling that after today there would be no turning back. That today would either be the day that everything changed, or everything remained the same for good. She no longer knew which one she wanted more.

* * *

Cassie sat stiffly at her desk; her shoulders ached from her ramrod position. But it was impossible to relax, not with *him* only mere feet away. In fact, as long as he was near, she was pretty sure that she was never going to relax again. Not after that dream. Unwillingly, she pressed her fingers to her mouth. She could still recall the heat of his lips against hers, the hard stroke of his tongue, and the press of his solid arms wrapped tightly around her. He had made her feel so safe and protected, and whole. It had been the strangest most realistic dream ever, and she desperately wanted to know what the real life experience would be like.

She had to force herself not to look at him, not to cast surreptitious glances his way. Not to stare at him. Not to relive every moment of pleasure he had given to her last night. It was impossible.

She clenched her hands tight. Her nails dug into her palm, her knuckles ached from the force of it. Her pen was clasped so tight that she feared it would snap. Her body crackled with electricity. Her pulse pounded in her ears, her heart slammed rapidly against her ribs.

She hadn't heard a word Mr. Maddox had said since class started. Unwillingly, her gaze drifted slowly over to Devon. He was sitting casually in his desk, his long legs stretched before him as he stared straight ahead. Those hands that had touched her so reverently last night were splayed before him, the long fingers lying upon the desk. Though his posture was relaxed, she sensed a current of tension and power just beneath his smooth surface. The power that ran through him seemed completely out of place for a normal teenage boy in history class.

She was completely confused by him. Baffled by everything that he represented, though she didn't know what that was.

Seeming to sense her focus, he turned slowly toward her. She knew that she should look away, that she should be embarrassed to have been caught staring, but she couldn't break the magnetic pull he radiated. Her fingers twitched, they longed to touch him. It took everything she had not to reach across the short distance between them, and seize him.

He didn't look away from her as he leaned slightly forward, shifting with an easy grace. His emerald eyes burned with intensity, and a hunger that left her breathless. The slow ripple of his muscles made her mouth go dry as her body erupted with tingles of electricity. She felt like a volcano bubbling beneath the surface, ready to explode in a torrent of molten lava that would certainly destroy her. But she was certain that for a few brief moments she would enjoy being buried beneath the heat.

Her world, her entire *being*, was focused upon him. She *needed* him. The strange thought, and the absolute certainty that accompanied it, left her shaken and frightened. But this time, she could not bolt, and she could not run. She could not turn away from him in order to do so.

Somehow, she didn't know how, but her pen was no longer in her hand, her hand was no longer clenched, and it was no longer upon her desk. Her hand was now in the middle of the aisle, reaching toward him.

She blinked, snapping out of the brief trance that had enshrouded her. Her face flamed red, heat burned down the back of her neck as the realization of what she had been doing crashed over her. He did not grin at her, did not look at all disgusted by her strange behavior as he leaned even closer.

She wanted nothing more than to reach toward him again, to feel him, but she could not bring herself to make such a forward gesture once more. She could not believe she had done it in the first place. It was not within her to make the first move, especially not with someone that she didn't even know, and who now probably thought that she was crazy. The few boys she had dated had *always* approached her first.

The loud ringing of the bell caused her to jump in surprise; she knocked her forgotten pen to the ground. Cassie groaned, disgusted with herself, and the entire situation. She needed to get her act together before she completely lost it. She couldn't continue to let some stranger disturb her life in such a way. She couldn't afford to be so badly distracted, so completely out of whack with *her* reality. People would get hurt if she was.

She shoved her book into her bag and bent over to retrieve her lost pen. But it was no longer where it had fallen upon the ground. Instead, it was held in a long fingered, strong hand that she recognized instantly. Her gaze traveled slowly from the hand, to the man now kneeling before her. His bright eyes clashed with hers. There was a fierce need radiating from him that caused her toes to curl, at the same time that fear tore through her. There would be no going back after this. If she took that pen from him, if she *touched* him, she knew that nothing would ever be the same again.

She could not move; she was frozen in place like a deer trapped in the headlights. A small smile curved the corner of his hard mouth; a twinkle of amusement lit his eyes. Anger spurted through her in the face of the challenge he seemed to radiate, he was daring her to take the pen back. Taking a deep breath, Cassie steeled herself. She was probably overreacting anyway, nothing was going to happen.

Though she knew she was lying to herself, she also knew that she could not simply leave this room, and him, with her pen.

Reaching slowly across, her heart hammered in eager anticipation as her fingers curled around the top of the pen, mere centimeters from where his fingers stopped. Though they were not touching, electricity shot through her, stunning her, leaving her breathless and shaken. Vivid images of the dream sizzled through her. He did not release the pen to her. He did not move as the smile slipped from his face and his eyes burned with the consuming need she had seen in him before.

And then he moved.

His fingers slid slightly up the pen, breaching the small gap between them. Cassie inhaled sharply, something inside of her locked into place, it froze her muscles and kept her immobile. The world disappeared as everything in it became him, became *them*. They were joining, their molecules blending and twining together in a sensuous dance that was soothing and beautiful. Everything suddenly made sense, everything became right. All of the loss, and ache, and loneliness did not hurt as much as his touch became the balm that soothed it all.

The dream last night had been wonderful and beautiful, but the reality was far better than anything she could have ever imagined. In that moment, she knew she had found her home in him. This was where she *belonged*, where she would always belong. Her life would never be the same, but she was no longer frightened by the realization. She was *exhilarated* by it. Everything would be ok now that he was a part of her.

His eyes darkened, his fingers tightened around hers as he clung to her; a tremor shook his powerful frame. A tremor that melted her heart and made her ache to reach out and caress his cheek. She longed to soothe the fear and confusion radiating from him. It did not make her feel better that he seemed just as mystified as she was by all this. No, it only made her wish to get closer to him, to ease the pain in him, to soothe the torment she sensed deep inside him.

She did not know where his torment and anguish came from, but she suspected it ran even deeper and further than her own. And somehow she knew that she could help him with his pain, just as he helped with hers. She could feel the strength running through him, the tight control he exerted over himself. She completely understood his feelings as they were the same ones rattling her too.

He released her suddenly, the loss of contact leaving her shaken and hollow inside. Leaving her broken and lost once more, but the feelings of hurt and confusion were not as consuming or as unbearable as before. He had healed something inside her, somehow his touch had put back some of the pieces of her broken soul.

For a moment he hesitated, his eyes burned into hers as something dark shifted behind his intense gaze. A small smile flitted across his hard mouth. He rose swiftly, with a grace that was breathtaking and stunning. Staring down at her, he was unable to suppress the small tremor racing through him, a tremor that warmed her heart. It was apparent that she affected and rattled him just as much as he shook her, and he hadn't even had the same wonderful dream that she had experienced last night. He reached his hand slowly out to her, a hopeful expression on his face that tugged at her heart.

She stared at his hand, her heart hammering fiercely as she took note of the perfection of his strong fingers. Heaving her bag onto her shoulder, she took a deep breath as she decided to throw her life over to fate. There was no stopping fate after all, and she was surprised to realize that she no longer wanted to. Sliding her hand into his, she clasped tightly hold of it, surprised to note the slightly cooler feel of his skin. She didn't have long to contemplate that thought though as the strange sense of comfort and peace descended over her once more, wrapping her within the warm cocoon of strength and power that he exuded.

He would keep her safe, keep her protected from the hurt and pain of the world; she knew that with every cell of her being. Although, given that she was not entirely human, she was probably stronger and far more capable of protecting *him*. Though, with him, she did not feel as if she were less than human, she did not feel abnormal and freaky. With him, she felt human and feminine and alive in ways that she had not felt in a very long time.

"Where to?" he asked softly, his deep voice sent a shiver of delight down her spine and caused goose bumps to break out on her hypersensitive skin.

The last thing she wanted was to go to another class, but she could not walk out of school with him, like she longed to do. However, she was pretty sure that she couldn't sit through another minute without touching him, and feeling him. Especially not now, not when she knew how wonderful, and right, the feel of him truly was.

Noise drifted to her, breaking through her turbulent, uncertain thoughts. She was surprised to find that the next class was already filtering in. Students glanced questioningly at the two of them as they took their seats. No one from their class remained. Cassie sighed heavily, knowing what she had to do, but wishing that she didn't. "I have Anatomy and Physiology now."

"Lead the way."

Taking a deep breath, she forced herself to start moving, before she couldn't. "What class do you have now?"

He frowned slightly as he dug into the pocket of his jeans and pulled out his rumpled schedule. Though he had been in school for nearly a week, he apparently had not learned it yet. But then again, it did change every day. "Study hall."

The frown on his face surprised her; he almost looked confused as he stared at the paper, his dark eyebrows drawn tightly together. For a moment it appeared as if he didn't know what study hall was, but that was impossible, every student knew what study hall was. Didn't they? "That's probably in the library, but some are held in classrooms," she said softly.

"Library."

"Do you want me to take you there?" she asked, certain that his confused expression was because he didn't know where to go.

He glanced up at her; a small smile curved his full mouth. Cassie felt her heart melt, her toes curled at the sight of that heart stopping grin. He appeared so much younger, more approachable, and nowhere near as hard when he smiled like that. She had thought that he was gorgeous before, but now, smiling, he was *magnificent*. It took all she had not to reach out and stroke his face, not to bury herself against him, hold him tight and shut out the rest of the world. Something she knew that he would be able to help her do.

"Trying to get rid of me already?" he inquired lightly.

Cassie couldn't stop herself from grinning back at him. "No," she answered honestly. "I just don't want you to get lost."

He shoved the schedule back in his pocket, his hand tightened around hers. "I've found you, how could I be lost?"

Cassie blinked in surprise, staring breathlessly up at him as her heart lurched with wonderful joy. It was the sweetest thing anyone had ever said to her, and though it sounded like a pickup line, his tone rang with sincerity and truth. If anyone else had said that to her, she probably would have laughed at them and blown them off as corny. But this was different. This was not corny, it seemed genuine. It felt right, and she realized that if *she* had been the one to say it to him, she would have meant it.

It would have been true.

Their hands fit perfectly together; his was stronger and larger as it wrapped gently around hers. His touch was everything she had dreamed it would be, and more. His presence alone had helped to fill the holes inside her, but his physical touch was like aloe on sunburn. His touch made it so she could move a little more freely, and breathe easier than she had in years.

She had never believed in love at first sight, never believed in soul mates. But maybe, somehow, her body and her spirit had known that he was out there, and it had been waiting and searching for him all along. And she *had* been completely miserable without him. But she didn't feel misery now; she felt a joy so pure that she kept expecting to float off the ground with the lightheartedness consuming her.

He was staring down at her, his emerald eyes stormy and intense. He was waiting for her to say something, waiting for her reaction. Cassie could not find words; she could only manage a simple, reassuring smile.

The tension eased from him. His eyes crinkled with the bright smile that lit his wonderful face. Cassie couldn't stop herself from grinning back at him. "I'll be fine; the library was one of the first things Melissa showed me the other day." He said easily, as if what he had just said to her had not left her as shaken as a baby's rattle.

Swallowing heavily, Cassie tried to calm the turmoil racing through her. If it had been just a pick up line, she did not want him to know that he had just caught her hook, line, and sinker. "Of course it was."

They reached her class far faster than she would have liked. Hesitating in the hall, she turned to him, reluctant to let go. "I'll see you soon," he said softly, his eyes rapidly scanning her face, seemingly trying to remember every detail of her.

Cassie nodded, not fully trusting herself to speak. She half felt like crying, which was completely crazy, it wouldn't be that long before she saw him again. She hoped. His hand tightened around hers, his skin burned into hers. He took a step closer, and for a moment Cassie was certain that he was going to kiss her. She held her breath in anticipation, her entire body clamored for the feel of his lips against hers.

Instead, he squeezed her hand briefly and released it quickly. Cassie felt the loss of his touch as acutely as a knife to her heart. Her entire being ached for it again. She couldn't move as he slipped away, disappearing into the remaining crowd.

CHAPTER 9

Devon folded his arms over his chest, leaning against the wall as he waited impatiently for the bell to ring. He had tried to sit through the whole study hall thing, but he didn't understand what he was supposed to be doing, or why he even had the class. But then again, he didn't understand any of this high school stuff. They were like rats in a maze, going through the same thing day after day.

He supposed education was a good thing; he simply had no use for it. Maybe if he was a human in this day and age he may have needed it, but he wasn't. When he had been human, he'd had schooling because he had been a member of the aristocracy, and it had been expected of him. But even before he'd died, he'd seen no reason to continue with his education. Even as a human he had simply taken everything he wanted, with no regard for whom he hurt in the process. And when he'd died he'd become even worse, far *far* worse. It was not a fact he was proud of, it was just a fact that he had to live with, and try to atone for, every day of his lonely existence.

An existence that somehow wasn't as lonely whenever she was near.

Now, staring at the empty hall, he wondered if he had missed out on something. His, had been a long existence. He'd thought that he had done everything there was to do; apparently he had forgotten one thing. He just wasn't so sure that he wanted the experience, it was tiring. He did want *her* though. He wanted to see her and touch her, and he wanted to be near her, and she spent a good chunk of her time within this building.

His dreams had been nothing compared to the reality of her, but he had known that they wouldn't be. Her skin was even softer, warmer, and gentler. The feeling of rightness she brought to him was amazing. It was something he had never expected to experience in his life, but now that he had it, he was not going to let it go. *Ever.*

Though he knew where his fierce possessiveness of her might be coming from, he was still unwilling to explore that possibility, or reality, yet. There was still a chance that he could walk away from her even if he didn't want to. Her safety was number one as far as he was concerned, and she could never be truly safe with him in her life. He needed to be able to walk away, but if what he suspected was true, there was a good possibility that he may not be able to.

He had meant what he'd said to her earlier, he was not lost when she was near. He was whole in a way that he had never been whole before, not even when he had been alive. When she was near, he did not feel adrift in a world where he was not welcome among humans, or vampires. She was an anchor in a world that was cold, uncaring, and cruel. If staying here, torturing himself in high school was the only way to be close to her then he was going to suffer through the classes like everyone else.

He shifted slightly, the discomfort in his veins growing by the second. He should have fed before he came here today, but he hadn't realized how hard it would be to keep control around her. She was a temptation that he couldn't resist, not anymore; especially now that he had touched her. And now that he had felt her, he knew he would never stop touching her.

The only problem was that the burning in his veins had kicked into hyper drive the minute his skin had brushed against hers. The sweet scent of her blood had slammed into him, causing his mouth to water and his body to burn with the fierce hunger that engulfed him. It had taken every bit of self restraint he had not to rip her against him and sink his teeth into her delicate white throat, draining the delicious blood that flowed through her veins.

He had not touched a drop of human blood in a hundred and thirty seven years, and until that moment he had never felt the desire so fiercely, or so acutely. He had never had his control nearly shattered, never nearly snapped and drained a person simply from touching them. But as much as she unsettled him, and rattled his firm restraint, she had also calmed him in a strange way. His baser instincts were held at bay as her delicate fingers curled around his. Touching her had locked the demon inside him back in its cage; it had calmed his raging urge to drain the blood from her even more than it had enticed it. Whatever spell she had cast over him had him completely ensnared.

Glancing at the clock on the wall, he shifted slightly, growing impatient to see her, growing completely impatient with the high school life. Over seven hundred years old and he was lurking in the hallways of adolescent teenagers, and all because of a girl. Granted, she was an exceptional girl, and he was captivated by her, but never had he gone to such lengths for a woman before. He had *never* thought that he would either. And he was fairly certain that this was only the beginning of what he would do for her.

The annoying bell rang suddenly, its sound was exceptionally sharp in his sensitive ears, but it was a welcome distraction from his disconcerting thoughts. Stepping away from the wall, his arms fell back to his sides as he eagerly waited for her to emerge from the class. Doors were flung open around him, chatter spilled into the halls as students emerged. He was barely aware of the humans as they filtered around him, the boys instinctively leaving a larger gap then they would with anyone else. The girls drifted closer, "accidentally" bumping into him, giggling flirtatiously as they openly admired him.

He ignored them, his attention fixed upon the people filing out of Cassie's class. He could smell her; feel the beat of her tiny, delicate heart. She appeared in the doorway, her mouth parting, her step faltering slightly as she caught sight of him. The small redhead that had been speaking to her broke off abruptly, her brown eyes widened in surprise.

He did not think about it as he instinctively reached his hand out to Cassie, relief filled him as her fine boned fingers slid into his, locking tight. The beast inside of him quieted instantly. The burning in his veins lessened as her presence soothed the edgy rawness in him. He could not separate from her again. If he did, he would not make it through the rest of this day.

Her smile was easy and bright as she stared up at him, the sight of her beautiful face calming him even further. "Um yeah, I'll talk to you later Cass."

Cassie glanced at the redhead, giving her a brief nod before turning her full attention back to him. "You got here quick."

He shrugged, unable to tear his gaze away from her. "I don't really see the point of study hall."

She laughed softly, the sound beautiful and sweet, like the gentle ring of wind chimes. It resonated through his body, shaking him to the marrow of his bones. At that moment, he knew that he would do everything in his power to make her laugh as often as possible. Her eyes twinkled merrily as the laughter broke off, but she continued to smile radiantly up at him.

"Most people look forward to study hall; it's their favorite time of day, other than lunch of course."

"I don't see why, there's nothing to do."

"That's exactly why."

Devon shook his head, realizing that he would never understand humans again. Though, he hadn't really understood them when he'd been human. There was no pleasure in doing nothing, it drove him crazy. "I see," he said, even though he didn't.

Her smile slid away as she frowned questioningly up at him. "Didn't they have study hall at your old school?"

"Of course," he lied smoothly, sensing that to do anything else would seem odd. "I didn't see the point of it then either."

She smiled again, shaking back a strand of golden hair that had slid into one of her exquisite eyes. Without thinking, he reached forward and brushed the hair aside. She froze, her breath catching in her chest, her eyes wide upon him as his fingers lingered on her silken skin. He found he could not take his hand away as he stroked lightly over the delicate contours of her face. He recalled touching her like this last night but it was nothing, *nothing* compared to this.

She did not move, did not even breathe as she watched him in silent, fascinated wonder. Her eyes searched his face in awe, her mouth parted slightly. In her gaze he could see her own recollection of the dream. Her heartbeat kicked up, her pulse pounded loudly through her veins. He did not feel a surge of hunger this time, felt no desire to drain her dry as he was completely ensnared and entranced by her.

"Cassie!"

She jumped slightly; his hand fell away as Chris's sharp voice broke through the odd spell encasing them both. He took a step closer to her, fierce possession tearing through him as Chris appeared at her side. Chris's blue eyes narrowed as he met Devon's gaze, his shoulders stiffened. "Hi Chris," she greeted, her voice sounding slightly strained and confused.

"Did you do the homework?"

Cassie rolled her eyes. "Yes, but there's not enough time for you to copy it."

"I know I just wanted to make sure you had done it also."

Cassie's forehead furrowed in confusion as she frowned at Chris. Devon was nowhere near as confused as Chris shot him a dark, warning look. Though Melissa felt that they were more like siblings, Devon was beginning to believe that Chris's feelings were not so platonic, and he did not like the competition that Devon threw into the mix.

Devon didn't particularly care what Chris thought, or wanted. Cassie was going to belong to him no matter what. He took another step closer, his shoulder brushing against hers, his hand tightening on hers. Chris's narrowed eyes followed him, his broad shoulders stiffened slightly. "Are you going to English now?" he asked sharply.

"Of course, I'll see you there." Though it had been a clear dismissal, Chris lingered for a few seconds more, his gaze was steady as he stared hard at Devon. Chris glanced briefly at Cassie before turning on his heel and disappearing into the thick throng of students. She turned back to Devon, confusion still evident in her features. "Ready for class?"

He fought back a groan, he wasn't ready at all. He wanted to stay here, with her, but he was in her world now, and unfortunately he had to obey the rules that came along with it. Even if the rules sucked. The only good thing was that he knew they had the same class now.

He followed her down the hall, taking note of the people surrounding him for the first time. Or at least taking note of the boys. Many of them didn't acknowledge his presence as they gazed eagerly upon her. His temper bristled at the obvious desire behind their stares. They did not care about his presence, would easily ignore him if they thought they had a chance to talk to her, to be near her.

It was a fact he didn't like, but would remedy very shortly. Following her into a classroom, he reluctantly released her hand when he slid into the desk next to her. He had been assigned a seat a few desks away from her, but he had no intentions of sitting there today. Though he could no longer touch her, he wasn't moving any further away from her than this. She watched him with wide eyes, her head tilted slightly to the side.

Chris and Melissa entered the room, their heads bent close together as they talked softly. Chris grew quiet; his eyes darted toward him and Cassie. Melissa quirked a dark eyebrow, a smile flitted across her mouth. She gave Devon a brief nod before sliding into the seat in front of Cassie. Chris sat next to Melissa. The boy who had been assigned Devon's seat hesitated for a moment, looking as if he wanted to argue with the new arrangement. Instead, he wisely closed his mouth and resigned himself to Devon's abandoned seat.

Cassie's grin widened as she chuckled softly. Unable to resist her any longer, he leaned across the aisle and took her hand. He was acutely aware of the fact that she had stopped breathing and was watching him in wide eyed wonder. She clung to him with a desperation that he recognized instantly, as it resided inside of him also.

He never wanted to release her again; unfortunately he didn't have a choice as the teacher breezed into the classroom. She dropped her books on her desk, and turned swiftly toward the chalkboard. Though she had not noticed them yet, it was only a matter of time before she did. He released Cassie's hand reluctantly.

Though they were separated, he kept his hearing attuned to every beat of Cassie's heart. He was well aware of the delicious scent that wafted from her skin and hair. Now that they were no longer touching the hunger began to kick in again. His mouth started to water, the burning in his veins intensified. For a moment it took all he had not to grab hold of her and taste her. The temptation was almost more than he could handle. Clenching his teeth, and his fists, he forced himself to relax, to keep restrained. The last thing he wanted was to hurt her, to take her against her will, to have her know that he was a monster. He would rather kill himself first.

Fighting hard against his baser instincts, and the raging demon inside him, he eventually regained control and was simply able to enjoy her soothing presence once more.

He was beside her again the moment the bell rang. Her touch soothed him further, easing the aching tension and hunger coiled tightly within him. Her soft smile warmed him. "Would you like to show me all of the town hotspots tonight?" he asked, unable to stop himself from grinning at her like a fool as they made their way slowly outside.

Her laugh was enchanting. "Well you've already seen the number one spot, B's and S's."

"Yes, and it was amazing."

She laughed again, shaking back her golden hair. "Well, their shakes definitely are. But I'd be happy to show you around town if you want."

"I do."

Her long lashes lowered shyly over her eyes, a dull flush stained her cheeks. "Great, I'll uh… oh crap." The smile slid from her face, her light brown eyebrows drew tightly together. "I forgot, I can't tonight, there's something that I have to do."

He tried to contain his disappointment as she stopped walking and turned to face him. Students milled easily past them, eager to get to their cars and escape the crowded parking lot. "Tomorrow night then?"

Her smile returned, but her eyes remained oddly troubled and distant. He could sense a fierce tension swirling through her, an odd sense of regret and loss seemed to fill her. "I would like that."

Though she said yes, he sensed something behind the words, disappointment maybe? Anguish?

"Cassie come on, let's go!"

She glanced over her shoulder to where Chris stood, leaning out of his car with his arm resting on the driver's door. Melissa was by the passenger door, her dark eyes narrowed slightly as she studied them. "I have to go."

Sadness still enveloped her as she met his gaze again. Her hand tightened around his before she released him, her eyes searching his face with an intensity that left him shaken. Loss seemed to envelope her as she took a small step back.

"I'll see you tomorrow then," he said softly, knowing he would see her before then.

He didn't understand what was going on with her, but she seemed to be releasing him, for good. He had no intention of letting her go though. Not now, not after he had finally broken through some of her barriers. Especially not now that he knew the reality of her was far better than the dream version.

"Yes."

She smiled wanly at him before turning and hurrying away. Glancing briefly back she hesitated for a moment, seemingly torn, before joining her friends and slipping into the beat up Mustang. Melissa and Chris watched him for a moment more, their eyes fiercely intense, piercing, and slightly unnerving. There was something strange about those two, something that he could not quite put his finger on. But strangely enough, their oddness was vaguely familiar to him.

He studied the car as they pulled out of the parking lot, wracking his brain for what it was about Chris and Melissa that plagued him. Deciding to put it aside for now, he headed to where he had parked his car. A group of students had gathered around it, most of them were female. He nodded and briefly returned their greetings, but barely paid them any attention as he hit the button on his remote. The car beeped in response and the locks popped open.

"Devon! Devon!"

He turned as Marcy hurried up to him, smiling brightly as she adjusted her books in her arms. "Marcy," he greeted tonelessly.

She chose to ignore his lack of a warm greeting as she reached out to touch his arm lightly. He moved away from her grasp. "I was wondering if you would give me a ride home."

He frowned at her, his eyes darting back toward the Mustang that was stuck in traffic at the entranceway of the school. He knew what Marcy was angling for, knew that she wanted to be seen pulling out of this parking lot with him. And though he was new to high school, he had quickly learned how fast gossip and rumors spread through the small social network. He didn't want those rumors starting about him. Not now that he had finally reached Cassie, not now that she was finally talking to him, and acknowledging his existence.

"What's the matter with your car?"

She frowned at him, her leaf colored eyes narrowing slightly. It was apparent she had not expected any kind of hesitance on his part. "Well I usually ride with Kara, but her car isn't starting."

Devon moved even further away from her, his hand rested lightly on his door handle. He didn't want to leave the girl stranded, but he also didn't want to let her in his car. He knew his affect on women, but there were some that were drawn to him even more than others. Marcy appeared to be one of those girls. It would not end well if he let her pursuit of him continue.

"I'm sorry Marcy, but there is something that I must do. I'm sure one of your other friends could give you a ride." It was not a lie; he did need to find a place to stay. He was tired of hotel rooms and floating about. He hadn't had any intention of remaining when he first arrived in this town, now he had *no* intention of leaving.

Marcy's eyes narrowed slightly, anger sparked through them. She turned briefly, her gaze darting toward the Mustang that was now at the front of the line. "I saw you speaking with Cassie."

Devon stiffened, his hand slid away from the door handle. Even if he had been human, he never could have missed the hostility in her tone, or her gaze. "Yes."

She chose to ignore the warning in his tone as her gaze slid slowly back to him. "It would probably be best if you stayed away from her."

"And why is that?" he grated through clenched teeth.

Marcy shrugged as she plastered a falsely sweet smile on her face. "You could do better."

"Like you?"

She blinked in surprise, than her smile widened. "Well, you never know," she responded, lowering her eyelashes flirtatiously. "If you play your cards right."

Devon stepped closer to her, bending down to make sure that his words were not overheard by the group surrounding them. He knew he had to nip this in the bud now, but he did not wish to humiliate the girl. "That is never going to happen Marcy. I'm sorry, but I have no interest in you."

She gazed up at him, her eyes wide with surprise before they narrowed furiously. He decided that was his cue to leave, before she lost her composure completely. Swinging his car door open, he slipped swiftly inside.

CHAPTER 10

Cassie moved slowly beside Chris, her feet dragged along the sidewalk. It used to be after a night of training that she would feel invigorated and pumped. Tonight, she felt bone weary and beaten. Though the night off had been needed, she was still unable to concentrate on any moves, could not throw a stake, or even defend the blows that Chris and Melissa had thrown at her. She had been the best of the three of them in training and fighting, but now she looked like a floundering newbie. She was just grateful it had not been a real fight, or she would be dead right now.

Luther was still frustrated with her lack of concentration, and ability, but his irritation was nothing compared to hers. Her entire body ached, but not from the beaten she had taken tonight. She ached for *him*. She ached to see him, and to touch him again. It was a physical itch that had gone deeper than her skin; it had imbedded itself into the marrow of her bones and taken hold of her soul.

She would never be free of him again.

Confusion, fear, and distress tore through her at the thought, and the certainty that accompanied it. For the past four years she had tried to keep things as simple as possible, but they were not simple anymore. She had spent the past years concentrating on four things, and four things only. And those things had been family, school, training, and hunting. Those four things were all that had gotten her through the years. Her focus upon them had not allowed her time to think about anything else, they had especially kept her from thinking about the future she could never have. She had no dreams of college, did not even plan to attend, and she had stopped daydreaming long ago of marriage, a family, and children.

Now though, she could not stop thinking about the future she couldn't have, the future that had been stolen from her four years ago. She could not stop thinking of Devon, and could not stop her mind from wandering and dreaming. She did not think of marriage and children, she would never allow herself to dream that far. But today her mind had wandered to dates, and dances, and even tomorrow. She was actually looking forward to tomorrow, simply because she was looking forward to seeing him again.

Before Devon, she had never thought of tomorrow. She had simply lived day to day, moment to moment, for she never knew when that moment could be her last. But he had made her forget all of that, and it had shaken her entire world. To hope could be dangerous; she had learned that long ago. Hope only led to disappointment and hurt. She was tired of being hurt; it was much easier to stay safely walled away from the world, safely protected from emotional pain.

But somehow he had managed to tear that wall away. She didn't understand how it had happened, but she knew that she could not keep him out. That he had officially wedged himself into her existence.

For now anyway.

She could not allow herself to hope to far into the future, not past tomorrow at least, for that was already a huge leap. It would be too painful when she lost it all. And she would lose him, just as she had lost so many things that mattered to her.

There were already plans for the three of them, and Luther, to leave after graduation. Though Cape Cod received its fair share of vampires, thanks to tourist season, there were many other places that had a much higher concentration. Areas where they were needed more. On average they only killed ten vampires a year, most in the summer. Though last year it had been fifteen, and this year they were on track to beat that record.

Luther believed that after graduation they would be trained well enough to go where they were needed more, to offer their help and protection somewhere else. Cassie didn't think much about it, she wanted to make it to graduation, she would *like* to graduate, but she did not plan for it. Neither did she panic at the thought of leaving the only town, and the only life she had ever known; for she didn't know if she would ever live to see it happen. She would worry about it if the day came, not a minute sooner.

But today, for one brief moment, she had found herself hoping, and dreaming, and planning for tomorrow. Then, she had gone to training tonight and was forced to remember why she had kept herself so shut off in the first place. She was still completely distracted and uncoordinated. If she had been in the field, she would have been killed. And she would have put Chris and Melissa in danger also.

Devon was a distraction that was risky to her, and her friends. Yet she knew she was not going to let him go. Devon was the only selfish thing she had done since Luther had disrupted her ordinary childhood, and she could not bring herself to give him up. Not yet anyway. If she couldn't find a way to balance her life with him in it, then she would let him go. She would have to.

But she was determined not to let that happen.

She needed the little bit of happiness, and the little bit of hope, that he brought into her life. She had known all along that she was unhappy and lost, but she had not realized just how much until he had arrived. She didn't know if she could stand to retreat behind her wall again. She was greatly afraid that it might destroy her, maybe not physically, but spiritually.

Shuddering deeper into her windbreaker, she wrapped her arms tightly around herself. Though it was not a cold night, there was a chill deep in her bones. The clicking of the tree branches, and the soft rustle of the leaves, did not help the melancholy that enshrouded her. It felt eerie out tonight, somehow wrong, or maybe that was just her.

"Are you ok?" Chris asked softly.

Cassie glanced up at him, noting the worry in his blue eyes. "I'm fine, why?"

He shook his sandy hair back. "You've been out of it for awhile Cass, slow, ungraceful, ill coordinated…"

"Thanks for the vote of confidence," she muttered.

"I'm just saying." He shrugged his massive shoulders and shoved his hands into his pockets. "You've been off, which is very unusual."

"I've got a lot on my mind."

"Hmm." They crossed the street, stepping briefly into the spill of streetlights as they reached the sidewalk. The soft rustle of a coyote in the woods caught Cassie's attention. It moved slowly through the shadows, staying low to the ground as it hunted a small rabbit. Cassie shuddered, an ominous feeling descended upon her. "Is this because of him?"

Cassie jerked as she tore her gaze away from the cruel reality of life. She knew how the rabbit felt because she also felt trapped, desperate, hopeless, with no way out. And there was no way out; no way to escape her heritage.

Chris was studying her intently, worry gleamed in his eyes. She should have known he would notice her strange reaction to Devon. Even if he wasn't using his ability, he didn't miss much. Guilt tugged at her, she had never kept anything from Chris, had never wanted to. But she wasn't sure that she wanted to talk about this now. These feelings were so very new to her, so very private and fragile, and confusing.

Shrugging absently, Cassie brushed back a straggling piece of hair. "I do have other things on my mind, besides a boy."

"Usually yes, lately no. You really like him?"

Cassie was silent, her eyes focused on her Nikes as they moved slowly along. She did not know how to answer that question, for she wasn't sure there was one. Yes, she really liked Devon, but it was far more than just like. She had *never* felt this drawn to someone before, never wanted to be near someone with as much intensity as this. She had never even imagined that feeling like this could ever be possible.

But it was also more. It was something almost primeval and instinctive. She could not say that it was love, for she hardly knew him, but he touched something deep within her soul. He touched something that she had never thought could be touched. Before she had met him she had never even known that this piece of her even existed.

"Yes," she finally admitted. "I suppose you could say that I like him."

Chris was silent for a few moments before sighing softly. "I could sense that he liked you too."

Cassie perked up, her head snapped around as an instantaneous smile sprang forth. "Really?"

He gave her a sad smile as he nudged her shoulder gently. "Of course, who wouldn't?" he teased.

"Chris," she groaned.

His kidding demeanor vanished, his smile faded as he became completely serious. "He definitely feels something for you."

"Did you sense something wrong with him?" she asked tremulously.

He glanced at her in surprise. "Are you actually asking about what I sensed from someone, again?"

Cassie shrugged absently, a dull blush stained her cheeks as she glanced quickly away. She never inquired about what Melissa and Chris knew; it seemed an invasion to her. She wouldn't want other people knowing about her life if they had access to two such gifted people, she felt they deserved the same right. She was also afraid to know what Melissa saw, as all of their futures were so very uncertain. If Chris sensed any danger in a person he would share it with them, whether they wanted to know or not, so there was never a need to ask him.

Sighing heavily, her shoulders drooped slightly as she shook her head. She could not invade Devon's privacy in such a way; she could not press Chris about what he had sensed in him. "No, I suppose not."

Chris draped an arm casually around her shoulders. "I didn't sense anything bad in him, just something different."

Cassie frowned as she glanced up at him, her curiosity was peaked. "Different how?"

"I don't know." His eyebrows drew tightly together; he frowned as he thought carefully before answering. "Just different. There was no harmful intent, but there was a strange sort of darkness inside him."

Cassie frowned, her hands clenched on her arms as she thought over Chris's odd choice of words. "What kind of darkness?"

"I don't know, not an evil one, maybe its loneliness or loss or pain. It's hard to say Cass; some people are just harder to read then others. But there is no ill intent in him; at least not toward you, of that I'm sure."

Cassie bit nervously on her bottom lip. "But toward others?" she asked worriedly.

"No, I don't think so. Why don't you ask Melissa if she has seen anything?" Cassie fervently shook her head, she may ask Chris a few questions, but she would *never* ask Melissa. That seemed like a dangerous path to tread. "You never ask her about anything she sees. Why is that?" She shrugged, not wanting to get into it with him. "Is it because you don't think you have a future?"

Cassie glanced sharply at him, anger boiled rapidly inside of her. "Did you read me?" she demanded fiercely.

Chris was taken aback, his eyes widened slightly. "Of course not Cass, I wouldn't do that to you. Besides, you know that it doesn't work like that. I can't tell what people are thinking, just what they feel and who they are. I don't have to read you to know that you've shut down since we found out what we are."

"I have not, I…"

Chris held up a silencing hand. "You go through the motions of living, but you don't truly *live* anymore. We've always been together Cass, I know the girl you used to be, and you locked that girl away the day that Luther and Melissa walked into our lives."

Cassie remained silent; her eyes darted over the wooded, shadowed streets. She saw nothing out there; no distraction from Chris's probing questions and keen insight. She'd thought she'd hidden herself well, kept her fear buried behind her wall. Apparently she had not. "Do you think you have a future?" she inquired softly, her eyes slowly coming back to his.

He looked sad and lost as he studied her worriedly. "It may not be as long as I had once hoped, but yes, I think I have a future. I often wonder about marriage and kids, and maybe one day I might even retire, and spend my days fishing."

Cassie huffed as she smiled softly at him. "You hate fishing."

"Not the point."

"I know," she sighed.

"But you don't think of those things, do you?"

"No," she admitted reluctantly. "I don't."

"You should. Look at your grandmother, she's a Hunter and she's still alive."

"She's the *only* one that has lived past fifty. Most of us don't make it to twenty, and the remainders usually die before they're thirty. I know some of our history too Chris, my grandmother is an oddity."

He rolled his eyes, his arm tightened briefly on her shoulder. "There's the optimistic Cassie I love," he teased lightly. She frowned at him, slightly wounded by his comment, but knowing that he was right. She was far too pessimistic most of the time. "But seriously, Luther thinks you are one of the best Hunters to ever come along, I'm sure that will make your lifespan longer."

"Yeah, you're probably right," she atoned just to get him to stop talking about it, but she was not fooled into thinking he believed her.

His arm remained tight around her shoulders as they walked on. "Just be careful ok." At her questioning glance he expanded further. "I don't want you to get hurt by him."

She bristled slightly over the fact that he didn't think she could take care of herself. "I won't get hurt."

Chris sighed as he shook back his shaggy hair. "I mean it Cass; you don't have much experience with guys so just take it slow here."

She shot him a fierce look. "I *have* dated before Chris."

He grinned annoyingly down at her, his arm slid forward to drop around her neck as he hugged her against his chest for a brief moment. "Yeah, but you've never really noticed guys before…"

"Of course I have," she interrupted sharply.

"Not like this. You've paid attention to them before, the same attention you would give a puppy, but you have never really *noticed* them."

Cassie's nose wrinkled slightly at his analogy. She did not treat boys like puppies, and of *course* she had noticed them before, she just hadn't felt anything for them. Not like she felt for Devon, nothing even close to that.

"Not like you notice him," Chris continued softly.

Cassie was pulled back as Chris stopped walking. His arm fell from around her as his intense sapphire eyes burned into hers. Cassie shifted uncomfortably, she and Chris shared everything, but this was a topic that had never come up before, and she had never seen him this concerned. "Chris…"

He held up a hand, fending off her words. "I just don't want to see you get hurt. I have to pull the older brother caring bit, even if I'm not your brother." Though he smiled, it did not reach his eyes. "Ok?" She managed a nod. "I would expect you to do the same."

She grinned up at him, but she did not feel lighthearted as she punched him lightly in the shoulder. "But you notice *all* the girls," she reminded him.

Chuckling softly, he draped his arm back around her shoulders and pulled her along. "That I do, that I do. You *are* going to have to pay more attention in training, and especially in the field."

"I know," she said softly. "I will. I won't ever let anything happen to you or Melissa."

He grinned at her. "Of course you won't, but you better not let anything happen to *you* either."

"I won't," she told him, knowing that it was a promise she couldn't keep. Anything could happen to them.

They walked the rest of the way in silence. Music drifted from Chris's house, the sound was muffled by the loud laughter braying from inside. Chris groaned in disgust, his arm fell away from her shoulders. "I'll have grandma make you a plate," Cassie told him.

He nodded before making his way tiredly toward his front door. Cassie watched after him, dismayed by the sad, weary slump of his shoulders. No matter what life threw at him, Chris retained hope. She wished that she could be the same way. She wished that she could have the inner strength that Chris and Melissa possessed, the fierce hope, and will of steel they radiated. She may be the strongest fighter, but she was by far the weakest of them.

Shrill shouts rang from Chris's house; his mother started screaming at him for some unknown slight. Cassie winced; her heart ached for him as the shouts propelled her faster to her house. She wanted to get his plate ready, the mattress out, and the baseball game on before he arrived. It would be another silent night, but she felt that they both needed it after today.

Running up her steps, she froze at the edge of the stoop as the hairs on the nape of her neck stood up. Her hand on the knob, Cassie turned slowly to survey the darkened night. Though she could see a hawk in its nest, and a fox at the edge of the woods, she saw no one amongst the tree cover. Yet she could not shake the unsettling feeling that something was watching her, that some*one* was watching her. It was the same feeling that had encompassed her the other night.

Though she sensed no hostility from the presence out there, she still hurried into the house. She was eager to escape the eyes she couldn't see, but knew were there.

***

Cassie pulse rate picked up, her heart trip hammered loudly as she watched the Challenger drive slowly by. She waited breathlessly, her hands resting lightly on the hood of Chris's mustang as the Challenger pulled into a spot three cars away.

The door opened and Devon slid gracefully from behind the wheel. His eyes were shadowed by dark sunglasses, but she knew the moment that they locked upon her. The constriction in her lungs eased and she was finally able to draw her first easy breath since they had parted yesterday. Closing the car door, he ignored the curious glances of the students as he moved toward her with mesmerizing, easy grace.

The strange urge to cry with joy took her over. Everything was better now; the hope was back, the world was finally right again. There was no hesitancy as he took hold of her hand, enfolding it in both of his. She breathed a sigh of relief, her hand tightened around his as she held him, desperately needing his strength and comfort.

The smile that lit his face revealed his perfect white teeth, and two small dimples she had not noticed before. Her heart lurched as she took an instinctive step closer to him, needing to be as close to him as possible. Chris studied them with a worried frown; his eyes were intent upon Devon. Melissa stood beside him, a small, knowing smile on her face.

That knowing smile caused Cassie's heart to plummet. The sudden, awful insight that Melissa had received a premonition about Devon filled Cassie. Worry crept through her, chilling the marrow of her bones. She did not want to be the object of Melissa's prophecies, and she certainly did not want Devon to be a part of them.

The last thing that she wanted was for him to be hurt, or wounded, because he had become a part of her life. Her selfishness not only put the three of them at risk, but could also get *him* killed. Her life was dangerous; no ordinary human could survive it.

The chill inside her grew; her body became hollow as the hope inside her curdled like three month old milk. It was just as sour as milk as it sat in a tight knot in her stomach. She could not risk him getting hurt; she could not drag him into this world with her. Her world was horror and death, it was cruel and brutal; it was not fair to him.

Melissa turned toward her, her gaze growing questioning and curious. Though she did not possess Chris's ability, Melissa's insight into a person was uncanny and she did not miss a thing. She especially did not miss the sudden terror that was suffusing Cassie. Cassie had not known that she had been holding her breath until it exploded from her. She inhaled sharply, drawing much needed air into her denied, burning lungs. Her clenched fingers began to ache, and she realized that she was holding Devon's hand so tight that her nails had dug into the palm of his.

She eased her grip, but did not release him as she was not ready to let go. Not yet anyway. She could feel his curious gaze upon her, but she did not look at him again. She was afraid she would start to cry, and never stop, if she did.

Feeling like a wooden marionette, she followed stiffly as they filtered slowly into the school. She knew that she was not going to make it through this day.

CHAPTER 11

Cassie escaped from the school the first chance she got. Bursting free of the large brick building, she sprinted across the baseball field and darted into the woods. Her lungs began to burn, but she kept going, leaping over fallen logs, dodging branches, and other dangers with the easy grace that those of her kind possessed.

Her kind, she thought bitterly. She wanted nothing to do with *her* kind. Other than Chris and Melissa, they were *not* hers, and her heritage had been anything but *kind* to her. It had robbed her and Melissa of their parents, taken Chris's father from him. It had destroyed his mother.

When Luther had found them, the revelation that their parents had not been killed in a car accident had been a shattering blow to both her and Chris. It was disheartening to learn that it had not been an accident that had taken their families from them, but a calculated mission to destroy their loved ones. A slew of vampires had gotten together to seek out the Hunter line and viciously slaughtered as many of them as they could find.

What was she thinking to expose Devon to such a life? To such brutality and death? Though it had been awhile, they were all still fearful that the vampires would band together once more and finish what they had started sixteen years ago with The Slaughter. She had no right to risk Devon getting hurt, or even worse, killed. She had no right to put him in danger, especially when he didn't even *know* about the danger she might inadvertently place him in.

Though she barely knew him, she did know that it would destroy her to lose him because of her selfishness.

Cassie darted past some briar patches, her arm got caught on one. She didn't notice the pain as it tore across her skin and spilled her blood. Though it was impossible, she continued to try and outrun everything that she was, everything that she had become. She did not recognize the person she was now, for it was far different then the young, hopeful, innocent girl she had been just four short years ago. That girl had dreamed big and loved every moment of her easy going, fun filled life. The person she was now was a stranger inside her body, it wore her skin, but it was no longer her.

Pushing herself harder, she tried to run from the twisting pain that wrenched at her heart, and shredded her insides. Stumbling out of the woods, her feet hit sand as she reached the beach. Sand filled her sneakers as she slipped in it, but she continued to push herself onward. Her lungs burned fiercely and her legs were beginning to ache, but she kept going, too frightened to stop. If she stopped she would have to think, and if she thought, she didn't know if she could survive it.

Her feet slipped out from under her. With a soft cry, her knees hit the sand, her fingers slipped into its grainy depths and dug beneath the surface. It was cool to the touch, wet from the incoming tide as it lapped against the shore. Her shoulders trembled, she labored for air. Tears finally slipped free, spilling onto the beach as sobs shook her body and soul.

She couldn't move, she could barely breathe as agony and pain twisted through her gut. She sobbed for all of the unfairness in the world, for all the loss and pain she had experienced. She sobbed for the parents she could not remember, and had never cried for before. She sobbed for Devon, who had come to mean so much to her in such a short amount of time, and whom she feared she would have to let go of. Once the tears started, they would not stop, and she had no control over the torrent that poured from her.

Memories rolled forth, old wounds were sliced open, leaving her ragged and torn. She recalled her early years, years spent on the run and moving constantly. Though she and Chris had been to young to understand the reason

behind the constant moving, it had been stressful and lonely
for them. Chris's mother had fled with them to Cassie's
grandmother in Florida, and from there they had moved to
Georgia, Iowa, Kansas, Oklahoma, Vermont, Pennsylvania,
New York, Maine, and had finally settled on Cape Cod
after six years.

She and Chris had never known that they were moving to
avoid being hunted by the same monsters that had
murdered their parents, until Luther arrived. They had been
given six wonderful years of peace in which they hadn't
had to move, and they had actually been able to make
friends outside of each other. Though she hated the fate that
Luther had handed them, she did take some joy in avenging
her parent's deaths by ridding the world of the monsters
that walked upon it.

Cassie rested her hands on her knees, her tears slowly
subsided as the gentle ebb and flow of the sea drew her
attention. A soothing calm settled over her, drying her
tears. She was surprised at how much better she felt,
surprised by the tranquility that settled over her. She hated
the path that fate had laid out for her, but there were many
people who had it far worse than she did. She may hate the
path, but she would walk it, and she would stop struggling
against it.

She had been given the ability to destroy some of the evil
in the world, given the ability to help people; she should
start to consider it a gift, not a liability. Though she had lost
a lot because of what she was, to continue to fight it would
only destroy her. She had to make a choice, either accept
her fate, or continue to live in misery for whatever short
time she had left.

Staring silently at the ocean, the strength within her
began to grow. It slipped out to her limbs and dried the
remaining tears on her face. Her parents had died to keep
her safe, had died to protect her, and the world. She could
not deny her heritage any longer; she could not deny what

she was. And with the strength finally came a calming peace that she had not experienced in a very long time. For the first time in four years there was serenity inside her, a sense of true tranquility. By finally beginning to accept what she was, her path seemed to unfold swiftly, winding easily along instead of being broken and fractured.

A car door slammed, Chris and Melissa appeared at the top of a sand dune. Chris's face was drawn tight with worry, Melissa looked aggravated. Cassie sighed softly, turning her attention back to the deep blue sea. Dark clouds had begun to roll in along the horizon, but it would be awhile before the storm hit.

"What are you doing?" Melissa demanded; her black flip flops appeared next to Cassie.

Cassie didn't look up at her as she patted the sand at her side for Melissa to sit. "Thinking."

"Thinking will get you in trouble," Chris remarked, trying to sound light, but the tension in his voice betrayed him.

"Are you ok?" Melissa asked softly.

Cassie glanced at Melissa as she settled beside her, drawing her legs up Indian style. "Yes, better actually."

"You've been crying."

"I have."

"I've never seen you cry." Chris knelt beside her; his eyes were worried as he scanned her face. "Never."

Cassie smiled reassuringly at him and squeezed his hand gently. "Once it started I couldn't stop," she admitted. "But I feel better now, different somehow, stronger and more peaceful. It's weird, but it's ok."

He nodded, but his eyes were still troubled as he searched her face. "Tears can be soothing." Melissa rested her hand lightly on Cassie's arm. "Are you sure that you're alright?"

"Yes. You've had a premonition about Devon?" It was a question but came out more as a statement.

Melissa blinked in surprise, the pupils of her dark eyes

dilated slightly. "Do you really want to know?" When Cassie nodded, she continued on. "Yes, I had a vision about him arriving here; I knew he would touch something within you. I just didn't know when, or how deeply, he would touch you."

Cassie was silent, her gaze focused on the ocean as the tide continued to roll slowly in. Her mind clicked along, recalling the night when she had first seen Devon at B's and S's. "When you said that it was "about time" that first night he arrived, you weren't talking about time to leave were you?"

Melissa gave her a small smile as she shook her head. "I've been waiting over a year for him to arrive."

Cassie and Chris both frowned at her, their brows furrowed in confusion. "Why were you waiting for him to arrive?" Cassie demanded.

"To wake you up of course." She grinned at Cassie, leaning lightly against her side. "I knew that he would shake you up, make you come alive again."

Cassie stared at her in surprise, confusion flowed through her. "Well, that he did," Cassie whispered. "I think I have to give him up."

"Cassie…"

She shook her head fiercely. "It's too dangerous for all of us, for *him*. I cannot bring him into this life, cannot put him, or us, into that situation. I've been distracted, luckily only in training so far. If I'm distracted in the field I could get us all killed. This is our fate, our heritage; he can't be a part of it."

Melissa sighed softly, her hand tightened on Cassie's arm. Cassie turned slowly toward her, fighting back the tears that threatened to fall. "There was a reason that I saw him coming Cassie, and I think that it was more than just to wake you up," Melissa said softly.

"What then?" she whispered.

Melissa shrugged, shaking her head slowly as her black eyebrows drew tightly together. "Unfortunately I only catch glimpses of the future, not the whole plan Cass. I don't know why it's important for him to be here, but it is. And I believe that it is *very* important for him to be in your life."

Cassie squelched the hope that bloomed momentarily in her chest. "So you think that I shouldn't push him away?"

Melissa shook her head as she bit nervously on her bottom lip; her face was composed in thought. "He's only been in your life for a week and already you're happier than I've seen you in years. You need that, we *want* that for you. We'll find a way to keep him safe Cass. The three of us can do anything together. Give it some time; you don't need all the answers right now. You just need to focus on being happy."

"And if something does happen to him?"

"We won't let it," Chris vowed.

Cassie fought back the tears of gratitude and love that filled her eyes. She was so very lucky to have two such wonderful friends in her life. "Should I tell him? Shouldn't he know about this danger?" she whispered.

Chris stiffened; her question touched a very sore spot in him. His mother had never known about his father. She had been human, and Chris's father had thought it best not to tell her what he was, and the danger that he faced every day. Mary had simply thought that Chris's father was working a second job at night in order to support his wife, and young son.

The harsh truth had not been revealed to Mary until the night she'd fled with Chris and Cassie. Over the years, whether due to the fact that she had lost her husband and feared losing her son, or to the fact that she could not handle the reality of everything she knew, Mary had retreated further and further into an alcohol induced stupor. And further and further away from Chris.

"You know my feelings on that," Chris said softly.

Yes, she knew that Chris would *never* keep such a secret from someone he loved; he believed it was what had destroyed his mother. Chris felt that Mary's resentment at being lied to, and cheated of the dreams she'd possessed, were what had made her the cruel drunk she was now. And he was very likely right. But Cassie wasn't in love, she couldn't be in such a short time, she hardly knew Devon.

"I think that you should tell him one day. But maybe you should get to know him a little better first." Melissa released her grip on Cassie's arm, needing her hand to clamp back her hair as the wind began to pick up.

"But I do know him," Cassie murmured. "I know that sounds crazy, and if it were one of you telling me this, I would be suspicious too. But I *do* know him. I know him in a way that I never thought I could know anyone. It's so strange, so different…"

Cassie broke off, unable to put into words exactly what it was that she felt for him. It would be impossible to explain to them, when she couldn't even explain it to herself. "I understand that Cass, but I think it's too soon. I think that you should wait for a little bit."

"Or until you find out how the hell he can afford such a kick ass car," Chris said softly.

Cassie rolled her eyes, but she had to admit she had wondered the same thing. As much as she felt she knew Devon, there was still a lot that she didn't know. But she was certain she knew his heart, his soul. Melissa's dark eyes were caring; Chris's were turbulent as they studied her. Nodding, she took hold of both of their hands, squeezing them tightly. "When you guys are ready for me to tell him, I will."

Their tension eased, their hands squeezed hers gently as their fears lessened. She understood their concerns about telling Devon, they didn't know him, or how deeply she felt about him. It was their secret, and their lives too, and it would also have to be their choice.

Cassie turned back to the ocean, her questions and doubts twisted her stomach. She didn't know what to say or do, but she doubted that all of the answers would come to her at that moment. They sat silently together until the tide washed in to their feet, and the sky was rumbling. Cassie was too comfortable to move. She found solace in their strength, in their presences.

"It's going to pour," Chris said softly.

"We should go," Melissa whispered.

Cassie sighed, not wanting to move, but knowing that they had to. The sky was about ready to split open and release a torrent of rain upon them. She climbed stiffly to her feet, wiping the sand off her legs and butt. She followed silently behind as they made their way over the dunes to the parking lot.

"How did you know I was here?" she asked softly.

"I had a glimpse," Melissa answered.

'Of course she did,' Cassie thought silently, trying hard not to roll her eyes. She may have discovered a new inner strength and tranquility, but she still did not like the idea of Melissa knowing her future, or her whereabouts.

Cassie reached the car as the wind picked up. She took hold of her hair, trying to keep it out of her face as she grasped the handle on the passenger side door. The hair suddenly stood up on the nape of her neck, the blood in her veins turned to ice as a chill swept down her spine.

Lifting her gaze, she scanned the empty parking lot. Sand blew across the numerous parking spaces, scraps of garbage skittered along with it. Past the parking lot wild trees, Rosa rugosa, beach grass, and sand dunes spotted with scraggly bayberry rolled forth. Though there were few places to hide, she knew that there was someone out there, some*thing* watching them. However, this feeling of being watched was not like the one she'd had last night. This feeling was something evil, something malevolent, and wrong. She could sense the hunger and bloodlust in the thing that she could not see.

Cassie glanced at Chris and Melissa. They were both frozen, their gazes locked on the wild area she had been searching. "You feel that?" she asked, pitching her voice above the rising crescendo of the wind.

They both nodded. "There is something out there," Melissa said softly, her nostrils flaring slightly.

"And it's not good," Chris agreed.

"Should we go look?" Cassie inquired.

They glanced briefly at her. Thunder shook the sky and rumbled the earth. Lightning flashed brightly, blazing across the dark sky as it sizzled to the ground with a loud pop that caused goose bumps to break out on her skin. The air was heavy with the scent of ozone as the sky split open and a deluge of rain fell upon them.

Cassie ducked into the car, already soaked as she slid into the backseat. Her gaze remained riveted upon the scraggly woods, but nothing fled from the rain as it pounded loudly upon the roof of the car. Chris and Melissa slammed their doors shut, but Chris did not start the car. They sat in silence, waiting for whatever it was to reveal itself.

It did not.

***

The ringing of the doorbell was diminished by the hard rain hitting the windows. Cassie frowned at Chris and Melissa as she uncurled herself from her bed. Chris didn't look up from the episode of Deadliest Catch he was engrossed in. "Awesome," he muttered.

Cassie shook her head at him as Melissa rolled her eyes. "Be right back."

Cassie hurried from her room, curious as to who could be at her door. Though she was popular at school, it had been a few years since she had invited anyone over. Plus the school day was still in progress, even though the three of them had opted not to return. Flinging the door open, she froze; her mouth went dry as her heart fluttered wildly in her chest. Devon stood upon her doorstep, his wet hair tussled and windblown. He looked heartbreakingly beautiful as drops of rain trailed over the hard contours of his face. His bright emerald eyes met hers; a small smile curved his full mouth.

"Devon," she said softly, surprised that her voice actually worked.

His smile widened enough to reveal his perfect teeth. "Melissa said you went home sick, I wanted to see how you were feeling."

She swallowed heavily, trying to regain control of herself but failing miserably. "I feel a lot better now." It wasn't entirely a lie; she did feel better than she had this morning. "Thank you."

He continued to stare at her, leaning slightly forward as he rested his hand on the door jam. "You look well."

Her face flared with heat as he perused her with a look that caused her toes to curl. "Who is it?" Melissa called as she pounded down the steps. She froze at the bottom of the stairs. "Devon, how are you?" She inquired as she walked over to stand beside Cassie.

"Fine. I just came to make sure Cassie was feeling better."

"Oh, that's really nice of you. Why don't you come in out of the rain?"

Cassie cast a sharp, panicked look at Melissa that she chose to ignore. "Cassie?"

She turned back to Devon, knowing her fear and distress was written all over her face, but she unable to keep her expression neutral. He was staring at her expectantly, his green eyes troubled and intense. She knew that she looked like an idiot, and a cold hearted jerk for not inviting him in, but her thoughts would not form a coherent sentence in her shaken brain. She did know one thing; she could not leave him out there in the rain.

"Yes, of course, come in," she managed in a choked voice, and somehow getting her feet to move out of his way.

Her heart hammered as he moved with easy grace into the house, his shoulder briefly brushed against hers. A tremor raced through her, causing her heart to lurch, and her body to hum with electricity once more. His powerful frame seemed to take up the entire foyer, her entire world. Fascination seized her as he ran an elegant hand through his damp hair, shaking the rain from it. Melissa nudged her, her eyes wide as she nodded slightly toward the kitchen in an attempt to make Cassie at least act somewhat normal.

"Do you want something to eat, or drink?" Cassie asked quickly, a little too quickly as she realized she sounded like a complete idiot. His close proximity was shaking her to the core though.

"No, thank you."

She nodded, her gaze darted to Melissa. She didn't know what to say or do. "Hey, grab me a Coke!" Chris shouted down the steps, apparently on commercial break.

"Please!" Melissa yelled back.

"Please!"

"I'll get it." Melissa headed for the kitchen, leaving the two of them painfully alone.

Cassie shifted uncomfortably, fidgeting nervously with the edge of her shirt. "You won't get in trouble for leaving school will you?" she asked softly.

He shrugged absently. "It's worth it to make sure that you're ok."

Cassie hated the heat that flooded her face, but she could not stop the fire that burned over her skin. "We were uh just watching TV and hanging out," she managed to stammer out. "Do you want to join us?"

He grinned at her, his dimples flashed as his head cocked slightly to the side. "Sure."

His gaze roamed over the house as she led him up the stairs. Her heart pounded loudly in her ears, her throat was dry as excitement and terror tore through her in equal waves. The heat of his body was fierce in the small confines of the stairwell. It burned through her clothes, heating her to the core of her being.

Chris did not look up as she pushed the door open, his attention was still riveted on the TV. "Who was it?" he muttered, shoving a handful of chips into his mouth.

Cassie shook her head at him in disbelief. He was like a zombie when TV and food were involved. He didn't even sense a new presence in the room. "It's Devon."

He turned slowly toward them, his eyes widened in startled disbelief. "Hey," he greeted dully.

Devon nodded to him as his gaze ran over Cassie's room. She glanced around, her eyes darting over her mahogany dresser with its assortment of jewelry boxes, knickknacks, and hair care products. The only thing decorating her cream colored walls was a picture of her parents. It hung above an overstuffed armchair next to the window that Chris climbed through. On the other side of the window were two large bookcases stuffed full of books neatly organized alphabetically. The nightstand, beside her queen sized sleigh bed, held only an alarm clock.

For the first time she noticed how sparse it was, how much it did not look like a normal teen's room with all the cluster, posters, and chaos that were usually present. Then again, she was anything but a normal teen. She looked back at him, not at all surprised to find his steady gaze focused upon her once more. She couldn't stop the blush burning into the roots of her hair.

"Here you go." Melissa breezed into the room; she tossed a can of Coke to Chris, who was still staring at Devon in disbelief.

Melissa plopped onto the bed and drew her legs up beneath her. "Do you want to sit?" Cassie asked Devon softly.

Melissa scooted over on the bed, making room for him as he sat on the edge of it. Cassie's heart fluttered, a strange sensation took over. She had never had a boy in her room before, unless she counted Chris, which she didn't. And Devon was most certainly not a boy, or at least not like any boy she had ever known.

"You like this show?" Chris asked Devon.

Devon turned slowly away from her, his forehead furrowed slightly as he watched the ship battling the fierce weather and sea. "Never seen it."

"Oh, you're in for a treat then, this show is the best!" Chris said eagerly, thrusting the bag of chips at Devon which he politely waved away. Apparently watching TV was Chris's favorite way to bond.

"Looks interesting," Devon replied. "Are you going to sit?"

Cassie's eyes widened as he patted the spot beside him on the bed. She glanced wildly at Melissa, but her friend was watching TV, an annoyingly bright smile on her face. There would be no hope from her, and Chris was already engrossed in the program again. Moving stiffly, she perched gingerly on the corner of the bed, unable to fully relax with him only tantalizing inches from her.

Her hands clenched upon her legs, her fingers dug into her jeans. She could feel the strength of his aura. Unknowingly she leaned closer to him, a current shooting through her as they touched briefly. His fingers intertwined with hers, locking tight as he pulled her hand into his lap.

She glanced up at him, her mouth parting as she found his emerald eyes on her. She knew that she try and slow her involvement with him, but she could not bring herself to move away, could not bring herself to put any distance between them again. She was mesmerized by him, enchanted like a cobra under the snake charmer's spell.

Resting her head on his shoulder, she fully resigned herself to the fact that she was not going to be able to stay away from him. She could not stand to part with him for more than a few hours, never mind the rest of her short life. She would just have to make sure that she kept him safe. That they *all* kept him protected from the dangers and brutality of their world. She did not kid herself into thinking it would be easy.

CHAPTER 12

Cassie sucked on the end of her straw, pulling the thick shake through it as she studied the group gathered around the picnic tables. The crowded area was loud as kids shouted, laughed, and threw things at one another. The football team had won their game tonight and it seemed that the entire school had turned out to celebrate.

Chris shifted slightly beside her, his large body was crammed into the tiny corner they had managed to snag. "Freaking mad house," he muttered.

"It's because you guys are so great, you should be happy," Melissa told him.

He rolled his eyes, but they gleamed with pride. Though he tried to play it off like it was no big deal, he loved being the star of the team. Cassie's gaze scanned the crowd as she waited impatiently for Devon to arrive. He hadn't been able to make it to the football game, but he'd said he would be here.

It was amazing how attached she had become to him in the past week. She itched when he was not around; her skin was uncomfortable when he was not there to soothe the burning that his absence created. She still didn't understand the strange power he had over her, the fierce connection that blazed between them, but she had accepted the fact that she had no control over it.

He had inserted himself permanently into her life, creating chaos where there had been none. But it was a chaos that she relished in, and needed as much as she needed air to survive. She would be completely lost without his strong presence, and the hope that he had brought to her life.

Her phone went off, the faint beep barely audible above the din surrounding her. Digging it out of her pocket, she flipped it open relieved to see the text from Devon saying that he was on his way. Flipping it closed, she shoved it back in her pocket, unable to stop the small smile that flitted across her mouth.

"Devon on his way?" Chris asked quietly.

"Yeah."

He nodded as his blue eyes scanned the crowd. Though he still wasn't completely relaxed around Devon, they seemed to have forged a strange friendship. They watched TV together every night when Devon came over to see her. They commented on this and that, laughing or groaning depending on what was on. They were both obsessed with The Deadliest Catch and Cassie found it highly amusing to watch and listen to them. She had grown accustomed to Devon's visits after school, looked forward to the time they spent together in her room before she had to go back to the grind of her nightlife. She was still not used to having Devon in her room, in her life even, but she had grown to like having him there.

A loud shout drew her attention to Jack Wells. The quarterback was standing on one of the picnic tables, throwing French fries at anyone unfortunate enough to be close to him. Cassie rolled her eyes as Melissa heaved a large sigh. "What an idiot," Chris muttered.

"Boys will be boys," Cassie said softly.

"Shoot me if I ever act like that."

"Oh, it's a guarantee, and don't forget I know how to use a crossbow."

He grinned at her. "Yeah you do."

Cassie scanned the crowd again; impatient to see Devon. Since she had made the decision not to fight her feelings, things had leveled out inside her, become more peaceful. She could concentrate on her training again; she was more settled, and more alive, than she had been in years. She was still a tumult of feeling and sensation when it came to him, and she was beginning to believe that that feeling would never change.

There was a ripple in the crowd, a slight shifting amongst the students. She knew instantly that he had arrived as his presence always caused a stir. The boys were still slightly wary of him, and the girl's eagerly followed his every move. The girl's had also started to give her angry, hate filled looks that she had not gotten used to receiving, and was perplexed by. She had done nothing to them; in fact she had considered most of them her friends. Until now. She knew it was jealousy over her relationship with Devon that fueled their anger, knew that they wanted him, but that fact didn't make the resentment from them any easier.

He walked gracefully through the crowd, not acknowledging the strange or lustful stares that followed him. Jack stopped tossing french-fries as Devon moved past, not even he was crazy enough to throw a fry at Devon. Though, Cassie thought it might be entertaining to see. Devon didn't even acknowledge the winning quarterbacks presence as he moved swiftly past. Until Devon had arrived, Jack had been the most sought after boy in school. Now Jack's all American good looks couldn't hold a candle to Devon's dark splendor.

Cassie bristled slightly as Marcy stepped in front of Devon, halting his progress. It was not jealousy that broke through her, for he did not look at other girls that way. In fact, Cassie knew that she was often the *only* person he saw. He conveyed that to her with every one of his searing looks and gentle touches, for even now as he spoke with Marcy, his gaze was focused upon her. The smile on his lips was for her only. No, it was not jealousy that tore through her, but aggravation that Marcy had stopped him from coming straight to her. She needed him to ease the aching tension clinging to her.

He spoke with Marcy for a few moments, but his gaze remained firm upon her, his eyes warm and caring. Some of the anxiety eased from her, a small smile curved her mouth as she watched him. The bond between them was fierce, and they still hadn't even kissed yet. In fact, they had done nothing more than hold hands and sit with each other. She ached for his kiss she just didn't know what would happen when he finally *did* kiss her. His touch was enough to drive her crazy, she couldn't imagine what his kiss would do to her, but she was dying to find out.

Yet, she did not rush it, did not try and make the first move. She knew it would happen eventually, and that it would be as thrilling as everything else with him was. For now, it was simply enough to be with him every day.

He nodded to Marcy, giving her a brief smile before stepping casually around her. Excitement tingled through Cassie as he came to her; her body instinctively leaned closer to his as his hand slid easily into hers. The burn and itch in her skin eased, allowing her to experience the bliss that he brought her. He was the only balm that could ease her discomfort.

He stood close beside her, his chest pressed lightly against her shoulder. The hand not holding hers wrapped possessively around her waist, and rested lightly upon her hip. A small shiver worked its way down her spine, her eyes closed briefly as she relished in the pleasure that his touch brought her. His scent engulfed her, filling her nostrils with the smell of fresh air tinted with the crisp hint of spices. It was a scent she had grown used to, and she welcomed it with every fiber of her being.

His hand lightly stroked her hip, his fingers set up a firestorm within her that only he could start, and put out. "You look beautiful tonight."

His soft words and gentle breath blew against her hair, ruffling it slightly. She shivered again, leaning closer to him as he gently nuzzled her neck. His lips brushed over her skin, briefly caressing the nape of her neck. For a moment Cassie feared that her knees would buckle as her legs began to tremble fiercely.

He chuckled lightly, his hand tightened on her waist. Pulling her closer against him, he gently supported her suddenly weak legs. Cassie's hand tightened around his. "Oh!" A loud shout echoed through the air, reverberating beneath the metal overhang of B's and S's.

Cassie looked up as Jack did a back flip off the table, landing perfectly on his feet. "What an idiot," Chris said, tossing his empty shake into the trashcan.

"He throws you the ball," Melissa reminded him.

"Yeah, but that doesn't mean he has a brain cell. The guy relishes in being the stereotypical jerk jock, one of these days I'm going to punch him."

Cassie grinned as she shook her head. "You'd be kicked off the team."

"Would be worth it."

Chants began as Mike Daniels jumped onto the table, preparing to do his own jump off. Cassie sighed heavily. "This isn't going to end well."

Melissa was already grinning brightly, a knowing twinkle in her dark eyes. Mike jumped off the table, spinning through the air. His feet hit the ground, the left one skidded out from under him as he slipped on one of Jack's discarded fries. He landed hard on his butt, a loud whoomph issuing from him as his breath rushed out.

Laughter filled the air; Cassie nearly choked on her shake as a satisfied gleam lit Melissa's onyx eyes. Then she glanced past Cassie, her forehead furrowed as her eyes narrowed sharply. Cassie stiffened, turning slightly to follow Melissa's gaze. Surprise riveted her to the spot.

Luther stood on the other side of B's and S's, his eyebrows raised disdainfully as he watched Jason climb onto the table. His glasses slid down to the edge of his nose to perch precariously upon the tip. The loose fitting jacket he wore hung off of his slender shoulders, making him appear even thinner than he was.

"What is he doing here?" Chris asked softly.

"I don't know. I'll go find out."

Melissa slipped past them, skirting the group gathered around the picnic tables. "Who is that?" Devon inquired softly.

Cassie shifted slightly, not at all sure how to answer that question. "It's Melissa's dad," Chris told him.

"I thought Melissa's parents were dead," Devon said.

"Adopted father," Chris amended, glancing briefly at Devon. "But he's raised her since she was a baby, so it's her dad."

"I see," Devon said softly, his eyes coming swiftly back to Cassie.

Cassie swallowed heavily, barely managing a slow nod. It was not entirely a lie. She should not feel bad, but she did. Tearing her gaze away from his, she tried to keep her breathing, and her heart rate, under control. "Were Melissa's parents with yours in the car accident?"

Cassie's mind fumbled with an answer for that, she knew what she was supposed to say, what they had been *told* to say, but her tongue could not get the lies out. "No, Melissa's family was in Egypt at the time. Her mother died in childbirth, and her father was killed in the line of duty."

Again, it was not entirely a lie, but it was Chris who uttered the words, not her. "Line of duty?"

"Yeah," Chris answered his gaze intent upon Devon's. "He was in the British armed forces, stationed in Egypt, where he met Melissa's mom. Luther and he were good friends, so Luther adopted Melissa when she was orphaned. There was no other family."

"I see." Devon nodded slowly, his eyes slightly distant as he gazed down at Cassie. "How sad for you all."

"My mother is still alive," Chris reminded him, unable to keep the bitterness from his voice.

"Chris…"

Chris's anguished eyes swung toward her. She knew Chris loved his mother, but there was so much pain and anger between them that Cassie feared their relationship could never be repaired. Her words trailed off; there was nothing that she could say. Though he was grateful that his mother had been spared the massacre of that awful night, she knew he would give anything to be free of her, and his household. He was eager to flee town as soon as they graduated.

A gentle breeze wafted over them, tickling the hairs at the nape of her neck, blowing strands of it across her face. Devon stiffened beside her, his hand stilled on her waist as he turned slowly toward the woods behind them. Nostrils flaring slightly, his eyes narrowed as he studied the shadowed forest. His jaw clenched fiercely, a muscle jumped in his cheek. The hand upon her waist tightened as he moved protectively closer to her.

Confusion swirled through Cassie. She turned toward the woods, her gaze intently searching the darkened interior for some hint of what had caught his attention and upset him so. She glanced back at him; his eyes had turned a dark leaf green color, the tight clench of his jaw looked painful. She frowned, not understanding what had him so tense, and focused upon the forest.

Cassie's attention was torn from him as Melissa came back toward them; she looked grim as she weaved gracefully through the crowd. A chill of foreboding traveled down Cassie's spine. Melissa's dark eyes met hers briefly, a strange hollowness radiated from her usually bright gaze. "Is everything ok?" Chris asked quietly.

Melissa shook her head, her attention turned briefly to Devon. He had turned away from the woods, but he was still wound as tight as a bowstring. "No, Luther just received some bad news. I'm afraid I have to go."

Cassie shifted, pressing briefly against Devon in the hopes of easing some of his rigidity, but he did not relax. He was so tense that he was not even breathing, she realized with a start. "Do you want us to come with you?" Chris asked.

Melissa sighed heavily. "Yeah, he's pretty upset. It would be nice of you." She glanced back at Devon. "You know he thinks of you as family and I think he needs all the comfort he can get right now," she added for his benefit.

A cold shiver ran down Cassie's spine again, it turned the blood in her veins to ice as her heart lumbered to pump it through. Swallowing heavily, she managed a small nod. "Of course." She turned slowly toward Devon, trying hard to keep the panic from her face as she met his fierce, dark gaze. "I have to go."

He nodded, but she could tell that his thoughts were elsewhere, and that he was still unsettled. Though he had started to breathe again, he was still as solid, and unbending, as a rock. His hand moved over her back, clenching briefly against her. "I *will* see you later."

Cassie blinked in surprise; the words had come out almost as a growl. The fierceness in his hard gaze and the intensity of his words caused goose bumps to break out on her skin. She did not know what was going on tonight with Luther, or with Devon, but her sense of foreboding kicked up another notch.

"Yes." She agreed simply because she didn't know what else to say. His eyes burned into hers, his hand was firm against her. For a moment he seemed to have no intention of letting her go, and then his hands slid away.

"Be safe."

She frowned in confusion, puzzled as to why he would say that. "Of course."

The intensity of his gaze did not lessen as she took a small step away. She thought he was going to grab hold of her again as he made a small motion toward her, but then he stopped. The quiet desperation in him tore at her, keeping her riveted. "Come on Cassie, we have to go," Chris said gently.

She nodded to him, swallowing heavily as she turned slowly away from Devon. She could feel his gaze boring into her back as they moved through the crowd. Another gentle breeze wafted over them, but this one carried the strange sense of wrongness that had been present at the beach the other day. Cassie halted; she turned slowly as the evil washed over her, and rooted her feet in place.

Melissa and Chris stopped beside her, their heads turned slowly as their gazes fixed upon the woods. Nothing stirred amongst the darkness, but she knew that something was out there. Knew that whatever it was it was evil, and it was thirsty. She shivered, her arms wrapped instinctively around herself in a useless attempt to fight off the ice in her veins.

The crowd of students moved and shuffled around her, their laughter loud in her frozen ears. Their joy was oddly out of place in the pulsing malevolence encompassing her. Whatever was out there, she could feel its eyes upon her. Feel it watching her.

"We have to go," Melissa said softly, her normally strong voice wavering slightly.

Cassie tore her attention from the woods; her gaze instinctively fell upon Devon again. He was no longer watching her as he had turned back to the forest. His attention was riveted upon the woods, his body taut once more. A jolt tore through Cassie as she realized that somehow, she didn't possibly know how, he felt the evil too.

CHAPTER 13

"I believe that an Elder is here."

Cassie's legs ceased their swinging motion on the island she was sitting upon as Luther slapped the paper down in front of them. The large headline blazed up at her in big black lettering. **ANOTHER WOMAN KILLED BY WILD ANIMAL.** Though she tried, she could not tear her gaze away from those words. The paper had been on her counter this morning, but she had thought nothing of it as she breezed by to grab a box of cereal. Then again, she had not thought about much since Devon had entered her life. But now, for the first time since she had met him, Devon was not foremost in her thoughts.

Horror and nausea rolled through her. Her stomach in a tumult, her body broke out in a cold sweat, and her temples pulsed with the fierce beats of her heart. For a moment she thought her life was flashing before her eyes, but then she realized it was just white lights blazing because she had forgotten to breathe. She inhaled sharply, the air burned through her tortured lungs.

"An Elder?" Chris asked softly, his voice tight and choked.

Luther nodded vigorously, shoving his glasses back up with his index finger. "Yes, murders are up, and animal attacks have doubled over the past couple of weeks. You know what that means. Now, it could be a young vampire, but I don't believe so."

"But you don't know for sure?" Cassie asked her voice higher pitched than she would have liked.

He nodded again, his gray eyes grave as they met hers. "I'm fairly positive Cass. This thing has been stalking people for a little while now. It's covering its tracks very well, something that younger vampires are not so discreet about, and tend not to do. I wouldn't have noticed the trend if I didn't follow the newspapers so carefully. I firmly believe that this thing is older, more powerful, and it *is* hunting here."

Cassie shivered; she wrapped her arms tightly around her middle again. The painful knot in her stomach only clenched further, seeming to twist her intestines. An Elder. They had never dealt with an Elder before, never even come close to one. And she had *never* wanted to.

It had been The Elders that had grouped together to destroy The Hunter line, determined to take them all out in one fell swoop. Though they had not completely succeeded, they had managed to slaughter hundreds of men, women, and children. Including their parents. The massacre had left The Hunter line straggling, broken, scattered and lost across the globe. The survivors had fled for their lives, moving about continuously in order to stay hidden and alive.

Before the carnage there had been almost six hundred Hunters. After, there were only thirty two known ones left. That number included Cassie, Melissa, and Chris who hadn't been old enough to walk, let alone fight for their lives when The Slaughter occurred. It had been left to her grandmother, Luther, and Chris's mom to keep them safe and alive.

Chris had been telling the truth when he'd said that Luther was good friends with Melissa's parents. Luther had also been their Guardian; one of the people entrusted to train and protect The Hunter line. His duties as a Guardian consisted of schooling them in the old ways, navigating them through Vampire and Hunter lore, and teaching them how to fight. When The Slaughter occurred Luther had fled with Melissa to Germany, then Japan, and finally to the U.S. where they had bounced around in search of survivors. During the carnage, Guardian's had also been slaughtered; there were only twenty one survivors that had been accounted for. Her parent's own Guardian, Brent, had been murdered with them when The Slaughter occurred.

All the Guardians had known where The Hunters had been located before The Slaughter, but in the aftermath, many had been lost, maybe forever. Luther continued to search for more survivors, but his journeys always came up empty handed, and Cassie knew he worried that he wouldn't find anymore.

With the small number of survivors, it was feared that The Hunter line would eventually die out. Cassie did not plan on having children. There was no way that she would leave them orphaned and alone after saddling them to this life. And if she didn't have kids, and the others did not survive to have children, then it was only a matter of time before there was no one left. It was Luther's biggest fear; after their deaths, of course.

Cassie tried to swallow the hard lump that had imbedded itself in her throat, but it was choking her, cutting off her air as it remained lodged in her windpipe. It seemed that their time had come, much sooner than she had expected, *far* sooner than she had wanted. Tears burned the back of her eyes. However, they were not tears of pain or sorrow, but of anger.

She was angry at fate, and this monster that had come into their lives. It was not fair that she had finally found something good in her life, and now she was going to lose it. She glanced around the room, her heart breaking for the only family she had ever known. Chris looked shell shocked, Melissa's gaze was distant and unfocused; Luther was frantic.

"What do we do?" Chris asked softly.

Luther turned toward him, the normally soft lines in his face hard and fierce. "We run."

There was a moment of stunned, breathless silence, before Cassie and Chris exploded at the same time. "What!?"

Luther nodded briskly, he folded his hands behind his back as he started to pace the confines of his kitchen. "None of you are ready to face an Elder. You haven't had enough training; you do not know the full scope of this creature's abilities. *No* one fully knows what an Elder is capable of. You cannot go up against that."

"The three of us…"

"Are not enough," he interrupted Chris sharply. "Your powers and abilities are nothing compared to what this creature may be able to do."

Cassie's head spun, her extremities went numb. She felt as if she could slide off the kitchen island and become a limp pool of body parts on the floor. There was nothing left to her. "How can you be so sure that this is even an Elder?" Chris asked softly.

Luther heaved a large sigh as he continued his relentless pacing. "I cannot. The biggest clue I have is the lack of evidence that the police have. This monster is killing for the pleasure, and power, of it. He is not turning them; he is leaving their bodies behind with no blood, when he leaves them behind, but he also leaves no hint of his mark upon them, which is something that new vamps tend not to do. The lack of blood at the crime scene is stumping police, but they are not digging too deeply into it. Probably because they don't want to know. Also, most new vampires do not survive their first month."

"What? Why not?" Cassie gasped in shock, breaking free of her paralysis.

Luther rolled his eyes as he shook his head. "You never listen to me," he muttered. "Most new vampires are killed in their first month."

"Why? How?" Chris demanded fiercely.

Luther shot him a fierce, disapproving look. "Either by Hunter's, especially when there were more of you, or by other vampire's." Cassie stared at him in stunned silence, her mind spun with the revelation. Luther shoved his glasses back up his nose and returned to pacing. "Older vampires don't want a lot of newbie's around. They do not want the human population to know that vampires are real, and young vampires tend to be careless about the conditions they leave their victims in, and the amount of bodies they leave behind. They tend to raise questions that the Elders don't want raised. Also, hunting and killing another vampire is more power than a human, and more thrilling for them. I imagine that they thoroughly enjoy it."

Cassie inhaled sharply; she found the brutal picture he was painting extremely disturbing. They fought amongst themselves in search of a more thrilling kill, and more power? She knew that they were monsters, awful, horrendous, and despicable, but this was far beyond her scope of disgust and hatred for them. Nausea twisted in her already sour stomach.

"How come we didn't hear about this fact before now?" Chris demanded.

Luther stopped pacing; folding his arms firmly over his chest he glared at him. "Because you and Cassie didn't want to learn about the lore, and the behavior of vampires, you just wanted to learn to fight."

Cassie had the grace to look chagrined, Chris did not. Melissa stood silently to the side; she already knew what Luther was talking about. Having grown up in the life, Melissa had been taught everything as a child. She also firmly believed that if she was going to know the future, then she needed to have a tight grip on the past. And Melissa was very much about the future and the things that were revealed to her. However, Cassie had resented her heritage as it was; she did not want to learn more about it. And Chris, well if it didn't involve food, girls, and action then he wanted nothing to do with it.

"Well it's all boring crap," Chris muttered defensively.

Luther's jaw clenched, his eyes narrowed slightly. "Well you just learned something new, and important, from that boring *crap!*" Luther snapped. Chris finally had the grace to look discomfited as he ducked his head. "So that is why I believe that we are dealing with an Elder now."

"The thing in the woods," Cassie said softly, looking wildly at Melissa and Chris. "That's what was out there tonight, and at the beach the other day."

"How could it have been at the beach? It was daylight," Chris argued.

Cassie shook her head, hopping off the counter as she began to pace rapidly. "It was overcast though, probably cloudy enough for them to come out at that point of the day."

"What are you talking about?" Luther demanded fiercely. Melissa quickly filled him in on what had happened the other day, and the strange feeling they had all experienced again tonight. Luther's face was grave and thoughtful, his eyes distant as he studied the far wall. "We may never know exactly what an Elder is capable of. The scope of their powers may be far beyond anything we can even imagine."

Cassie's stomach rolled over again, and she was very fearful that she was going to throw up her strawberry shake before this night was over. "If it is watching you, then it's likely that this creature knows what you truly are. It is also likely that the three of you may have drawn it here. It may have sensed your powers, and abilities, and it also may have noticed the deaths of its brethren do to you. That's why we *must* leave. It will hunt you until it destroys you."

Cassie abruptly stopped pacing; she nearly tripped over her own feet as she stared at him in disbelief. Melissa slid limply off the island; she rested her hand against it as her legs buckled slightly. Chris took a step forward, his eyes turbulent, yet blazing with a fiery determination.

"No," Cassie said softly, swallowing heavily as she tried to wet her parched throat. "No, I am not leaving," she managed more firmly.

Luther looked at her in surprise, his eyes blinked rapidly behind his Lennon style glasses. "What do you mean no? You don't understand Cassie…"

"I understand that you think this thing will kill us, and you may be right. I also understand that we may have led this thing here; I will not abandon the town, and the people I have known since childhood, to this monster. It may kill us, but we are also the only defense that they have against it. I will not leave them to be slaughtered because of us."

"Neither will I," Chris said firmly.

Melissa wet her lips nervously before straightening her slender shoulders. "We can't Luther. Cassie's right, this thing may be far more powerful than us, but we are the only defense here. We can't abandon them; it would be like leading the lambs to the slaughter."

Luther stood silently for a moment, disbelief and something akin to pain bloomed in his eyes. "I understand your desire to stay, and I commend it, but I cannot allow that to happen. There are not enough Hunter's left to risk your lives. I *must* keep you safe. You cannot stay here."

"I will not allow innocent people to die because of us!" Cassie retorted fiercely.

"They die every day. Your lives are more valuable, you do far more good alive than you do dead." Cassie stared at him in surprised disbelief, she felt as if she had been slapped. She could not believe that he had just said that. "I'm sorry to sound cruel, but it's true. If you are killed, then even more innocent people will die, you must weigh everything before coming to this decision. Sometimes we have to do things that we do not want to in life."

Cassie took a step toward him as fury blazed through her. "I am already doing something that I don't want to do *every single day*! I did not ask for this, but I will *not* run from it! Not now. I am staying, if you wish to flee then do so, but I will not!"

Pain and anger flared through Luther's gray eyes, making them even brighter behind his glasses. "I do not *wish* to flee! It is the best for you. My only charge in life is to see that you are prepared to fight, and to keep you safe."

Cassie's anger melted in the face of his anguish and hurt. "You cannot keep us safe forever, it's not possible. You have done your best to train us Luther; you have to have faith in that."

He glanced at their determined faces. His eyes were troubled and wide behind his glasses, his hands fisted tightly at his sides. Heaving a sigh, his set shoulders slumped in defeat. "Fine, but you cannot go hunting alone anymore. The three of you must stick together, and you must wait for me to go with you. No more running off on your own. Also, I want to know every time you have the same feeling that you had tonight." He turned to Melissa, his eyes intense and fierce. "Have you had any premonitions about this?"

She glanced over them quickly, her dark eyes sad and distant. "No."

"Have you had any lately?"

She shook her head. "Nothing to do with vampires. I knew we would win the game tonight, and I know that tomorrow, at lunch, Marcy is going to announce the nominee's for homecoming queen. Congratulations by the way," she added with a wary smile at Cassie.

Cassie lifted her eyebrows, but refrained from commenting. The last thing she cared about was homecoming, or being queen. Maybe at one time she would have, but no longer. Her entire life had become focused upon her friends, her survival, and Devon. Her heart gave a mighty thump as her attention returned to him once more. They had left him at the side of the woods, within close proximity of that *thing*!

Panic tore through her as she whipped out her cell phone, sliding it open she frantically dialed his number. She turned her back on them, pacing swiftly away as she listened to the endless ringing. It clicked over to his voicemail; she did not leave a message. Sliding the phone shut, her hand shook with the terror suffusing her. Taking a deep breath she tried to calm herself as she texted him quickly, asking him to call her as soon as possible.

Turning slowly back to them, she knew she was unable to keep the horror from her face. "What is it?" Melissa asked softly.

"We left Devon standing there, and he's not answering his phone," she answered tremulously.

Worry flitted over their faces as they quickly exchanged looks. "He's fine," Melissa assured her gently. "I'm sure of it."

"How can you be so sure?" Cassie demanded. Panic tore through her, nearly choking her as she struggled to remain somewhat calm. "If that thing is stalking us, wouldn't it go after him if he saw us together?"

"It's ok Cassie." Chris grasped her arm gently; his touch only slightly soothed her tumultuous emotions.

She turned from him, pacing rapidly back and forth, her fingers still clenched around her phone. She had left him there, she had involved him in this, and she had *left* him there. She had been too selfish to set him free, and now she may have cost him his life. Pain and anguish tore through her nearly crushing her with the ferocity of it.

She didn't think she could survive without him. In such a short time he had become a part of her, she needed him even more than she needed her own extremities. She couldn't lose him; she would lose the best piece of herself if she did. She would hunt that thing down and destroy it if it hurt him, even if it meant destroying herself in the process.

Her phone went off; the ringing jarred her as she jumped in surprise. Relief flowed through her at the sight of his name and number. Opening her phone, she walked swiftly away from them. "Is everything ok?" he demanded immediately.

Cassie took a deep breath, fighting the tears of relief that burned her eyes. "Yes, yes I... uh I just wanted to say hi," she lied badly, feeling like a complete idiot as her face flamed red.

He didn't speak for a moment, and she could hear the wind rushing past his car as he drove. "Are you sure?" his voice was still fierce, the tension in it unmistakable.

"Yes, I'm sure."

"Are you still with Melissa and her father?"

"Yes."

"How are you getting home?"

"Chris will take me."

"I could pick you up."

Cassie licked her lips nervously, she glanced briefly at everyone but they were engrossed in their own conversation. She desperately wanted to see him again, to make sure that he was safe and that he stayed that way, but this was going to be a long night, and it would be better if he went home. Where he would be safe until morning.

She sighed heavily. "No, that's ok; we're going to be here awhile."

There was another long stretch of silence. "Ok, let me know when you get home safely."

She frowned at the command, surprised to hear him so worried about her safety again. She suddenly recalled his strange reaction earlier, the tension in his body as he had turned toward the woods. She recalled him still watching the forest intently after she had walked away. With a sudden jolt of surprise, she realized that he had sensed it to, that he had felt the evil and hatred that had permeated the air around them.

Her hand tightened around the phone. She knew, of course, that there were humans with their own special gifts. There were those with ESP, telekinesis, telepathy, and many other strange abilities that manifested in them. She suspected that perhaps Devon was one of them. She didn't know exactly what his ability was, but it seemed to be somewhere along the lines of Chris's talent.

What surprised her most was the fact that Chris had not picked up on it. He had sensed no power inside of Devon, no special gifts. He would have told her if he had. She thought that Chris would have recognized it immediately, especially if Devon's gift was similar to his own. Instead, he had felt nothing except for a strange darkness. Maybe that darkness was Devon's gift. Maybe because their abilities were so similar that Devon's acted as a block against Chris's own power.

Sighing softly, Cassie closed her eyes. She rubbed her temple as confusion and angst tore through her. This was one more thing that she simply could not deal with at the moment. There was already too much on her plate to even attempt to put the pieces of this puzzle together right now.

Pushing aside all questions and doubts, she focused upon her conversation with him once more. "I will," she promised softly.

He was silent for a moment more, and she could almost feel the tension radiating from him through the phone. "Good night Cassandra."

He purred her name, making her shiver in delight as she closed her eyes, savoring in the sound of his voice. "Goodnight Devon."

She reluctantly hung up, hating the loss of connection between them. Slipping her phone into her pocket, she turned slowly back to the others. She had no intention of telling them what she had just discovered about Devon. They had more than enough to deal with right now. Besides, she wasn't one hundred percent certain that she was right, and she didn't want to divulge something about him that he probably preferred to keep private. Maybe *he* wasn't even sure that he had such a gift.

"He's fine."

"Good," Chris said briskly. "Now, do you think we should tell your grandma and my mother about this?"

Cassie sighed heavily as she was drug back into the harsh reality of her world.

CHAPTER 14

Devon stepped around the back of the tree, folding his arms over his chest as he watched Cassie disappear safely inside. He breathed a sigh of relief as the door closed behind her, the click of the lock reached him even at his distance of two hundred feet. Crossing his legs, he leaned against the tree, prepared to stay there for the entire night.

He was not going to leave her unprotected until he knew who it was that had been in the woods tonight. He knew *what* it was, as he had recognized one of his kind immediately. He also knew that they were angry, hungry, powerful, and power thirsty. It wanted blood, and Devon had felt its fierce interest in Cassie. He had also felt the intense desire the creature directed at her. For that reason, he was more inclined to believe that it was a male.

Anger bristled through him as he shifted slightly. He did not want anyone else looking at her, or wanting her in such a way. Let alone someone that wanted to hurt her. As soon as he found who was out there, he was going to destroy them. They could not be allowed to run free, not in this town, and not with Cassie present. They would go for her, and he could *not* have that. No one was going to touch her, no one was going to hurt her, and absolutely *no* one was going to taste her blood, or turn her.

She was his, she belonged to him, and as long as he was alive he would keep her safe from any harm. Including himself.

Hunger sparked in his veins, burning through him. His canines pricked, feeling heavier and sharper as his thoughts turned briefly to feeding. He'd had no time to hunt tonight, not food anyway, as he had been too busy trying to find the creature that was stalking the town. Now, with thoughts of Cassie on his mind, the hunger sparked to life with a vengeance. He ran his tongue over his teeth, surprised to find that they had lengthened on their own. He usually had control over such a thing, unless he had gone to long between feedings and was extremely hungry, or primed for the kill. He was neither of those things now. It was simply thoughts of her that excited him so.

Heaving a large sigh, he ran his hand absently through his hair. It was going to be a long night, as he had no intention of leaving in order to satiate his hunger. The light in her room flicked on. He waited, anticipation clutching at him as she moved in front of the window, her lithe body was outlined by the curtains. She peered out for a moment, her gaze scanning the woods. Though he knew that she could not see him, he slid into the shadows, hiding behind the large oak once more.

When he came back around, she had disappeared from view. He leaned against the tree, trying not to think about the fact that this was what he was doing at the moment. In all his seven hundred and fifty two years, he had never thought that *he* would be standing outside of a girl's room, watching her, keeping her safe. Humans were only good to feed off of, to hunt, to stalk, and he hadn't done that in over a hundred years so he had simply taken to avoiding temptation.

His gaze drifted back to the window. She was no longer in sight, but the knowledge that she was there soothed the aching loneliness in him. She was all that he needed to get through the endless days and nights of his solitary existence.

His thoughts turned to Luther. It was the first time he had seen the strange man that Cassie had spoken of in her dream. Confusion twisted through him as he recalled the strange, thin man, standing in the shadows of the restaurant. Why did Luther have such a pull over her, such an effect on her, on all of them?

Devon's hands clenched on his arms as he recalled the confusion and slight fear that had eclipsed her in their dream, recalled the hesitance that had filled her when she had spoken of Melissa's father. And tonight, the minute the man had appeared they had all swiftly disappeared to follow him back to his house. A house they all spent a fair amount of time at, a *strange* amount of time at.

What the hell was going on with them?

He dropped his head into his hand, he rubbed the bridge of his nose as he thought over all of the strange things that seemed to circle around the three, no *four*, of them. A strange niggling began to take hold of him. It was all oddly familiar, and yet strangely unfamiliar. Frustration filled him; he was so close to putting a finger on it, yet the answer continued to elude him.

He lifted his head, frowning as the light in her room went out, though the flicker of the TV could still be seen. Glancing over at Chris's house, he was surprised to find that he appeared to have no intention of leaving for the night. After a few minutes the light in his room also went out. Devon waited, leaning against the tree, but Chris did not emerge.

Devon shoved aside all of his doubts and questions as a fierce desire claimed possession of him. He slid from the shadows, moving swiftly across her open yard. Not fully understanding what drove him, he grasped hold of the tree he had watched Chris climb before. He made his way quickly up the branches, climbing with the agility and grace that only one of his kind could possess. He paused outside her window, not sure what he had been thinking, not sure what to do. He just knew that he wanted to see her again. He *had* to see her again.

There was something out there that wanted her with a ferocious hunger. Something that wanted to take her away from him, and he could not have that. That knowledge spurred him into action; he couldn't be separated from her for a moment longer. Not pausing to think about it, he reached out and rapped lightly on the window.

His breath caught when she appeared before him, a beautiful angel silhouetted against the dark night. Her golden hair tumbled around her shoulders in thick waves that framed her exquisite face. The long blue t-shirt she wore fell to mid thigh, baring her creamy skin. His baser instincts leapt to life, his mouth watered as his hands clenched the tree branch. This was quite possibly the biggest mistake he had ever made, but he couldn't bring himself to care. Not when he got to look at her like this.

Her stunning eyes widened when she caught sight of him, her rosebud mouth parted slightly as she stared in astonished silence. Then, she was moving swiftly, unlocking the window, sliding it up as she leaned toward him. Her sweet scent of strawberries and spices assailed him, the beat of her heart pounded in his ears, instantly arousing the hunger that was ever present whenever she was near.

"Devon," she breathed, her husky voice causing a small shiver to run down his spine.

Her eyes raked over him, the desire radiating from her caused his own to intensify tenfold. He had felt her want for him before, but it was stronger tonight, deeper and more urgent. He didn't know where it had come from, what had caused it, but he wasn't sure he could resist it. His hand tightened around the branch, he had to stop himself from tearing it from the tree as he fought the fierce urge to seize hold of her and ease the burning hunger raging through him.

This had been a mistake; he never should have come here, not as tumultuous and unsettled as he was. He could hurt her; he *would* hurt her if he lost control. Though he knew that he should go, he did not move. He couldn't leave her.

She took a small step back, turning slightly to allow him access to her room. He hesitated, knowing that if he went through that window there would be no turning back. If he entered that room, he knew he would never be able to separate from her again. And he did not care. He did not care about anything but holding her, feeling her, being with her.

Hunger and need burned through him, but he could control it. He *would* control it. He could deny himself anything to be near her, to be with her, to keep her safe.

He moved swiftly through the window, rising slowly to his full height before her. She gazed up at him with wide eyes that gleamed in the glow of the television. The light played over her perfect features, robbing him of all reason as he simply gazed at her, unable to move. He sensed a strange vulnerability about her tonight, a wealth of sadness and fear that he had never seen before. He did not know what had happened with Luther, but it was obvious that it had troubled her greatly.

"What are you doing here?" she asked, slightly breathless.

He didn't know what he was doing here; he just knew that this was where he was supposed to be. Where he was *always* supposed to be. "I had to see you," he said honestly.

Her eyes widened even more, tears filled their bright depths. Those tears broke his paralysis. Reaching out, he wrapped his hand gently around the back of her head. The feel of her instantly soothed the raging beast, instantly calmed the fierce urges clamoring loudly inside him. He pulled her against him, relief filling him as her body melded against his, fitting perfectly, completing him.

Though no air came out, he breathed a sigh of relief, his fingers stroked through her silken hair as he caressed the back of her head. He had to remember to be careful around her, remember to pretend to breathe, and to keep her away from his nonexistent heartbeat. He had to remember to be gentle, to keep his strength restrained so as not to hurt her. But he found it difficult to concentrate on such things whenever he was around her.

"Cassie," he murmured, dropping his head into her hair, nuzzling her softly.

A fiery ache for her spread through his whole body. His grip on her tightened, his body hardened as he held her. Her arms wrapped around him, clinging to him as her fingers dug into his back. He did not know how long he held her, simply taking pleasure in the feel of her. The rightness of her body against his robbed him of all sense and reason. Time had no meaning in heaven, and he knew that this was as close to heaven as he was ever going to get. This was the only bit of heaven he would ever know in his world of death and destruction.

The flow of light from the moon drew his attention to the fact that it was getting late. He did not want to leave her, but he could not keep her up all night. She needed her rest, needed her sleep. She was far more fragile than he. She was a breakable, *mortal* human. The thought seized hold of him, sending a fierce bolt of bloodlust surging through him.

His fangs sprang free. Shaking, unnerved, he struggled to keep hold of himself. He fought fiercely to keep the demon inside, though it was bursting to get free of its cage. It was bursting to sink its teeth into her, bursting to drain the sweet, pure blood that pounded deliciously through her veins. It clamored to deplete her, and change her, and make her his forever. It clamored to make her immortal, and strong, and safe from the world of imminent death she resided in.

A tremor wracked through him, his grip tightened upon her. "Devon," she said softly.

He realized that his hold upon her had become painful. She did not strain against him though, did not complain. He fought to regain control, fought not to think about the appealing blood he could hear pumping through her veins. He knew she would be wonderful, a powerful rush unlike any he'd ever known. Then he would turn her, make her his forever, and keep her safe from the ultimate finality of her fragile life.

The temptation was so fierce, so overwhelming that he dropped his head to the side of her neck. He caught the scent of her blood, fierce and strong. The enchanting smell assailed him, causing uproar inside of him. The bloodlust shook him, the beast screamed to be soothed by her, appeased by her. His lips pulled back. His teeth were painful with their need to be sated, throbbing with their desire to pierce her. They were heavy and sharp and aching to bite down, aching to sink deep into her tender flesh and feast upon her.

"Devon?"

A tremor tore through him again, shaking him. He could not be denied, he would *not* be denied. And then she caressed him. Her delicate fingers stroked over his back, soothing the beast inside of him. He shuddered, burying his head in the side of her neck as he struggled fiercely to regain control of himself. Reason began to return as her gentle touch lulled him, slowly returning the monster to its cage.

What had he been thinking? He had been about to condemn her to his world. A world of darkness and brutality. He had been about to take the light from her. Had been about to rob her of her purity and goodness, of her innocence, and he had been about to do it against her will. He had to get away from her, stay away from her. She rocked his self restraint, his control, and in his world those were two things that he desperately needed to keep under wraps, or he *would* kill someone.

Shuddering, he caressed her hair once more. He would watch over her until the threat was gone, but he could not be near her anymore, could not hold her again. The thought tore through him with a burning rage that seared the inside of him, and left ashes in its wake. Agony blazed hotly in him, he felt the loss acutely, even though he still held her against him.

She tilted her head up, her bright eyes gleaming in the light. Her beautiful face broke his heart, shaking him completely, leaving him rattled and lost to her forever. In that moment he knew he could leave her, that he could go to the opposite side of the world, but she would be with him for eternity. She would remain burned into his heart, his thoughts, and every fiber of his being. He would never be without her, never be free of her; *never* escape her.

And he didn't want to be. Even if he could not be beside her, he wanted to carry her with him everywhere he went, no matter how far.

"I should go." His voice was tight, but he had regained most of his control.

She simply stared at him, the longing in her eyes almost more than he could stand. "Don't."

He blinked in surprise, not sure what to say, or do. Her long lashes lowered over her eyes, heat flared through her creamy cheeks. A soft groan issued from him. Her eyes came back to his, hesitant and shy. Her sweet simplicity was heart wrenching. She was far too good for him, and everything that he was. He was a monster and a killer, and she was an angel.

When he did not speak, her face flushed even redder, fire climbed high into her cheekbones. "I uh... I didn't mean..."

Her voice trailed off, she ducked her face, hiding it from him. Brushing back her silken hair, he cupped her face gently, feeling the heat of her skin against his palms. Her eyes flitted up to his. "I know," he said gently, hoping to ease some of her embarrassment. "I know what you meant."

He traced his thumb gently over her lip, relishing in the soft fullness of it. He could stay with her, lie beside her, and keep her safe as he held her through the night. He could control himself for that. He could give himself this, and then he would leave tomorrow. Even as he thought it, he knew he lied.

He was not leaving her. It would *never* happen. His feelings for her were to strong, to powerful, and he was acutely aware of the fact that he knew what that meant. That he knew what she was to him now, what she would always be, and how this would all end. He just did not want to think about it. Not now, because the ending was something that he didn't want for her. The ending was something that she would not want for herself, and he hated the fact that he may end up forcing his life upon her.

Now, he simply needed to hold her and protect her and keep her safe. Even if he may end up being the most dangerous thing to her.

He would just have to learn to control himself around her, and he would have to make sure that he was well sated whenever she was near. But he could not leave her; he did not think he could survive if he was unable to touch her, to know that she was safe, and that she was with him. To lose her would destroy him. On some primitive level, he knew that he could not survive without her.

"Beautiful," he whispered. Her lashes swept the delicate curve of her cheek as she ducked her face once more. He gently nudged her chin up again. When her eyes met his, he bent slowly, wanting to give her time to deny him. Wanting to give her time to come to her senses and flee while she still could.

She didn't move, didn't even breathe as he bent slowly over her. His lips brushed over hers in a butterfly caress that nearly shattered him as the glorious feel of her suffused him. The touch of her lips healed every broken bit of him. It soothed the loneliness of his life, made him forget the hunger and ruin of his existence. Though she did not make right the many deaths that stained his soul, she greatly eased the pain that resided permanently inside him.

He deepened the kiss, needing more of her. Light and warmth suffused him. Whiteness embraced his essence, pushing out the black as his hands tightened in her hair. He was trying to go slow, trying not to scare her, but he wanted more. He wanted *all* of her.

The fiery hunger tore through him once more. Pulling away, he struggled to regain control as he met her wide, stunned eyes. Slowly, she lifted her fingers to her mouth, gently touching them to her lips in awe. "Are you ok?" he asked worriedly, frightened that he had gone to fast and scared her.

She smiled tremulously. "Yes."

He clutched her tightly to him again, needing her warmth and strength as he struggled to maintain restraint. "It's late, you should lie down," he ground out. She gave a small nod, but did not look at him again. "Come on."

He led her slowly over to the bed. The blankets were pulled back from where she had laid before he arrived. He stared at the bed, wanting nothing more than to crawl in beside her and hold her tight. She sat down, her head bent, her golden hair tumbling forward in luxurious waves.

Sliding her legs onto the bed, the t-shirt she wore pulled back slightly to reveal a mouth watering view of her creamy thigh. Devon tightened everywhere, stiffening as more than just bloodlust tore through him. Then she looked at him again, her face bright red, her innocence almost intolerable.

Lifting her hand to him, she moved over. "Lie with me for a little bit."

For a moment he could almost feel his heart trip hammering, almost feel it turning over in his chest with a fierce slam that shook the place where it had once beat. She was testing the very limits of his control, nearly destroying the small thread he still had upon his self restraint. Then her gaze darted to the window, and he saw the fear that crossed her face, flashed swiftly through her eyes as she gazed at the dark night.

He turned slowly, searching for any hint of danger with his far superior eyes, and with every ounce of his vast power. Though he knew that the monster was still out there, he could not sense it now. It was either far away, or it was strong enough to mask itself at a distance. His stomach turned slightly. Though he was more powerful than most vampires in existence, Cassie was not. The thought of something that strong out there pursuing her, made the decision for him. If he stayed with her tonight, he would know that she was safe, protected.

Turning from the window, he kicked his sneakers off. She slipped further over as he climbed onto the bed beside her. Her eyes were wide as he laid back, wrapping his arm around her shoulders and pulling her gently down. She curled up like a sweet kitten against his side, nuzzling him gently as her hand rested lightly upon his chest. He grasped hold of her hand, keeping it away from the empty hollowness of where his heart should beat.

Devon remained stiff, unable to relax due to the fire burning through him. He stared unseeingly at the pictures flickering across the TV, holding her tight as she eased against his side. Soon, her breathing evened out, her hand relaxed against his. He felt the moment when she fell asleep.

Her trust in him was absolute as she gave herself over to him in her most vulnerable, helpless stage. He nuzzled her hair; his fingers gently stroked the nape of her delicate neck. He did not deserve her trust, for she did not know what he truly was. If she did, she would probably run screaming into the night. The thought terrified him.

It was something that he would have to make sure *never* happened. He could not lose her, nor could he shatter her innocence by being the one to tell her that the world was truly cold, heartless, and filled with monsters. Though he knew that one day he would have to leave her in order to keep her protected, he could not bring himself to let her go now. Not yet anyway, he would leave soon, return to his post outside at a safe distance from the vast temptation that she was. And one day, no matter how much it might destroy him, he would leave for good.

Maybe he could just tell her…

He instantly squashed the thought. How could he shatter her innocence? How could he destroy the sweetness in her with the knowledge of the true horrors that walked their world? He couldn't. He could *never* do that to her. And even if he did, what guarantee did he have that she would stay with him? He was a monster. Why would anyone want to stay with a monster?

His grip on her tightened, self loathing washed through him. He was not strong enough to leave her, and he was too much of a coward to risk losing her. He had done many awful things in his life, but this was by far the worst. He couldn't let her go, but even he realized that by keeping this from her, he was keeping the biggest part of himself hidden. The caring and trust she gave him was not complete.

It couldn't be complete without the truth he could never reveal. She would hate him if he did. And that would destroy him.

CHAPTER 15

Cassie woke slowly the next morning; her mind was still groggy from the deep, dreamless sleep that had claimed her. Memories of the night assailed her; she stiffened slightly as she realized that Devon was still beside her, his arm draped over her waist, his body melded against her back. Pleasure swept through her; heat warmed her body, causing her toes to curl against his jeans.

His kiss had been everything she had known it would be. It had filled her entire being, warming and melting places she had long thought frozen and dead. He had healed all of the jagged and torn pieces of her soul; filled the holes with his soothing presence. He made her stronger than she had ever thought she could be, stronger than she had ever imagined being.

He completed her.

He was everything that she needed, and she would willingly die to keep him safe from the evil within their town. His hand tightened upon her waist as she nestled closer to him, needing the strength of his body. "Don't move."

The words were groaned in her ear through his teeth. She instantly stopped moving, holding her breath as he stiffened around her. She did not know what was wrong with him, but it had almost sounded as if he were in pain. He moved so suddenly, and swiftly, that she didn't even have time to blink before he had rolled away from her, and was on his feet.

Cassie gasped in surprise as she sat up, but he had his back turned to her. His gaze was focused upon the window, and the rising sun. His hands were clenched tightly at his sides, the muscles of his forearms bulged with the tension that coursed through him. He seemed to be waging a silent battle, over what she had no idea, but she was disturbed by the tension radiating from him.

"Are you ok?" she asked softly.

He turned his head toward her; his emerald eyes were dark in the early morning light. His hair was tussled from sleep, giving him a boyish appeal that melted her heart. Silhouetted against the morning sun he was the most splendid man she had ever seen. "Fine."

Some of the stress seemed to be easing out of him; his voice was not as tight. Music suddenly blasted into the room, Cassie jumped in surprise, her heart leapt wildly. It took her a few seconds to pinpoint the source of the racket. Turning swiftly over, she hit the off button on her alarm clock. Dismay filled her as she realized that the world was intruding upon them, crashing down on the blissful peace she had found in his arms throughout the night.

"I need to go." She turned back to him. He had turned fully around again, his stance wasn't as rigid, his hands unclenched at his sides. He had taken a step closer to her. "I'll see you at school."

She nodded, not knowing what to say. She didn't want him to leave, didn't want to be apart from him for even a moment, let alone an hour. He took a deep breath, seeming to brace himself before striding over to her. Bending down, he dropped a soft kiss upon the tip of her nose. Smiling brightly up at him, her hand lightly stroked over his forearm, taking note of the thick, corded muscles that flexed beneath her touch. She marveled at the feel of his skin and the dark hair sprinkled over it. She could have stayed in bed, touching and feeling him all day long.

He hesitated for a moment, and then pulled quickly away. Slipping his sneakers back on, he moved with startling grace, and speed, to the window. Casting a quick glance over his shoulder, he smiled softly at her before disappearing swiftly outside. Cassie gaped for a moment before tossing her blankets aside and springing to her feet.

She hurried to the window, surprised to find that he had already disappeared from view.

Frowning, Cassie realized that she had not heard his car start. Had he walked over here last night? The sudden realization hit her that she didn't even know where he lived. It was more than a little disturbing. She was falling helplessly in love with him, seemingly bound to him in a way that she had never wanted to be bound to anyone, and had never thought possible. Yet, she knew nothing about him. She felt that she knew what kind of man he was, but that was all she knew. Leaning her head against the window, Cassie took a deep breath in order to try and calm the disquieting thoughts racing through her.

Sliding the window shut, she threw the lock and hurried to the bathroom to get ready for the day. She tried not to dwell on her upsetting realization about Devon as she went through her morning ritual. But try as she might, she could not keep the endless questions from running through her mind. Brushing her hair out, she clipped it up to keep it off the nape of her neck.

Hurrying downstairs, she braced herself for the conversation she was going to have to have now. Her grandmother was already at the stove, humming happily as she danced around the kitchen to Toby Keith singing about America. Her strawberry blonde hair had been pulled into a ponytail that bounced against her shoulders. She was a small woman, barely five foot, but she was slender with an athletic, fluid grace.

She turned to Cassie, her beautiful face lit up as her sky blue eyes landed upon her. The lines around her eyes crinkled merrily as she slid a bowl of oatmeal to Cassie. "Brown sugar and crème, the way you like it."

"Thanks grandma." Cassie took the bowl, but she did not sit, or grab hold of the spoon. This was a conversation she was certain would turn into a battle, but it was inevitable; she had to warn her grandma, she could not leave her unprepared, and vulnerable. She returned to singing merrily as Montgomery Gentry came over the radio. "Grandma, we need to talk."

Her grandmother turned back to her, the merry smile slipped from her face. Her light eyebrows drew sharply together over the bridge of her delicate nose. Her eyes darkened, going from sky blue to deep brown in an instant. Cassie was not unnerved; she was used to this trait of her grandma's. Though some people thought it was a genetic flaw, it was in fact what happened when her grandmother reached out to her spirit friends, communing amongst them.

Cassie sighed and plopped onto the stool. Sometimes her grandma would talk to her spirits for long periods of time, even forgetting that other people were present. Cassie played with her oatmeal as she waited. Though the three spirits that visited her grandma had become her grandma's friends over the years, her grandma had never known them in life, and she had never been visited by someone that she had known. Sometimes through her three "friends", her grandma was able to communicate with other people's loved ones, but never her own.

Cassie found it a cruel twist of fate for her grandmother to have her husband, and her daughter ripped away from her, but never be able to speak with them again. Cassie's grandfather had been killed three years before her mother; he had lost a battle to a vampire. Just like they all would. Her grandmother did not think it was cruel. She had once told Cassie that it would have been more painful if she had been able to speak with her loved ones.

"Something has come to town," she said softly.

Cassie dropped the spoon; she focused on her grandma's once more blue eyes. This time however there was no humor in them, but a grave sadness. Though she spoke often with her "friends" they were never able to tell her anything that might impact the course of her fate, or Cassie's. Telling her grandmother that something had come to town was their vague, roundabout way of trying to warn her of the danger that had arrived.

"Yes," Cassie answered. Sliding off her stool, she rested her hand on the countertop. "Luther believes that there is an Elder here."

Terror flashed across her grandmother's delicate features. She took a small step forward before leaning back against the counter. Cassie reached for her, afraid that her grandmother was going to collapse. Then, she straightened her delicate shoulders and stepped away from the counter. "Does it know that you are here?"

"I don't know, but it looks that way," Cassie answered honestly.

"You cannot stay here. You must leave. All three of you must get somewhere safe."

Cassie had known that this was coming, and she had been dreading it, but she had not changed her mind. In fact, after last night, she was more convinced than ever that she could not leave. She would not let the town go unprotected, and she could *never* leave Devon unprotected. Taking a deep breath, Cassie braced herself for the battle that was about to ensue.

"No grandma, we aren't going anywhere."

Her grandmother's mouth dropped. "What do you mean you aren't going anywhere?" she demanded fiercely.

"We can't abandon this town, we cannot leave everyone to face this danger alone, and unprotected. The Hunter's were made to protect innocent people; it's what we were created for. We have been prepped for our shortened life spans, for the threat of death that constantly overhangs us. We cannot simply run because this may be a difficult time."

Her grandmother stared at her in startled disbelief. "*May* be difficult? *May* be difficult?" Cassie winced at her grandma's hysterical tone and the raw panic in her voice.

"Cassie, if this thing finds you, if it figures out what you are, it *will* kill you! There is no difficulty in that!"

"Grandma…"

"Don't you grandma me! You get up those stairs and get your bags packed, *now!* I have lost my husband, my daughter, and my son-in-law to these monsters! I will not lose my granddaughter!"

Cassie's heart ached for her, and the losses that she had experienced, but she couldn't back down. No matter how much she hated the anguish in her grandmother's eyes, she could not leave this town. "You wouldn't leave if it were you grandma. Think of all of the innocent people that will lose their lives if we do."

Her grandmother's eyes flashed brown for a brief moment before she focused her full attention on Cassie again. "I left with *you*. I left innocent's behind then."

A knife twisted in Cassie's chest. She could not argue with that. She had given up everything for Cassie, and now, when her grandmother desperately wanted her to, Cassie could not return the favor. That fact was killing her, but she couldn't back down, she simply couldn't.

"I'm only telling you about this so that you are aware of the danger, and you can stay safe."

"Cassandra…"

Before she could finish the sentence, Cassie stepped forward and hugged her tightly. Tears slid silently down her face as she clung to her grandmother's slight frame. "I'm sorry grandma, you know I would do anything for you, but I can't do this. You know that this is right; you know that we cannot leave them. I know that you are scared for me, *I* am scared, but we must stay."

Her grandmother shuddered, her head dropped to Cassie's shoulder. "You will be safer, more aware out there."

"Always," Cassie vowed.

Her grandmother squeezed her tight and pulled quickly away. Her bright eyes shimmered with tears, but her cheeks remained dry as she met Cassie's gaze again. "My brave girl, just like your mom."

A cold chill went through Cassie. She had been told she was just like her mother her whole life. She looked like her mother, she moved like her mother, and she acted like her mother. The only difference was that Cassie was not gifted and her mother had possessed the powerful ability to move objects with her mind. Cassie didn't mind looking and acting like her mother. She did not, however, want to die young like her mother. Yet, right now, her life seemed to be heading along that same path. Only she would be seven years younger than her mother's twenty four when she died.

Cassie fought the bone wracking shudder that tore though her, she desperately wanted those seven years. They may not seem like much, but they would be precious, and she had a very bad feeling that she was going to be cheated of them. "There are times I wish that Luther had never found you."

Cassie tried to push aside the cold terror, and aching hurt, that was firmly embedded in her belly. "There are times I wish that too," she admitted softly.

If Luther had never found her that day, then she and Chris never would have known that they were Hunter's. Chris's mother, and her grandmother, had decided to keep the truth hidden from them. They had been determined to keep them safe, and to raise them as normally as possible. Until Luther arrived, Chris's power had been passed off as a psychic ability that some normal people may have possessed. At the time, Cassie's grandmother believed that they were the last of The Hunter line, and that no one would come looking for them.

They had been wrong.

"You will be safe, right?" Cassie asked worriedly.

Her grandmother smiled, but it did not reach her eyes. "Don't worry about me dear, don't you ever worry about me. You don't get to be my ripe old age without knowing how to take care of yourself."

Cassie nodded, but she was not completely soothed. She knew her grandmother; she was not one to sit idly by, especially if she thought she would be keeping Cassie safe. She could only hope that she didn't do something crazy.

"Eat your breakfast dear, Chris is on his way over."

Cassie glanced back at her bowl of oatmeal, but she had no appetite. "I'll see you tonight grandma, I love you."

She dropped a quick kiss on her soft cheek as she grabbed hold of her bag and slung it over her shoulder. "Love you too dear. Have a good day."

Cassie glanced back at her, but she was still staring out the window, a distant look on her pretty features. A chill of apprehension slid down Cassie's spine.

CHAPTER 16

Cassie played with the applesauce on her plate, twirling it over on her spoon; her thoughts were distant and distracted. She could not get the lonely image of her grandmother out of her head, or shake the foreboding that had seized hold of her. Devon took hold of her hand, his touch soothing some of her tension.

Looking up at him, she managed a wan smile as she met his troubled gaze. "What is wrong?"

Shaking her head, she dropped her spoon; seizing hold of his hand she once again noted that it was abnormally cold. She frowned as she ran her finger over his skin, savoring in the feel of him. His circulation had to be poor for him to be this chilled. Either that, or he had just come from outside as it was a little brisk for September.

Shrugging it off, she managed a small smile for him. "Nothing, just not that hungry."

He didn't seem to buy it as he stared hard at her. "Are you sure?"

"Yes." She studied him carefully for a moment, her questions from earlier returning to her. "Devon, where do you live?"

Quirking an eyebrow, a small smile flitted across his full lips. "Is that what has you so distracted?"

Cassie shrugged absently. "I just realized that I don't know much about you."

Something flickered in his eyes. It was a quick flash, but she was certain that she saw it. She couldn't be sure what it had been though, but for a moment she thought it was fear. But why would her question cause him fear? "Well, we will have to remedy that," he said softly, his hand tightened briefly around hers. "My place is in Oyster Hills."

Cassie blinked in surprise; she didn't know much about

Oyster Hills, except for the fact that it was very expensive, and highly upscale. "Wow. What do your parents do?"

His jaw clenched tight, a muscle jumped in his cheek. "They're dead."

Cassie gasped, horror filled her. "I'm so sorry; I know how awful that is."

He shrugged absently, his finger caressing her hand lightly. "It was a long time ago."

"But the hole never heals," she whispered.

His distant gaze came back to hers, tender and loving as he studied her. "I suppose not."

Swallowing heavily, she leaned closer to him, hoping to ease some of the pain she knew such a passing left. "Do you mind me asking what happened?" she inquired softly.

He hesitated for a moment, before shrugging. "They were killed."

Cassie's eyes widened, anguish filled her as she studied his hard countenance. Though curiosity filled her, she decided against pressing further. She knew how much it could upset someone; how the wound never completely healed. No matter how much time passed. "I'm sorry, I didn't mean to pry."

He smiled at her, kissing her hand gently. "Anything you wish to know, you just ask."

Leaning closer to him, she was surprised to realize that she had completely forgotten about the noise and confusion of the cafeteria. He had a way about him that made it very easy to forget that the rest of the world even existed. He had a way that made it impossible to focus on anything, except him. She rested her head on his shoulder, savoring in his scent as he gently caressed her hair.

Closing her eyes, she allowed herself to drift into him, relishing in the comfort that he brought her. "Would you like to see my place today?"

She glanced up at him, grinning brightly as she nodded. "I would."

His eyes twinkled merrily as he dropped a chaste kiss upon her forehead. The memory of the passionate kiss they had shared last night assailed her, leaving her longing for more. For a moment a tremor of fear trickled through her. What would happen if they went to his place alone? Though the thought did arise some fear, she couldn't stop her pulse from racing with excitement.

A new commotion snapped her eyes to the center of the cafeteria. Marcy had grabbed a chair and was pulling it into the center of the room. Mrs. Kindel shook her head, but didn't stop her as Marcy brought forth a microphone and climbed onto the chair. Cassie had no idea where the microphone had come from; she didn't want to know either.

"Hello, testing." Everyone in the room winced as the microphone squealed loudly. "Ok, I have some announcements to make," Marcy continued when the noise died down.

Cassie glanced at Melissa, who smiled superiorly back at her and gave a quick wink. Groaning inwardly, she slid slightly down in her chair, hoping that she could somehow be overlooked. Devon was frowning in confusion; his dark eyebrows were drawn tightly together as he studied Marcy like some strange bug.

"What's this about?" he asked quietly.

"Homecoming nominations."

Uncertainty swirled in his eyes. Cassie stared questioningly at him, but he didn't say anything more. For a moment, she could have sworn that he hadn't known what she was talking about. But that couldn't be possible, no matter how small a school he had come from, they would still have homecoming, wouldn't they?

He leaned slightly back, his emerald eyes darting to Marcy as a mask of indifference slipped over his face. Cassie's hand tightened briefly around his as doubt continued to swirl through her. He glanced back at her, his eyes darker and more intense than normal. Their eyes locked forcefully, Cassie's heartbeat picked up. All of her doubts vanished as she was lost to him once more. His thumb stroked over her skin, causing her body to heat everywhere. She could not *wait* to be alone with him later.

"Now, when I call your name please come up here. Thanks. Nominees for homecoming king are Mark Young, Hector Rodriguez, Jack Wells, Chris Tempen...."

Cassie beamed happily, clapping loudly as Marcy called off Chris's name. Chris's fair skin blazed red as he stood to a raucous chorus of cheers and whistles. He bowed and waved to everyone as if he were royalty. Marcy frowned angrily, her voice breaking off as the cheers continued. Chris and Jack were pounded on the back by the rest of the football team as they made their way to the center of the room, and Marcy.

"Ok, settle down!" Marcy called into the microphone. She waited impatiently, her foot tapping, and her arms folded across her chest as the cheers slowly died down. Marcy rolled her eyes but as she glanced down at the piece of paper in her hand, a sly smile played across her lips. A feeling of foreboding stole through her. "The final nominee is Devon Knight."

Cassie's mouth parted slightly, shock coursed rapidly through her as cries of delight, and loud clapping sounded through the room. It was mostly the girls that applauded and shouted, making it apparent which side of the nomination he had received. Cassie turned slowly back to him. He was sitting stiffly in his chair, a blank expression on his face, but a hard gleam in his eyes. This was not his thing, not at all, and it was more than obvious that he didn't want it. She wasn't entirely sure he even knew what it meant.

Then he moved swiftly, sliding elegantly from his chair as he rose gracefully. He glanced down at Cassie, warmth momentarily melting the ice in his eyes. Gently releasing her, he moved swiftly and elegantly to stand beside Chris. The cheers grew louder, the higher pitch of the girl's voices reverberated in the large cafeteria. Though some of the boys clapped, including Chris, most did not.

This time, Marcy did not urge everyone to quiet down as she smiled brilliantly. Instead, she waited patiently for the commotion to stop. Anger filled Cassie as she glanced around the cafeteria, taking note of all the girls staring ravenously at Devon. Marcy was the worst offender, as her crush on Chris had obviously switched to Devon. Though Cassie knew that Devon did not want any of them, she still didn't like the fact that they all wanted *him*. And not a one of them gave a damn that he was already with her.

"It's ok," Melissa said softly, leaning forward to be heard over the commotion.

"I know."

"Then why are you glaring at every girl in this room like you want to hit them?" she inquired.

"Maybe not *every* girl."

"Just Marcy?" Cassie couldn't stop the laugh that escaped her as she shook her head at Melissa's teasing.

Cassie tried to catch Devon's eye, but he did not look at her again as he studied the other boys. Jack and Hector were playfully pushing each other; Mark was wearing a goofy grin and flexing his muscles. Chris was standing quietly, his arms folded over his chest, but he was beaming from ear to ear as he winked at the girls closest to him. They all looked so young and immature, Devon seemed vastly older and out of place amongst them.

Cassie's heartbeat picked up, her hands curled on the table. Who was he? She wondered again. Why did he seem so far beyond her age, and everyone else's?

"Now the nominees for homecoming queen," Marcy continued when the noise finally quieted down. "The nominees are Amanda Jenkins, Sharon Crosby, Kelly Standish, Cassandra Fairmont..." Loud cheers and whistles erupted around the room as she rose, but unlike Devon, her appreciative audience was mostly male.

Cassie flushed hotly as she slipped from the table. She tried to keep her shoulders straight as she hurried to stand beside Kelly. The dark, angry looks from most of the girls in the room followed her, along with the leering stares of the boys. Her skin crawled with the mixed emotions blazing against her. Trying to keep as collected as she could, she kept her face expressionless, but inwardly she was a seething mass of turmoil.

Marcy sighed loudly, tapping impatiently at the microphone to get everyone's attention. Slowly the caterwauling died down with only a few whistles and shouts still piercing the air. Devon's face had become even harder, his jaw clenched tight as he met Cassie's gaze briefly. It was apparent that he disliked the attention of the men toward her, almost as much as she did. She wished that she could reach out and touch him; she desperately needed the comfort that he always brought her.

"And finally," Marcy continued with a bright grin on her face. "Myself."

There was more applause, but it was not as enthusiastic, and Marcy was unable to hide her annoyance. "Here are your nominees for king and queen, voting will begin in two weeks. Everyone, consider your candidates carefully and vote on the people you think deserve it most. Thank you all."

Marcy dismounted from her chair, eagerly accepting the congratulations she received as she made her way through the crowd. Cassie wished she could be as thrilled as Marcy, but she had never wanted popularity, never wanted the attention that came with it. Unfortunately she had been launched into the role during her freshman year, when puberty set in.

It had taken her awhile to learn how to deal with the sudden influx of interest. Over the years she had gotten a lot better with it, but she still did not like being thrust into the spotlight. And she most certainly did not want to be swamped by a bunch of people trying to congratulate her. She was not surprised that most of them were boys.

Devon was also surrounded by a group of well wishers, most of them girls, but a few of the guys had appeared to shake his hand. He looked highly uncomfortable as Ariel Drake grasped hold of his hand, clutching it tightly, nearly falling over him as she leaned close. Cassie fought back a smile of amusement as he gave Ariel a wan smile while discreetly trying to free his hand from her death grip. He finally succeeded but Janet and Jenna Howe immediately pounced upon him. Cassie heaved a sigh, realizing that she would have to rescue him if he was ever going to get free of the swarm of girls. And from the look on his face, he was in desperate need of rescuing.

Mark Johnson stepped swiftly in front of her, blocking her attempt at reaching Devon. Fighting back the fierce urge to groan and roll her eyes, Cassie met his dark, stormy gaze. "Hello Cassandra, I've been trying to get you alone for the past few days, but you're always busy."

Cassie glanced back at Devon, but now he was encircled by Linda Drake, Helen Potts, and Marcy had reappeared. He was never going to get free on his own now. "I'm sorry Mark…"

She tried to move around him, but he sidestepped, swiftly blocking her path. She frowned up at him, aggravated by the interruption. "I just wanted to congratulate you Cassandra." Mark always called her by her full name; she suspected it was because he thought it would separate him from everyone else in her life. It did not. His eyes sparked as his gaze ran appreciatively over her. Unable to stop herself, she took an involuntary step back. She hated the way his leering look always made her feel as if he could see right through her clothes. Her skin began to crawl in disgust. "Maybe you'll be my queen."

As much as the idea made her stomach turn, Cassie managed a brief nod. "Maybe."

She tried to sidestep him again, but once again he blocked her path. Her aggravation level mounting, she folded her arms firmly over her chest as she stared fiercely at him. "I was thinking that maybe we could go to B's and S's tonight," Cassie was already shaking her head, but he continued on. "Maybe catch a movie."

"No Mark, I'm sorry."

He blocked her path once more when she tried to escape him. This time however, there was no amusement, or leering, in his fierce gaze. Cassie was stunned by the depth of anger that radiated from his deep brown eyes. "Is this because you've become the new guy's toy?"

Cassie blinked in surprise, and then anger flared through her. "I'm nobody's toy Mark!" she snapped.

"Slut then?"

The word snapped all the anger out of her as shock and horror rolled forth. She had never been called that before, *never* been verbally attacked like this before. Oh, she had been called many things over the years, but never this, and not with this much anger, and hatred. It was the hatred that shocked her most, leaving her speechless and shaken. She had never been hated before, never thought it would feel like this. It left her hollow and uncertain.

She took a step back, just wanting to escape now, but he followed her. His eyes burned as he bore down upon her, his mouth pursed, and his large shoulders set stiffly. She did not fear for her physical safety, she didn't think he would do anything here, and she knew that she was stronger than he was. If she could fight off a vampire, she could fight off one very angry teenage boy, but it was the last thing that she wanted to do in a crowded cafeteria. However, she was concerned about what he would say next, and she was certain that she didn't want to hear any more of it.

"You know what you are Cassandra, you're just a tease. You're a twisted bitch that loves to tease people, playing with their emotions and wrapping them around your little finger."

Cassie's mind stuttered, searching for words that momentarily failed her. Swallowing heavily, she tried hard to think of something that would somehow ease the tension of the situation. "I have never led you on Mark," she said gently, fairly certain that he was about to explode.

"You walk around here, strutting around like you're better than all of us!" he snapped.

Bile rose in Cassie's throat, her stomach turned and knotted painfully. The words stung like a whip, but it was the cold fury radiating from him that made her want to throw up. She did not know what was wrong with Mark, what had sparked this fury inside him, but she did know that he was swiftly losing control. She looked quickly around; searching for some kind of help, but everyone was busy congratulating the nominees, or escaping for their next class. She couldn't even see Devon anymore, Mark completely blocked him out.

She was on her own.

"Mark, I'm sorry, I…"

"You're a whore!"

Cassie's mouth dropped open as shock and horror once more slammed through her. Her arms encircled her stomach in an effort to try and keep her lunch down. She wasn't entirely certain that it was going to work as her stomach lurched threateningly. "Mark…"

"A no good whore," he growled. He reached for her, but Cassie turned aside, just barely dodging his beefy hand. Disgust filled her, slowing her to the point that she could hardly move. Rage blazed through his eyes, it flared his nostrils. For the first time, she was afraid of the fury that suffused him. She was not entirely sure that she could beat someone that was as crazed as Mark obviously seemed to be right now. "Whore! Giving it away to everyone…"

Mark was suddenly ripped back; his feet came off the floor as he was pulled two feet up and away from her. Cassie's eyes widened in surprise, her mouth dropped. For a stunned moment she didn't know what had happened, who had grabbed hold of him. And then she saw Devon as he shoved Mark against the wall, his hand wrapped fiercely around Mark's throat. His green eyes were dark and dangerous, his lithe body taught with the anger that radiated from him.

"Don't you ever talk to her like that again!" he snarled, his hand tightening around Mark's neck. Mark coughed, beginning to struggle within Devon's grasp as his eyes bulged. "Do you understand me?"

Mark nodded enthusiastically, coughing again as he struggled to breathe. His fingers clawed at the tight hold Devon had upon him, but Devon's grip did not lessen. Though Devon was slightly shorter and not as broad as Mark, it was more than obvious that he was quite capable of beating Mark in a fight. In fact, Cassie was fairly certain that Mark wouldn't stand a chance.

Devon's hand tightened briefly, causing panic to flash across Mark's features. "If you ever even *talk* to her again," Devon growled his voice pitched so low that even Cassie had to strain to hear him. "I will make you pay for it, and I will make this look like it was a good time."

A chill swept down her spine at the threat, a threat she was certain he would make good on. Mark managed another brief nod, his gaze darted briefly toward Cassie, his eyes rolled with panic. Devon shoved him back hard again, releasing him at the same time. Slumping forward, Mark rested his hands on his knees as he gasped for air. Devon took a step toward her, putting his body effectively between the two of them.

Cassie peered around Devon's back, too flabbergasted to fully comprehend everything that had just happened. Mark's face was beet red, either from lack of oxygen, or anger. His shoulders were set tightly, but he did not look at either of them as he stormed into the crowd. Cassie's eyes widened as she took in the students still present to witness what had just happened. Though the cafeteria had emptied a lot, there were at least twenty of them still gathered about. It would only be a matter of time before this incident was all over the school. Oh well, she thought with a sigh, she hadn't wanted to campaign for homecoming queen anyway.

Devon turned toward her, his eyes fierce and dark, his hard jaw clenched tight. "Are you ok?" Cassie blinked at him in surprise, unable to get her malfunctioning brain to work correctly as she tried to focus her full attention on him. "Cassie, are you ok?"

He seized gently hold of her, pulling her a step closer to him. The touch she had always found so soothing, now only served to confuse and disorient her more. What she had just seen, it couldn't have been possible, could it? She studied him carefully, her mind spinning. Could a human be that strong?

But what else could he be, but human?

She scanned him rapidly, feeling slightly sick. "Who are you?" The words popped out in a choked whisper before she could stop them.

The hands on her arms tightened briefly as his body hardened subtly. A look of resignation filled his eyes and Cassie had the gut sinking feeling that she had somehow managed to push him away from her. "Did he hurt you?" he asked, the words coming through clenched teeth but carrying no hint of anger.

Cassie shook her head, trying to clear it of the stunned fog that clung to her. "No," she managed to whisper. "No, I'm fine," she said with a little more conviction.

His gaze ran over her, but it did not warm. "Let's get you to class."

Panic tore through Cassie. This was not the Devon she knew. This was not the man that gazed at her warmly, and touched her reverently. This man was hard and cold and distant, and *she* was the one that had caused this change in him. He had been trying to protect her, and she had pushed him away with her confusion and doubts. She may not know as much as she would like about him, but he was new to town, and part of the fun in a relationship was supposed to be getting to know the other person. Wasn't it?

Her gaze darted to where he had pinned Mark against the wall, lifting him as if he weighed no more than a feather. The strength it had taken was amazing, startling. It was a strength she had never seen in a human being before. She turned slowly back toward him, tilting her head to study him as her doubts slowly started to build into full fledged panic.

Who was he? *What* was he?

He gently took hold of her arm, but she could feel the cold distance that lingered in him. Slowly, she looked toward Melissa and Chris. Melissa's head was tilted curiously to the side, her dark eyes intense. Chris stood stiffly, his arms folded over his chest. He gave Devon a brief nod of approval, one that Cassie instantly recognized as a "guy" thing. Chris found nothing wrong with what had just happened, he was just impressed that Devon had stood up for her, and that he had beaten Mark in their brief encounter.

Cassie rolled her eyes at Chris as she heaved a sigh. She would never understand men, and their vast amounts of testosterone. "Come on Cassie," Devon urged, though his tone was gentle she could still hear the tension in it.

She followed him slowly out of the cafeteria, so lost in her own thoughts, and doubts, that at first she didn't notice the whispers and glances cast their way. Slowly, they penetrated her haze. Every student they passed shot them looks while whispering behind their hands. Cassie frowned fiercely; her pride shoved aside her hurt and confusion as she straightened her shoulders and determined to ignore all of their gossip.

CHAPTER 17

Cassie played idly with a blade of grass, pulling it lazily from the ground before letting it drop back down. She was tired, achy, and more than a little chilled. The sudden drop in temperature that had started earlier in the week, had made the night far cooler than she was prepared for with her light windbreaker. She huddled deeper into her coat, knowing that it was not only the night that chilled her, but also the events of the day.

She had seen Devon only briefly at the end of the day. He had still been cold, detached, and not completely himself. He had not mentioned coming over to his place again and neither had she. She had needed to get away from him for a little bit, to clear her mind, but it was not working out as well as she had hoped.

She tried not to think about the distance that had lingered around him, or the doubts that continuously plagued her now. She tried to keep herself focused on the here and now. But her mind would not cooperate as it kept jumping back to the tenderness and wonder of last night. Then she would recall her extreme lack of knowledge about him, and the strange strength that he had possessed today and her stomach would turn and her mouth would go dry.

She shuddered, huddling deeper as she flipped her collar up. "It's not that cold out," Chris muttered, his gaze rapidly scanning the cemetery.

Cassie shrugged absently before she returned to picking at the grass. She wanted to get home as soon as possible; she hoped that Devon would come to her room again tonight, but she was doubtful that it would happen. Her heart lurched in her chest, her pulse pounded in her ears as excitement and desire tore through her. No matter what had happened today, no matter her doubts and confusion, she *desperately* wanted to see him again. She did not care about anything other than seeing him, and easing the distance she felt between them now.

It was unreasonable, unnatural the way she felt. Her concerns should slow her down, should make her warier of him, but they didn't. She cared more about seeing him than she did about the possibility that there might be something wrong with him. That there may even be something truly deadly, and off, about him.

Cassie shivered again, huddling deeper into her light coat, hating the chill in her bones. Melissa threw aside the English essay she had been working on. For a moment Cassie thought that something had arrived. That a fight was finally about to ensue, and Cassie was spoiling for a fight. Then, Melissa pinned her with her intense, steady gaze.

"Ok, what's up?"

Cassie blinked in surprise. "Nothing," she answered automatically.

Melissa gave her the 'I'm not an idiot look,' and lifted her dark eyebrows almost to her hairline. "Come on Cassie, we all know you better than that. Something's on your mind and it has you pretty upset. Now spill."

Cassie glanced quickly over them, noting the inquisitive looks that Chris and Luther gave her. Heaving a big sigh, she tossed away the remaining blades of grass she had picked and climbed swiftly to her feet. Though she felt as if she might be betraying Devon by talking with them, she knew that Melissa and Chris were the two people that would have the most insight into him.

She paced slowly back and forth, not sure how to begin. Finally, she just decided to jump in. "What exactly have you seen about Devon?"

Melissa stared at her in surprise, her dark eyes becoming turbulent and distant. Shaking back her black braid, her eyes focused on Cassie once more. "Aside from his arrival, I've seen nothing else about him."

"What did you see about that then?" Cassie demanded, a sense of urgency filling her.

Melissa tilted her head curiously. "Not much Cass, I just saw him coming, and I saw brief glimpses of the two of you together. I knew that he was coming for you."

Those last three words caused a chill to run down Cassie's spine. Coming for her, he was coming for her. But why? What did he want with her? Cassie shuddered, feeling like a turtle as she tried to pull all of her exposed skin into her jacket. It was a poor attempt at trying to hide from the world. "You saw nothing wrong with him though?" she asked softly.

The three of them exchanged surprised, wary looks, before focusing their attention on her once more. "No Cassie, not at all. I would have warned you if I had. Why are you asking this?"

Cassie chose to ignore the question as she turned to Chris. "And what did you feel from him?" she asked softly.

Chris looked briefly confused before shaking his head. "Not much," he admitted slowly. "I told you I can't really read him."

Cassie absorbed this information slowly, not knowing what to make of it. Chris could get a glimpse of everyone. He was one of the main reasons she had never dated Mark. Chris had sensed something off about him, although Mark had never done anything wrong, never acted badly in any way before today. His doubts about Mark had been spot on though.

"Why is that?" she asked softly, the chill in her becoming an ice storm that seemed to freeze the blood in her veins.

Chris shook his head, looking thoughtful and distant. "I don't know Cassie, I really don't. For the most part there is an impenetrable wall around him that I can't pierce, and believe me I have tried. That guy is a challenge that I would love to master, but I can't."

She swallowed heavily, trying to huddle deeper into her jacket, but there was nowhere for her to go. There was nowhere for her to hide anymore. Chris's words only caused her doubt, and confusion, to escalate higher. What did that mean? How did a human keep Chris at bay? Unless, of course, he really did possess the same ability as Chris, and somehow it did keep Chris blocked out.

Then, she caught something that he had said. "For the most part?" she inquired softly.

He nodded, folding his arms over his chest as he leaned against a white oak. The leaves were still mostly green in the tree, almost black in the dark night, but a hint of color had made its way into the outer leaves. That hint of color was now the shade of blood. Cassie's stomach rolled with that realization.

"There is one thing that he can't keep blocked out."

"What's that?" Melissa asked eagerly when Chris did not continue.

Chris's gaze pierced Cassie. "His feelings for you. He can't keep those hidden, they radiate out of him like a lighthouse beacon calling home the ships. It's why I kinda like the guy. I know that he cares deeply for you, and he would do anything for you. I have to like someone like that."

Warmth swept through Cassie, slightly melting the iceberg that had enshrouded her. "Really?" she whispered hopefully.

"Yes."

Tears burned the backs of her eyes, but she would not shed them. Not here, not in front of them. Her doubts and fears lingered, but Chris's words had warmed her to the tips of her toes. "Why are you asking this Cassie?" Luther inquired softly.

"I was just wondering," she tried to bluff.

It was more than obvious that he didn't believe her. "You never just wonder, now what is going on?"

She paced restlessly back and forth, not sure how much she wanted to say. Sighing heavily, she spun to face them. "Didn't you find the incident in the cafeteria today odd?"

Chris's face darkened with anger, Melissa nodded eagerly. "I cannot believe Mark said those things to you! I was going to punch that guy myself if Devon hadn't got there first!" Chris spat.

"He was wicked quick to defend you."

Melissa's eyes took on a dreamy look. Cassie sighed loudly; apparently Melissa had decided to jump on the "I love Devon" bandwagon also. But that was not what frustrated her right now. Was she the *only* one that had noticed something off about what had happened today? And just how quick had Devon been? The last time Cassie had seen Devon, he had been across the cafeteria, and then suddenly he was there, tossing Mark around like a rag doll.

"Another reason I like the guy," Chris muttered.

Luther studied them all carefully before piercing her once again with his intense gray eyes. Nothing ever slipped past Luther, and he often saw far more than she wanted him to. "There is more, isn't there?"

"Yes." Taking a deep breath, Cassie decided to just plunge in. She needed to unload some of her confusion, doubts, and burdens on someone. And she trusted these three with her life. "I've come to care for him, a lot." That was the understatement of the year, but she did want to keep some things to herself. "And I realize that I know nothing about him."

"Well, he's new," Melissa defended. "It takes time to get to know someone."

Cassie licked her lips nervously, turning she began to pace again. "I know that, I understand that. What I don't understand is how he sensed that evil presence the other day…"

"What?" Melissa interrupted sharply.

"He knew that it was there, even before we did. I felt it in him, felt the tension that took hold of him moments before *we* even felt it. He knew it was there…"

"There are humans with special abilities," Chris interjected.

"Yes, I know that, but this was different Chris. I don't know how to explain it, but it was. It got me thinking about how little I really do know about him. Then today, in the cafeteria, the strength he displayed. What human could do that?"

They exchanged quick glances. "Some humans are very strong."

"*That* strong Melissa?" Cassie demanded sharply. "He lifted Mark with one hand, and Mark is not exactly a light weight. *One hand!*" Cassie realized her voice had taken on a slightly hysterical pitch, but she could not rid herself of it.

Silence met her. Their gazes became distant. "What are you trying to say Cassie?" Luther asked gently. "Do you think he might be a Hunter also?"

"I don't know. That's why I'm talking to you guys about this. But wouldn't you know if he was?"

Luther frowned, shrugging absently. "I don't know. I would like to think so, but things are so different now. I can look for Hunter's, but there is no guarantee that I will know them when I find them. Melissa had a premonition about yours and Chris's location. You were easy enough to find as I had met your mother once, and you look a lot like her. However, even with the few premonitions Melissa's had about other locations, I have never found another Hunter. I don't *know* if I would recognize him if he is one."

Cassie digested this slowly, she supposed that would make sense, but it still did not ease the anxiety clutching at her. "He said that his parents had been killed, but he didn't say how, maybe they were actually killed during The Slaughter. But if he does have Chris's ability, wouldn't he be able to sense us? Wouldn't he come to us? Wouldn't he want to be with people like him, instead of on his own?"

"He may not know what we are," Melissa said gently. "If he is keeping Chris blocked, then Chris may be doing the same thing to him."

"Maybe," Cassie muttered, still not completely convinced.

"I don't understand where you're going with this," Melissa said gently. "What do you think he is?"

Cassie threw her hands impatiently up as she resumed anxiously pacing once more. "I don't know!" she exclaimed in exasperation.

"You don't think there is something wrong with him, do you?"

Cassie frowned, biting her bottom lip gently. "I... no... I don't know," she finished lamely.

They inhaled sharply, their foreheads furrowed with doubt and confusion. "No Cassie, I would have seen that," Melissa said, though her voice was hesitant and not quite as confident as normal.

"And the way that he feels about you." Chris shook his head, stepping away from the tree. "No. No one can feel that strongly about someone if there is something wrong with them. What he feels is very pure and it's... well I have never felt anything like it before. I know that *I've* never felt that way about anyone. It's amazing Cassie, that's the only way I can describe it, and it's the only thing that gets through."

Tears burned her eyes again. "Really?" she breathed.

He gave her a lopsided grin, his shaggy hair falling into one of his sapphire eyes. "Would I lie to you?"

She managed a wan smile. Though they had managed to ease some of her fears, she could not shake the doubts that clung stubbornly to her. There were just so many things that she didn't know. Though, she *did* know that all she really wanted was for him to come to her room again tonight. Maybe if she talked to him she would feel better about this whole situation.

A flash of movement amongst the trees caught her attention. Her head snapped to the left, her eyes narrowed as she searched the shadowed woods. Though Luther had not wanted them to come out here tonight, they had insisted upon it. Some of the stories in the paper had led Luther to believe that there was an Elder out there; today's news had led them all to believe that there was also a young vampire on the Cape again. Two bodies had been found, mauled with little or no blood left in their system. It had taken a lot of persuasion, but Luther had finally conceded to let them come to the cemetery in the hopes that it would wander this way. The monster needed to be put down before it did anymore harm.

"It's out there," she whispered.

Luther straightened, his eyes narrowing sharply as he scanned the woods. "Is it The Elder?" he demanded sharply.

Cassie shook her head as Chris answered him. "No."

Another flash turned Cassie to the left. She braced her legs, setting her shoulders as she prepared for the imminent attack. It did not matter that they outnumbered the creature; it would still come for them. It would wrongly think that they were easy targets, and a buffet that it would want to partake in.

The woods exploded in a flurry of violent motion. Leaves exploded outward, scattering across the grass of the cemetery. The creature rushed them in a blur of motion that would have been imperceptible to the human eye, but Cassie picked up on it instantly. She braced herself, clenching tighter to her stake as she bounced on her heels in preparation.

Though her thoughts had been focused upon Devon during training, she found all of her doubts, worries, and concerns melting away. Years of breeding and training took over as adrenaline coursed through her, and anticipation for the fight consumed her. The monster went for Chris first, running in a headlong charge. Chris braced himself, turning slightly to dodge out of the way as the monster reached him.

Swinging out, Chris caught hold of him as he slammed a fist into the things shoulder. The young vampire, a man, grunted loudly as he staggered forward beneath the force of Chris's blow. Though he was off balance, and caught by surprise, he was still hungry, and volatile. His reddened eyes latched upon Cassie, his lips pulled back in a snarl as he caught scent of what he thought would be the easier prey.

Cassie grinned at him invitingly, welcoming the fight, needing to rid herself of her pent up, frustrated energy. It snarled as it lunged at her, its hands curled into claws as it aimed for her neck. A small chuckle escaped her; the thing was stupid that was for sure. It did not stop to think that it might be outnumbered and that a retreat should be considered. Instead, all it could think about was blood and feeding, and destroying life.

It launched itself at her, leaping into the air, its hands outstretched as it looked to devour her. Thrusting her hand up, she used the palm of her hand to smash upward. His head snapped back, his blood red eyes rolled back in his head as his teeth bit into his chin. Blood spilled down his face, but he did not completely slow in his rush. He seized hold of her arms, his hands tightening in a painful grip as he dragged her eagerly forward.

She did not panic, did not even feel a spurt of fear as his lips pulled back. His fetid breath washed over her, causing her gag reflex to react instantly. Lifting her leg, she slammed her knee into his groin. He howled as he bent over, the pain finally breaking through his bloodlust as he released her. Fisting her hands, she drove them hard into his back, knocking him to his knees.

The attack was so fast that Chris, Melissa, and Luther had not had a chance to react. Now they moved swiftly, converging on the creature that was trying to get off his knees. He stumbled up, but Chris got to him first. Driving the stake deep into its back, the creature grunted in surprise as Chris twisted it deeper and harder.

Cassie winced, trying to turn off her guilt as the creature mewled in pain and fear. Shock coursed through her as it met her eyes for a moment. They were no longer red, but a soft brown. They pleaded for mercy, but it was already too late, and no mercy could be given in this situation. Cassie swallowed heavily; remorse filled her as the young man released another low moan before collapsing before them. She should not feel remorseful; he would have killed her instantly if he'd had the chance. It was survival of the fittest after all, and luckily this time they had been the fittest.

But as they moved the body into the woods she couldn't stop herself from thinking that before he had become a monster, he had been someone's son, maybe even someone's brother or husband. She could not stand to think about the hurt that his family had gone through. Could not stand to think about the fear and pain the man had probably suffered before he had been killed the first time.

Cassie inhaled shakily, trying to rid herself of the lingering remnants of shock and remorse that clung to her. She had to shake them off, had to lose them. It would eat her alive if she didn't. She could never allow herself to glimpse the man behind the monster again. She couldn't do this anymore if she was unable to separate the two, and if she didn't do this than people would die.

Cassie shuddered, she felt hollow and shattered. She desperately needed to see Devon; she knew that only he could ease the aching coldness permeating her bones. Even if he couldn't know about this aspect of her life, he could help to ease the choking loneliness and guilt clinging to her.

She sighed heavily, now that they were done all she wanted was to escape the cemetery and return home as soon as possible.

A chill shot down her spine, the hair on the nape of her neck and arms stood on end. Fear and disbelief crossed Chris and Melissa's faces as they turned slowly toward the area where the evil suddenly seeped from. Turned toward the area where they had just left the body of the defeated young man.

Luther stepped closer to them all. "It's out there," Chris whispered.

"Yes," Luther agreed. "Let's go. We need to get you out of here. Now!" he snapped, when none of them moved right away.

"Why doesn't it just come after us?" Cassie asked softly.

"I don't know, but let's not tempt it. Come on, we have to leave *now*," Luther urged fervently, pushing at Chris and Melissa as his gaze worriedly scanned the forest.

Cassie's eyes narrowed as she stared hard into the shadowy interior. She could make out the different elms, oaks, tupelos, and locusts, but she could see nothing hidden amongst the trees. Not even an animal stirred, apparently scared away by the evil in their midst's. "Do you see anything?" Chris asked softly.

Cassie shook her head; frustration caused her hands to fist. "We need to go!" Luther hissed.

Though Cassie did not want to turn tail and run from the monster in the woods, she found herself moving swiftly along as they hurried toward Luther's Toyota Camry. She slid limply into the backseat, her gaze instantly turned back to the window. She half expected to see it standing at the window, its face twisted into a hideous snarl, ready to pounce, eager to slaughter them all.

But there was nothing there.

Searching the night beyond, she tried to pick out as many details as she could. Cassie's teeth rattled as ice encased her once more. Though Luther started the car, they did not move. She felt pinned beneath the wave of hostility and malevolence enveloping them.

"It's playing with us," Chris said softly.

Cassie turned slowly toward him, shocked by the paleness of his complexion, and the hollowness his cheeks and eyes had taken on. "Chris?" she asked worriedly.

His hand trembled as he lifted it toward her. He desperately needed to touch her, to connect with something other than the evil overwhelming his ability. He was shaking when he clasped hold of her hand, his fingers dug tightly into hers. His shoulders heaved as he inhaled a sharp breath. He looked sickly in the glow of the dashboard lights.

"Chris, what is wrong?" she demanded sharply, fear tightening around her heart. She had never seen him look so awful, so shaken.

"Drive," he ordered in a gruff voice.

Luther jolted slightly, shifted the car into drive, and slammed on the gas. Cassie was thrown against the seat, but she did not lose her grip on Chris's quivering hand. Luther peeled down the road, kicking up a spray of dirt and rocks that rattled off the undercarriage of the car. They fishtailed, the back wheels lost traction as the car spun sideways. Cassie had a brief glimpse of headstones only inches from the car before the wheels finally caught on the road once more.

Luther sped down the loosely graveled road at speeds far beyond what was safe, but nowhere near fast enough for Cassie. He barely hesitated before he shot onto the main road. Chris shuddered again, but his eyes seemed to clear slightly, and his face had regained some color.

"Are you ok?" she asked sharply.

He nodded, inhaling shakily as he nodded again. "Yes, yes, I'm fine."

He sounded as if he were trying to reassure himself as much as her. "What happened?"

Another tremor wracked through him, his hand convulsed upon hers. "I caught a glimpse of it. It let me inside for a moment, I think, on purpose. I wasn't trying to probe it when suddenly I found myself sucked in. The maliciousness…"

He broke off, his gaze flew toward the window. "It was just awful. Whatever that thing is, it's enjoying toying with us, playing with us, batting us around until it's ready to pounce. It takes joy in the hunt, and it is hunting us, stalking us." He shuddered again, his whole body heaved with the convulsions that wracked him. "We can't abandon anyone," he whispered.

"And we're not going to," Cassie assured him, trying to ignore the pain his clenching hand caused her.

"It's playing with us for now, but when it's ready, it *is* going to kill us. Before then though, it's going to wreak a lot of havoc on this town." He turned slowly toward her, his eyes oddly bright in the dim interior of the car. "It *is* going to destroy us."

Though Cassie could not get words past the lump of terror in her throat, she knew that Chris was right.

CHAPTER 18

"Looks like you have company."

Cassie's mouth parted slightly at the sight of the sleek Challenger sitting in her driveway. At the vast amount of relief that filled her, she realized she had truly feared she would not see Devon tonight, or ever again. But there he was, sitting at her house, doing God only knew what with her grandma. "I'll be," she murmured.

Chris managed to give her a shaky smile, but it was nowhere near the normal, self assured, cocky grin that she loved. Nor was there the familiar, jovial light in his usually merry eyes. She was truly frightened that she may never see either again. His eyes looked older, more worn and tired than she had ever seen them. His confident aura seemed to have vanished, replaced by one that seemed beaten. She didn't want this Chris to stay, but she was terrified that this was who he was going to be from now on. He seemed to have aged twenty years in the past hour.

For the first time Cassie was truly grateful that she had not received any of the "gifts" that had been bestowed upon Chris and Melissa. It had to be draining and painful to know far more about the world than one desired to. What Chris had seen tonight, what he had been drawn into, had wounded him badly. It was impossible to know just how deep those wounds went.

"Chris…"

"I had better get going," he interrupted, turning away from her as he shut off the car.

"Are you going to come over tonight?" she asked worriedly, despairing over his abrupt dismissal of her.

He sat silently for a moment before shaking his head. "No, I had better stay with my mom. She may need my protection."

Cassie glanced at his house. All the lights were on, music and loud laughter poured from the open windows. There were five cars in the drive that Cassie did not recognize. A party was in full swing. These were the nights that Chris always fled from.

"Did you tell her what was going on?"

He shrugged absently, his hand already rested on the door handle. "Yes, but you know her, if she can drink it away than it doesn't exist."

"Chris..."

"Go on Cassie, I'll be fine. You have company."

"After he leaves..."

He turned back to her, the haunted look in his eyes robbing her of her breath. "I'll be ok."

Before she could say anything more, he flung the door open and climbed swiftly from the car. Cassie was too stunned to move for a moment. Then, she threw her door open and joined him in the brisk fall night. She desperately needed the refreshing air as she greedily inhaled gulps of it. She could not rid herself of the worry that she was losing Chris. She feared that she had already lost the innocent, relatively carefree man he had always been. The best friend she had always known and relied on. She needed to reach him before he retreated farther into himself.

"Chris..."

"I'll see you in the morning."

He didn't look at her as he shoved his hands in his pockets and hurried forward. She watched him disappear into the house, her heart breaking for him. Whether any of them wanted it, or not, they had been forced to grow up even more rapidly tonight, and Chris had received the blunt force of it.

Cassie closed the car door, tears slid silently down her face as she made her way slowly back to her house. She paused at the door, wiping away her tears as she valiantly tried to regain control of herself. It took her a few minutes, but eventually the tears dried up and she felt stable enough to enter. Taking a deep breath she shoved the door open, and stepped into the bright, airy kitchen. The warm aura of the room seemed out of place with the dark cloud surrounding her.

Her grandmother was nowhere to be seen. The wonderful scent of roasted chicken and banana bread filled the air. Cassie's stomach rumbled eagerly in response. But she was far more ravenous to see *him* then she was for food. Moving swiftly through the kitchen, she eagerly followed the drifting voices coming from the dining room.

Stepping through the threshold, she blinked in surprise to find her grandmother and Devon sitting at the oak table. A plate of banana bread and a deck of cards sat between them. Her grandmother glanced up, a bright smile lit her pretty face as her eyes gleamed with amusement.

"Cassandra, you're home!" The vast relief in her voice caused Cassie a twinge of guilt. "Your friend stopped by."

Cassie braced herself before turning her full attention to Devon. Her heart knocked against her ribs and her breath froze as his emerald eyes seared into her. He was sitting casually in the chair; his cards were held loosely in his long fingered hand, his long legs stretched before him. Though his posture was one of relaxation she could feel the tension vibrating through him. There was a hum of power in him that was out of place with a normal human, but she couldn't resist it.

"Cassie." She loved the sound of his voice, the melodic flow of it. It did not wipe away the awful events of the night, but it helped to soothe some of the raw hurt, guilt, and fear that had taken up residence in her soul.

"I told you she'd be home before ten, that's when the library closes." Her grandma threw a card onto the table, reaching forward she moved some pegs on the cribbage board. "Your dinner is still warming in the oven dear, why don't you grab it while I finish beating your friend in cribbage."

Cassie's eyes flew back to Devon, widening in surprise. He was playing her grandma in cribbage? She stared at him in disbelief as he grinned back at her. "She thinks she's going to beat me, but she's wrong."

"Oh, but I will."

Cassie shook her head, turning slowly away. The whole night had been surreal, but this part of it seemed absolutely ludicrous. The object of her obsession, solace, and turmoil was sitting at her dining room table playing cribbage with her *grandmother* for crying out loud! She wondered if she had somehow managed to fall asleep in the cemetery, she felt that would make more sense than this.

Though she was no longer hungry, she robotically gathered the warm plate of chicken from the oven. The extra plate still sitting there, waiting for Chris, caused a tug at her heart. Her gaze darted to the window, but nothing had changed across the street. Turning stiffly away, she gathered silverware and napkins. She was reaching for a glass when she felt him against her. She started slightly, for he had been as silent as a ghost, but the feel of him was instantly soothing to her raw nerves. His chest pressed lightly against her shoulder, his hand reached slowly around her to grab two glasses from the cabinet.

Cassie instinctively melted against him, needing the strength of his body to wash away the ragged wounds of the night. Seeming to sense her fierce need, he brushed her hair gently back; his long fingers caressed her neck as he kissed her temple gently. "How did studying go?"

She had been so lost in his touch that the question took her by surprise. "Huh? Oh ah, fine, it was fine."

"That's good. Your grandmother would like a ginger ale."

Cassie took the glasses from him. Turning she met his fierce, heated gaze. Ripples of pleasure shot through her. It took all she had not to throw her arms around him, bury herself in his embrace and forget all the worries of the world. But she couldn't do it. Not with her grandmother in the next room, not with Chris across the street wounded and broken, and not with some monster hunting their town.

"Ok." She moved reluctantly away from him, opening the fridge she removed the ginger ale and root beer. "How long have you been here for?"

"Not long. I wanted to check on you after today, maybe take you for a walk."

Cassie shuddered at the thought of being outside again, exposed to that evil, vulnerable to it. "That would have been nice, little late now," she mumbled in response.

"Hm." He was studying her intently when she turned back around. Before she knew what he was doing, he reached forward and plucked a blade of grass from the arm of the coat she had forgotten to take off. His eyebrows lifted questioningly as he held it up.

"Gym," she lied poorly.

He smiled softly, but she had the feeling that he didn't believe her for a second. "Didn't realize it was that cold out today," he said softly.

"I chill easily."

His smile widened as he took the glasses from her. "I'll have to keep you warm then." Cassie's mouth went dry, her toes curled at the promise in his husky words. "Come watch me whoop your grandmother in cribbage."

Cassie swallowed heavily, managing a small nod. Settling down at the dining room table, her nose involuntarily wrinkled at the sight of the board. Try as she might, she had never caught onto cribbage. It was a fact that her grandma found very disappointing, as she loved the game and always wanted Cassie to play with her. "Thank you Devon, very kind of you."

Her grandma shot her a pointed look; there was a suggestive tilt to her eyebrows as she took her glass from him. Cassie fought against the fierce blush creeping up her cheeks. Focusing on her plate, she picked absently at the pieces of chicken and mashed potatoes. She watched silently as they continued the game, trading quips and laughing softly as their pieces progressed around the board. Cassie didn't have the foggiest idea who was winning, but from the smile on her grandma's face she assumed it was her.

With a cry of joy, her grandma moved her peg again and leaned victoriously back in her chair. "I believe that is game."

Devon grinned at her, his black hair fell boyishly across his forehead. Cassie's heart warmed and melted, her fingers itched to brush it back for him. "And a very good one, I wouldn't mind a rematch some time."

"That would be nice. My cribbage team only plays every two weeks, and I wouldn't mind a few practice games in between."

Devon turned his charming grin on Cassie. "Don't you play?"

Cassie shook her head as she pushed her plate away. "Cassie has never liked cribbage," her grandma explained.

"Truly? It is a very interesting game, when played right."

Cassie frowned over his words, they sounded so grown up, so outdated. Who said *truly* anymore? Her doubts reared back to painful life, crushing any of the small bliss she had found in the last hour. Her fingers clenched around her glass as she tried to rid herself of the nagging, awful suspicions lurking in her mind.

"I never really grasped it," she admitted slowly, searching his gaze, looking for answers that she knew weren't there.

"Then I'll have to teach you one day." Though he grinned at her, his eyes were darker, more intense. "You'll enjoy it once you learn."

"I've tried, but it's not my game."

"But if you want a rousing hand of rummy, poker, or spades, Cassie is your girl," her grandma chimed in merrily, apparently unaware of the sudden tension in the room.

"Interesting," Devon replied, his gaze never leaving Cassie's. "Spades and Faro are two of my favorite games."

Her grandma perked up. "You know how to play Faro?"

Devon turned slowly away. Cassie found herself able to breathe again as she inhaled sharply. She hadn't even realized that she had stopped breathing until her lungs greedily gulped down air. "Yes, my grandfather taught me."

"How fascinating, I love Faro! Though, I know almost no one that can play it."

"I have the same problem, it's a lost game."

Cassie couldn't stop herself from wondering how lost it was. She had never played the game, never even *heard* of it before. Who was this man sitting in her dining room with her and her grandmother? Her gaze darted to her grandma, fear turned through her as she realized that she may have also put her grandma's life in danger by allowing this stranger into their lives.

The thought was ridiculous, she knew that. He had never done anything but prove himself to her. Yet here she was, suddenly very suspicious, and slightly frightened of him. It was absolutely ludicrous, he had never hurt her before, and he'd had plenty of opportunities to do so. In fact, he had protected her today, kept her safe from Mark's anger, put himself in between her and Mark's crazed advance. He had risked his own safety in order to keep her protected.

She was being unfair, she knew that, but she couldn't stop her doubts and worries. No matter how hard she tried, they would not shut off.

"But a very interesting, entertaining one!" her grandma said brightly. "We must play sometime, I'm sure Cassie would love it. She enjoys all of the gambling games, and she's very good at them."

"I would like that. A card shark huh?" His intense, penetrating gaze swung back to Cassie. "Wonders never cease."

"Just lucky," she mumbled.

"Exceptionally lucky. If she ever hits Vegas, she'll break the place."

"Let's test that luck." Devon grabbed hold of the deck of cards, his long fingers shuffled so swiftly through them that Cassie could hardly see the cards flashing by. He was amazingly talented with them. "What do you want to play? Three hand spades? Seven card? Dealer's choice?"

"Dealer's choice," her grandma piped up. "I'll get the pennies."

Her grandma leapt gracefully to her feet, heading into the kitchen where she kept the jar of pennies they used when they played cards. There had been many nights when Chris would join them, and almost as many, when Luther and Melissa would come over. Those nights had become few and far between over the past year, a fact that Cassie hadn't realized until now.

A stab of guilt hit her as she realized just how distant she had grown from her grandma over the past year. She turned toward Devon, thankful for giving her this opportunity to spend time with her grandmother, especially now, with the danger and death that lurked around them. There may not be many of these nights left to share with each other.

She met his gaze, her doubts slipping away as she found herself charmed by the small smile he gave her. "Are you feeling lucky tonight?" he inquired softly.

Her toes curled, her face flamed. She hadn't been feeling lucky at all, not until now, that is. "Maybe," she responded with a teasing grin.

His eyes twinkled merrily in the light. "I hope so."

Her mouth went dry, her fingers clenched at the innuendo beneath his smooth tone. "Here we are."

Her grandma arrived again, happily slapping the jar of pennies down in front of Cassie. "Count them out dear, a dollar each." Cassie dove at the pennies, grateful for the distraction they offered from the man sitting beside her. "Maybe Chris would like to play with us."

Cassie shook her head, pausing at twenty three to look at her grandma. "He's staying home tonight, he's tired."

A knowing, sad gleam came into her grandmother's eyes as she leaned back in her chair. "I see."

Cassie couldn't stop herself from glancing back at Devon. He was smiling knowingly at her, a promising gleam in his eyes as he leaned forward. "Get those pennies counted."

She swallowed heavily, her heart hammering with the knowledge that he would return to her room tonight. She thought her head would explode from the blood pounding rapidly through it. Anticipation filled her, causing her fingers to shake as she returned to counting the copper mound before her. She had to recount them three times as she kept losing her concentration, but finally she was able to get one dollar together.

Devon took mercy on her, taking the jar away to count out the remaining two dollars. When he was done, he leaned elegantly back in his chair, dealing the cards swiftly out to them. "Five card stud, penny ante."

Cassie took hold of her cards, but her thoughts were not on the suits before her. She didn't think she would ever be able to concentrate on anything when he was near. He squashed any reasonable thoughts that filled her mind; instead it was filled completely with him, and his presence.

After a little while Cassie found herself relaxing, laughing and joking with them both. The horrifying events from the night were not forgotten, but they did not burn as brightly inside her. The comforting company of the people beside her helped to ease the wounds and pain that the night had inflicted. She hadn't realized how badly she needed to have a relaxing, easy night, until now.

They played for almost two hours, until somehow Cassie managed to win all of the pennies. Tossing in the last hand, Devon leaned forward as Cassie happily scooped up her winnings, which would be returned to the jar. "I guess you are lucky," he remarked, his eyebrows lifted boyishly.

Cassie grinned back at him. "I suppose so."

"Well kids, it is getting late, don't forget that you have school tomorrow," her grandma said gently.

Cassie shook her head. "Subtle grandma."

"I try dear," she replied brightly. "Devon it was a pleasure to meet you." She extended her hand to him, grasping tightly hold of his. "You must come by more often. We will get everyone together to play next time. Perhaps we'll teach them Faro, maybe it will be the one game that Cassie can't win."

"I doubt it." He flashed the beautiful smile Cassie was sure had melted many female hearts before, and her grandmother appeared to be no exception. "But it will be fun to see if we could beat her."

"Yes, yes it would. Goodnight kids."

Her grandma kissed her lightly on the cheek before slipping from the room. "I suppose I should be leaving," he said softly.

Cassie nodded, licking her lips nervously. "Yes."

She followed him to the back door, standing anxiously by as he opened it slowly. She stood silently, impatiently, her body screaming for his touch. Bending low, he wrapped his hand gently around her neck, caressing her briefly as he bent to her ear. "It will be easier if you just leave your window open for me tonight."

Cassie froze, trapped like a dear in the headlights as his words seared into her. There was no describing the feeling of longing that slammed through her. She had never felt this hopeful, wanting, confused, helpless, and needy before.

In that moment she knew, that for him, she would do anything. No matter how many doubts she had about him, she knew her feelings for him would always win out.

She did not know how to feel about the complete loss of control she had over herself around him, but in that moment she couldn't bring herself to care. She could only manage a small nod as his fingers stroked lightly over her cheek. "See you soon," he said softly, brushing a light kiss on the bridge of her nose.

He pulled reluctantly away, turning swiftly and heading out the door. She watched him until she was sure that he made it safely to his car, wishing she could go with him to make sure he arrived safely at home, or wherever he was going until he came back. Her heart pounded with worry, but it also took all she had not to flee to her room to eagerly await his return.

Her grandmother was leaning against the doorway of the dining room, smiling softly when Cassie came back through. "He seems like a very charming, very nice man."

Cassie stopped, trying to keep her face as impassive as possible while her heart pounded like a jack hammer. "Yes, he is."

Her grandmother's grin widened, a knowing gleam shone in her bright eyes. "You seem to like him very much."

"I do," Cassie admitted.

She stepped away from the doorway, moving with brisk agility as she came forward to clasp hold of Cassie's hands. "I'm glad for you dear, but you must be careful."

Cassie sighed heavily, squeezing her hands tightly. "I know grandma, I am being careful, I promise."

She smiled brightly. "I'm not talking about out there dear." She nodded toward the windows. Slipping her hands free she pointed to Cassie's chest. "I'm talking about in here."

Cassie swallowed heavily, knowing that it was already too late to be careful with her heart. It was no longer hers to be careful with. "I will," she said hesitatingly.

Dropping a kiss on her grandmother's soft cheek, she forced herself not to run as she quickly left the room. Her heart pounded eagerly with every step. Reaching her doorway, she froze, her legs locking in place. He was already standing by her window, his arms folded over his chest as he leaned casually against the sill. His eyes were dark in the night; his hair tussled across his forehead. He looked utterly tempting and wonderful.

She did not know how he had gotten there so fast, nor did she care. She was just glad he was there. He unfolded himself, his muscles rippled mouthwateringly. Power and desire radiated from him as he took a small step forward. A small twinge of fear shot through her, but it was also filled with excitement. Her doubts wanted to surge forth once more, but she shoved them aside. Her need for him far outweighed any misgivings she had.

Closing the door, she made her way swiftly forward. His arms enveloped her, pulling her tight against him. She clung to his hard body, needing the strength that he gave her, needing the comfort he provided. All of her hurts and aches and fears were forgotten as his hands entwined in her hair, cradling her head gently against his shoulder.

"Cassandra." He sounded like a starving man who had just been given a meal. She shivered, her fingers dug into his hard back as she tried to pull herself closer to him. He shifted her slightly holding her more firmly against his right shoulder, but she could not get close enough. She would *never* get close enough.

CHAPTER 19

Devon was standing by the window, staring at the night when she woke early the next morning. The sky was still dark, but the stars had blinked out and the moon had disappeared. Though she didn't make a sound upon waking, he turned toward her. A small smile played over his full mouth, but his eyes remained hard and distant.

Frowning, Cassie tossed back her blankets and climbed swiftly to her feet. She was surprised to realize that she had fallen asleep with her clothes on. She padded silently over to him; the hardwood was cool against her bare feet. His arm wrapped around her waist, pulling her tight against his side.

"Anything out there?" she asked quietly, trying to sound light but knowing that she failed. There really might be something out there, lurking within the shadows, watching them.

"Just a few early birds." His fingers tightened upon her waist, he briefly nuzzled her hair. He inhaled deeply before kissing her temple lightly and straightening from her.

Cassie studied the early morning; the sky was lightening to gray, a few birds were already chirping. She could see nothing wrong with the morning, or sense anything evil out there. Still, she moved closer to him, her fingers entangling in the soft cotton of his shirt. His hard muscles rippled beneath her touch.

They stood silently together, watching as the sun rose over the horizon and the sky flamed with a brilliant array of colors. It was one of the most beautiful, wonderful, serene moments of her life. The light played over his magnificent face, highlighting the hard planes of it, and illuminating his stunning eyes.

He kissed her gently, his lips brushing briefly over hers. A firestorm of emotion and feeling boiled through her, crashing over her like waves on the sand. She felt the loss of his kiss as acutely as she would have felt the loss of a limb. "I'll see you at school," he said softly.

Cassie managed a brief nod, her body already ached from the separation that was about to ensue. He kissed her briefly again, reluctantly releasing her. Swiftly, with startling grace, he moved through her window. Grasping hold of the tree limb he swung himself rapidly down. Cassie watched in awe as he leapt from the tree, still ten feet from the ground, and landed effortlessly upon the ground.

Cassie lifted an eyebrow, his agility left her breathless with wonder. Turning away from the window she hurried to the bathroom, eager to go to school.

***

Devon slid his car into park, his eyes slowly drifted over the students gathered by what had become his parking spot. They were mostly female, but there were a few boys that had followed the girls. Devon ignored them. He had no interest in any of them.

Throwing the door open he climbed swiftly from the car, not noticing the longing stares that followed his every move. He found her instantly among the crowd; her aura was like a homing beacon that he could not ignore. His fingers twitched slightly, his need to hold her again was almost consuming.

She looked up at him, smiling brightly. She radiated a life force that lit her from the inside out, causing her fair skin to glow, and her exquisite eyes to gleam in the bright morning sun. The tightness constricting his chest since he had left her, relaxed. In all of his many years, he had never come across someone as unique and magnificent as she was; her outer beauty was only dimmed by her inner beauty.

He had never felt this way about someone before, never knew it was possible to need someone so much that he could hardly think. He recalled Annabelle, and her unwavering feelings. He understood her better now, understood what she had needed and desired. Understood now what he could never have given to Annabelle, what she had truly been feeling, what she had needed, and that realization terrified him.

But he knew that it was too late to do anything about it now. He could try and leave, but he would not get far without Cassie. And if what he suspected was true, Cassie would be greatly hurt, if not destroyed, by his disappearance. He had not wanted Cassie so ensnared in his life, so entrenched in his world of darkness and monsters. But once he'd met her, he'd had no choice in the matter. It had instantly been taken away from him. And unfortunately, if what he suspected and feared might be true, she no longer had a choice either.

"Devon, I'm so glad that you're here! I wanted to talk to you about your nomination." Devon regretfully tore his gaze from Cassie. Marcy was standing before him, her pretty face lit with a bright, eager smile. Though she was as annoying as a gnat, he managed to offer her a small smile in return. "I think that you are going to win, and since there is a good possibility that I will win queen, I think we should coordinate our outfits, or maybe even go together."

He frowned at her, not at all surprised by her brazenness, or the fact that she would not accept his refusal of her. He had come across more than a few women like her in his long lifetime. He *was* surprised by the fact that she still couldn't realize that Cassie was the only woman he wanted. The only one he even *saw* anymore.

"I don't think so Marcy." He moved to walk around her, but she sidestepped quickly, putting herself back in his way. Aggravation spurted through him; he just wanted to get to Cassie, to touch her, to ease the crawling, burning sensation that enclosed him whenever they were apart.

"Well why not?" She planted her hands on her hips, her delicate brow furrowed angrily.

"Because I will be taking Cassie to the dance."

"After what happened yesterday?"

He frowned at her in confusion. "What happened yesterday?"

"With Mark Young," she reminded him impatiently. "That was awful. I can't believe she led him on so badly. I always liked Cassandra, but I never realized what an awful person she truly is. I can't believe you would want to be associated with someone like that. I mean..."

"Enough!" he cut in sharply, his gaze darting swiftly to Cassie. She was still standing by Chris's car, her eyes fixed upon them. Though she was well out of hearing range, she was frowning intently, her eyes were narrowed fiercely. He turned his attention back to Marcy, trying to control the anger surging through him. "Yesterday was not her fault, and I don't want to hear one bad word you have to say about her. Ever!"

Marcy's eyes widened, her mouth parted slightly. He moved swiftly around her, disgusted by her pettiness and cruelty. Cassie watched him warily as he approached, her bright smile was gone. "What was that about?" Melissa asked softly, nodding toward where Marcy still stood with her mouth agape.

"Nothing."

The last thing he wanted was for Cassie to know anything that Marcy had said to him. Though Melissa did not look appeased, she did not press him farther. Cassie gazed up at him, a wounded look in her eyes. He glanced back at where Marcy stood, about fifty feet away. A group of girls was now gathered around her, seemingly trying to console her. Though *he* could hear what they were saying, and did not like it, there was no way that Cassie could hear them above the noise of the other students, and the radios. No human could.

Hurt radiated from her as she continued to stare at Marcy, but there was also a spark of anger in her gaze. Though she could not hear them, she must have assumed that they were talking about her. That had to be it, he decided. Otherwise, if she could hear them, then that would make her something... Well, it would make her something other than human.

Devon studied her carefully, trying to decipher the mystery that she suddenly seemed to offer. She was most certainly not a vampire, he would have known that instantly, and she would not be here. Not in broad daylight, and not with a bunch of high school students. He was the exception to the rule, on both counts, for the most part. He also would have smelled it on her, would have sensed it in her blood.

No, she was definitely not one of his kind. But then, what was she? She couldn't be a Hunter, he'd heard that they had all been killed off, and he suspected that he would have sensed that in her too. But if she had heard his conversation...

The thought trailed off in the face of the distress she emitted. Wrapping his hand gently around her neck, he pulled her close in an attempt to ease the pain enshrouding her. She had to be human, that was all she could be. He was making far more of it then he should.

Glancing around the car, he was surprised to realize that it was only Chris and Melissa standing with her. Usually there was a crowd gathered around, mostly males, causing a raucous as they humiliated themselves while vying for her attention. Today, there was a wide berth around them as glances and whispers were cast Cassie's way. Even with him over here, the girls did not approach.

"I have become a pariah," she said softly, giving him a wan smile.

He glanced back at the crowds gathered together; her tried hard but was unable to ignore the whispers directed her way. Somehow, what had happened in the cafeteria yesterday had been twisted, and turned against her. He didn't know how it had happened, for he wasn't entirely sure how the minds of teenagers worked, but somehow they had cast her into the role of villain, and they were keeping her there. He thought it was partly due to jealousy on behalf of the girls, and resentment on behalf of the boys, but he also knew that he played a large role in it.

Due to what he was, he had a stronger allure to women. He was like a Venus flytrap, luring in its prey, moments before snagging it and draining the life from it. Though he did not kill anymore, the powerful lure was still there, ever present, and unable to be turned off. This draw had pulled in a good amount of the female population in town, and had also caused anger and resentment toward Cassie to fester. They wanted what she had, and they did not like the fact that she had it.

And the boys did not like the fact that she had rebuked them all, disdaining their advances over and over, and then accepting his. Their pride had been wounded, their ego's bashed, and they were not happy about it. Though many of them had never liked him, they had also turned on her now. Anger curdled inside him. He did not care what they thought of him, but she did not deserve their disdain and spite.

His protective urges surged forth. He wanted to take her from here, shelter her from the cold anger that radiated from them. Protect her from the inane cruelty of the foolish human race. However, he knew that he could not. Though his life was not tied up in these people, and this school, hers was. She had to live out this part of her life, had to fulfill her dreams and her hopes, and her future. Unfortunately, he had caused her this pain, and he wanted nothing more than to take her away in order to keep her safe from it.

"Ridiculous," Chris muttered.

Devon glanced over at him as he pulled Cassie a step closer, wrapping his arms tenderly around her waist. Chris met his gaze, his eyes distant and far older than they had been yesterday. Devon was shocked by the expression in those eyes, and the hopelessness that filled them. He didn't know what had happened to Chris between yesterday and today to cause such a change, but he was certain that it was far worse than what was going on with the student body now.

Cassie shrugged, her fingers curled into his back. "It's alright," she said softly. "Let them believe what they want."

Melissa sighed heavily and bent into the car to grab her backpack. "They're a bunch of jealous idiots Cass."

Cassie bit into her bottom lip; her eyes were troubled as she managed a brief nod. "Well, whatever they are, I don't care. I never wanted to be homecoming queen anyway."

"We know."

Cassie and Melissa exchanged a small smile before Cassie turned to look up at him, her eyes gleaming with a teasing light. "I won't make you coordinate, but you probably *will* win king."

Devon started, his hands tightened upon her. He glanced back to where Marcy still stood, tuning his ears in order to hear what they were saying. He had to sort through all of the background noise before pinpointing the exact conversation. It took him only a second to do this, but *no* human ever could. It was not within their capabilities. Only one of his kind would be able to pick up the conversation, and Cassie most definitely was not a vampire. The sweet blood pumping through her veins was a constant, tortuous, tempting reminder of that fact.

He glanced back down at her. Her head was resting trustingly against his shoulder, her hand on his waist. She could *not* have heard that conversation, it was impossible; it was only a coincidence that she had mocked Marcy's statement.

"Marcy always did want it though," Melissa said softly.

"Yes," Chris agreed.

"And now she has it. Good for her, she'll do better with it than I would." Cassie uncurled her hand from his waistband as the bell rang loudly, echoing throughout the parking lot. "Time for school."

He gathered her books from the roof of the car, tucking them beneath his arm as he led her into the large brick building. Students stopped to watch as they passed, they whispered loudly behind their hands. Melissa walked beside her, her shoulders thrown back proudly, her dark eyes raking over the worst offenders. Many of them shrank from her scathing glare.

Cassie walked proudly beside him, her chin thrust defiantly forward. She stared straight ahead, not bothering to look at anyone else. If it weren't for her death grip upon his hand, he would have thought that none of this affected her at all. But her tight hold, and the small tremor wracking her, told him that she was hurt by the cold hostility of her classmates.

It took all he had not to destroy every one of them.

***

Cassie walked stiffly through the cafeteria. She tried to ignore the whispers and comments that followed her, but most people were not discreet. In fact, she knew that every one of them wanted her to hear what they had to say. And none of it was good.

She had been called every name in the book today, a few of which she had never even heard of. Titters and whispers preceded, and followed, everywhere she went. Though she tried to play it off as if it didn't bother her, inside she was a mass of raw emotion and seething nerve endings. She had never been hated before; she had never expected to be hated. Disliked, maybe, but not hated.

And she was *hated*. It beat against her in waves of anger that made her stomach turn, and her body ache. She hadn't thought that people could turn against someone so quickly, and so effectively. And she didn't even know what she had done wrong. Mark had attacked *her*, not the other way around. She had done nothing to merit this treatment, and because of that fact she was swinging between fierce bouts of anger, and trying hard not to cry as she struggled to keep up a nonchalant appearance.

Her hands shook slightly; she had to take a calming breath in order to steady her tray. She was greatly relieved that Chris was already at the table, his distant gaze scanning the crowd. Dropping her tray on the table, she slid limply into the seat beside him. His tray was loaded with mounds of food that he had not touched yet, which was highly unusual for him.

"You look exhausted," he said softly.

"Rough day," she muttered, shoving the tray away from her. She wasn't in the least bit hungry; other than habit she didn't even know why she had bothered to stand in line.

"And these are the people that you want to stay and protect."

Her eyes widened at the cynicism, and anger, in his voice. "Chris." He turned toward her; the bleak look in his eyes was almost more than she could bear. "They need us," she finished lamely.

"And they are showing you that need now."

"Chris, you wanted to stay too."

"That was before."

"Before what?"

"Before I saw into what is out there, before I saw into a soul of pure malice and deviance. Before all these people turned against you like a pack of rabid, hungry hyenas."

She was stunned breathless for a moment, too shocked to move. "You want to leave?" she managed to choke out.

His hard gaze scanned the cafeteria one more time. Finally, his shoulders slumped as he shook his head. "No, I don't want to leave. I don't understand what is going on with everyone, but we have to protect them. I know that, I'm just aggravated with these idiots." He turned back to her, his hand clasped hers tightly. His action caused the buzz in the cafeteria to increase, becoming a dull roar in her ears that was impossible to ignore. "But I also caught a glimpse of what that monster is out there Cass, and all it wants is to play with us, torture us, and then kill us. There is no stopping that kind of determination."

A chill swept down her back, her hand tightened around his. She could feel the fear that ran through him. What he had seen last night had changed him. It had permeated his bones, seeped into his soul. Her hand tightened around his, trying to give him strength as she sought desperately to ease the pain he radiated.

"*We* can," she said more firmly than she actually felt. "Together, we can do anything Chris. We have survived so much, we can, we *will,* survive this."

"When did you become the optimistic one?" His smile was wan, but she saw an easing in his eyes that relaxed her slightly. She laughed softly as she leaned against his side.

"How many men does she want?"

Cassie turned at the nasty hiss, her gaze locked fiercely with Marcy's. Deliberately, defiantly, she lifted Chris's hand and squeezed it harder. She turned slowly back around, trying to control the anger humming through her body as she focused on Chris again.

"Sure you want to stick around?" Chris's eyebrows were raised inquisitively, a teasing light reappeared in his sapphire eyes. No matter how awful this day had been for her that gleam in his eyes made it all worth it.

"I'm sure," Cassie replied, grinning brightly.

"Jerks," Melissa muttered slamming her tray on the table. "Bunch of idiotic, useless, jerks!"

Cassie and Chris grinned at each other before turning toward Melissa. Her jaw was locked tight; her eyes spit black fire as she glared around the cafeteria. "Tell us how you really feel," Chris said, issuing the first laugh Cassie had heard from him all day.

Cassie chuckled along with him, squeezing his hand tighter. He was going to be alright, she was certain of that now. Whatever he had experienced last night had rattled him greatly, but he was going to be alright. His spirit was too strong to be beaten down for long. Devon was suddenly behind her, his hands gently grasped her shoulders. Relief poured through her, her tense shoulders sagged as he gently massaged her. She turned toward him as he bent over her, brushing a quick kiss on her cheek. His breath was sweet and tantalizing; it warmed her to the tips of her toes.

His eyes darted to the hand tightly entwined with Chris's on top of the table. Lifting a questioning eyebrow, he turned toward Chris. Cassie stiffened slightly, unsure how Devon would handle her connection with Chris. He knew that they were friends, but he probably didn't realize just how good of friends they were, or how strong the bond between them was.

"Trying to steal my girl?" he inquired, his tone far lighter than Cassie had expected from him.

Chris grinned back at him, snorting slightly as he shook back his shaggy blond hair. "No worries there she's too much of a pain in the ass for my liking."

Cassie shot him a fierce look as he released her hand. He grinned back at her before eagerly pulling his tray over to attack his tuna fish sandwich. Devon chuckled softly as he slid into the seat beside her, turning sideways to face her. A dull flush of excitement crept through her as he leaned toward her, his closeness causing her body to heat.

"How are you doing?" he asked softly, wrapping his hand around the back of her neck to massage her gently.

It took her a few moments to answer, as the thump of her heart made speaking difficult. "Fine," she murmured.

And she was surprised to realize that with Chris's smile, Melissa's unwavering loyalty, and his solid presence, she *was* fine. Nothing else mattered, not the cruel whispers, not the waves of anger and hatred, not even the monster that lurked within their town. As long as she had these three standing beside her, she could survive anything.

She hoped.

CHAPTER 20

Cassie's stomach curdled as if she had eaten something rotten. A ball of nausea had wedged itself into her throat, choking her. She leaned over the counter, breathing heavily, her gaze locked upon the large headline before her.

THIRTEENTH PERSON REPORTED MISSING FROM HYANNIS.

Her blood pumped heavily in her veins, feeling almost painful as it lumbered through her system as she read the article. The woman had gone missing from a bar on Main Street; no one had seen her since. And they probably wouldn't again, Cassie realized with a sinking sensation in her stomach.

It was smart, whatever was out there it was smart. It was definitely covering its tracks. And it was their fault that it was still out there killing, destroying innocent people, and their families. It was her, Chris, and Melissa's responsibility as Hunter's to protect the innocent, and they were failing miserably at the task. Thirteen was far too many people, and these were only the ones that had been reported, and weren't already reported as dead. There were probably even more that had gone unreported, that had no one out there to love and miss them.

Her hands trembled as she closed the paper, her gaze darted to the bright day beyond the kitchen windows. The bright sunlight was completely out of place with the emotions rolling through her. It should be dark out, cold, foreboding. It should match the hollow chill that had encased her from head to toe.

Taking a step away from the counter, she began to move slowly from the room when something about the article clicked into her mind. Turning slowly back, her throat went dry; her heart seemed to stop beating as her legs became suddenly shaky, wooden. She reached out quickly, grasping hold of the counter before she fell to the ground.

She inhaled great, heaping gulps of air in an attempt to ease the shaking that wracked painfully through her bones. She was trembling so hard that the teeth rattled in her head. Her gaze went slowly back to the paper. It now seemed malevolent to her, awful, wrong, out of place in what used to be the warm comfort of her kitchen.

Taking another deep breath, she used the counter to support her as she moved slowly back to the island she had left the paper on. She did not want to look at it again, did not want to touch it, but she knew that she had to. She needed to see it, to know for certain if what she had seen was right. To see if what she feared was true.

Releasing the counter, she stumbled to the island, nearly hyperventilating as she grasped hold of the paper and pulled it close. She was shaking so badly that she could barely get the pages open. Her gaze scanned over the article, coming to rest on the date of the first disappearance. September fifteenth, Megan Keller, twenty-two, had vanished from a park in Sandwich.

Cassie grasped the paper; sliding limply to the floor she pressed it tight to her chest. The wrinkled pages crinkled loudly as her fingers curled into it. Devon had arrived on the thirteenth. He had strolled into her life two days before the disappearances started.

Her mind began tripping over everything that she had been trying to deny. Little pieces of the puzzle she'd always had, but hadn't wanted to assemble, suddenly began to fall swiftly into place. Devon's speed and agility, the strength he exhibited when he lifted Mark easily, effortlessly, off the ground. He hadn't even broken a *sweat*! She thought over the way he spoke, it was so old and elegant, *so* outdated. He knew the card game faro, a game *no* one knew anymore. She had definitely never heard of anyone *her* age ever having played the game.

Though the puzzle horrified her, once the pieces began slipping together, she could not stop them from assembling the picture. Melissa had seen nothing about Devon, other than his arrival, and Chris could not read him. Both of which could be explained by the power that radiated from him, far more power than a *human* would possess, and she was beginning to believe it was even more power than *she* possessed.

A chill ran down her spine, her body shook with the fierce tremors wracking it. Closing her eyes she tried to stop the images tumbling swiftly together, but no matter how hard she tried, they would not stop. He was *always* slightly colder than normal, a fact that could be explained by the weather, or bad circulation, but neither of those explanations seemed right to her now.

She had been irresistibly attracted to him, pulled to him like a magnet to metal from the very beginning. All of the girls were drawn to him, so much so that they had turned against her in the hopes that they would get him. It was something that she had known all along, that her attraction to him was fierce, and something that most people did not experience. But she had chosen to ignore that fact in her desire to be closer to him, to be *with* him.

As the last pieces of the puzzle slid into place, Cassie's breath locked in her chest as panic clenched at her. Every single one of those pieces, *every* single one of those oddities, was abilities or traits, of vampires. Abilities that her worst enemies and most hated foe's possessed. Now that the puzzle was in place, she fully realized that it was a jigsaw straight from hell.

He had sensed the evil in the woods, but what if *he* was that evil? What if he had let his guard down briefly, allowing the evil to slip free, allowing it to permeate into them? 'It's playing with us,' Chris had said softly. 'Playing games with us, before killing us.' What better way to play games with her than to make her fall in love with him, before he tried to kill her?

Tears streamed down Cassie's face, pain twisted in her chest as she tried to inhale heaping gulps of air through the agony consuming her. Her gaze darted to the window, and the bright sunlight beyond. Her forehead furrowed tightly in confusion as a piece of the puzzle did not slide into place. Devon walked about in the day, unaffected by the light of the sun. She had *never* known a vampire to do that before, it was impossible. Sunlight killed them.

The day was for humans, their time to be safe, and not to have to worry about the monsters lurking in the shadows.

Hope ballooned briefly inside her, and then swiftly deflated as she recalled Luther's words. 'We do not know what an Elder could be capable of. The powers that they might possess.'

One of those powers may very well be the ability to stroll about in broad daylight, a monster among humans. It would be a perfect disguise to fool any Hunter. If Devon was an Elder, than he was more than just a normal vampire, he was one of the most powerful and one of the most hated. He would have been one of the ones to help mastermind the destruction of her parents, one of the ones that had helped to eradicate her race.

Her body lost all strength; the paper fell limply from her hands as she slid to the floor. Her heart was shattering into a million pieces, her world crumbling around her. She gasped, shaking and crying; her head fell forward into her hands. He breathed, she thought desperately, she had felt him breathe, but what if he only pretended to breathe in her presence? She tried to recall if she had felt the beat of his heart, but try as she might she could not remember ever feeling the reassuring pulse of life within his chest.

She tried to convince herself that she was wrong, but though she tried to hide behind a wall of denial, she could not. Not anymore. Her mind, her *soul*, knew that she was right.

He was not human. He was not a Hunter. He was not even a human with special abilities.

He was *the* monster. He was the one hunting them, stalking them, playing and toying with them. And he had been very good at it. She had fallen helplessly in love with him. She had allowed him into her soul, taken him into the very essence of her. And the entire time he had been playing with her, plotting her death, her murder, and the murder of the ones she loved.

The past two nights, when he had held her gently, making her feel safe and protected, had all been part of his game. He was good, excellent even, she had to give him that much. His game had succeeded in crushing her, from the inside out. There was nothing left to her. No hope, no wonder, no life. She was an empty shell of the person she had been, wounded and beaten.

And yet, somehow stronger. She would not let him win. She was stronger than that. He may have destroyed her, but he would not hurt anyone else. He would not take her loved ones from her.

Wiping the tears from her eyes, Cassie placed her hands on the floor and shoved herself up. She could not sit here and cry. She didn't have time for that. There was a monster out there, and she was one of the few people that could stop him. She stood shakily for a moment, numb and deadened. Then, like a phoenix rising from the ashes fury blazed hotly forth and burned away the devastating hurt that had encased her. He may have destroyed her, but she was also going to destroy him.

She strode forcefully from the kitchen, pounding up the stairs to gather her weapons. She was tired of running, tired of hiding, and very tired of being frightened. It was time to take a stand. It was time to do some hunting, instead of being the hunted for a change.

***

Devon sat completely still on the tree branch, all of his senses tuned to the night beyond. It was the exact same thing he had been doing every night for the past week while Cassie had been occupied with studying, or at Melissa's. Probing with his mind, he sorted through the few brains close enough for him to pick up on in the area. It was one of his talents, the ability to sift through people's minds in order to pinpoint the one that he wanted. The mind he would then latch onto, track down, and destroy; the one that stalked this town, and its inhabitants, especially Cassie.

Thoughts of Cassie caused him to tense. Whenever he came out here, he had to shut his mind off of her; otherwise he would be disrupted from his pursuit. He could pick up her mind from miles away; it was as bright and as welcoming as a lighthouse beacon to him. But now, here, her mind was a distraction to him, and one that he could not have if he was going to succeed in destroying his prey.

Tuning his senses to the night, he strained to feel anything out there, to *find* anything out there. Then, he felt it. For the first time, he picked up on a small flicker of power in the night. A power that he recognized instantly as belonging to the one he sought.

Slipping easily from the tree, he moved swiftly through the woods, faster and more graceful than any cheetah. Leaping over fallen logs, and effortlessly dodging branches, he darted swiftly through the trees, hunting the power that he had sensed. He could feel it moving deeper into the woods, running from the pursuit that it had sparked.

Devon broke out of the woods, racing across the cemetery, jumping stones and tombs with smooth, easy leaps. Whatever he was pursuing was slower than he was, not as fleet in its retreat. He was gaining ground on it.

Leaving the cemetery, the woods encircled him once more. He poured on the speed, becoming nearly a blur as he chased his prey. Excitement and bloodlust pounded through him. It had been so long since he had pursued any real game, any real kill. Animals didn't amount to the same thrill as a human, or another vampire. Both of which he had not touched in a very long time.

A scream echoed loudly through the air, a young girl's voice penetrated the dark night. Devon realized that the creature had not been fleeing from him, but had been hunting its own prey instead.

***

Cassie had just stepped out of Luther's car when the terrified scream echoed throughout the night. It rang off the headstones and echoed throughout the eerily still night. Chris and Melissa stiffened, freezing in mid-step as their mouths parted in surprise. The thick silence that followed the scream was even more nerve wracking.

"It's out there," Chris said softly.

"Let's go."

Cassie took a step forward, but Luther grabbed hold of her arm, halting her. "Wait."

She spun on him, anger fisting her hands as it tore through her. "We have to stop him!" she snapped.

Luther's eyes narrowed sharply upon her, the light gray of them inquisitive and keen. "Him?"

She realized her mistake instantly, they had always referred to the monster as *it*, and Luther had not missed the fact that she had called it *him* this time. Cassie glared fiercely at him, she didn't have time to explain her newfound knowledge, nor did she want to. She didn't want to hear their gasps of shock and surprise; she did not want them to dissuade her from what she knew. She was right, she had no doubt that Devon was in those woods. Just as she had no doubt that *she* would be the one to take him out.

Though he had fooled all of them, it was her that he had focused upon. It was *her* that he had teased with promises of love and hope, only to rip it all cruelly away. She hated him the most for making her hope and dream. She had been surviving well enough, hiding behind her wall, safely protected from the hurts of the world until he had walked into her life, tossing it upside down, and shredding it to pieces.

Cassie ripped her arm away from Luther, spinning back toward the woods. Her blood was boiling with the fury pulsing through her, she knew that she was reckless right now, but she couldn't bring herself to care. She didn't care about anything anymore, except for keeping the people surrounding her safe. Her gaze rapidly scanned the forest, trying to pinpoint where the scream had come from. Another scream shot through the air, bloodcurdling, pain filled, and terrified. Horror filled Cassie, her heart leapt wildly in her chest; she had never heard anyone make that sound before.

And it was entirely her fault.

Her love for Devon had completely blinded her to the fact that he was a monster. Her stupidity and ignorance had allowed him to continue to kill. He had destroyed the lives of many innocent people, and she was not going to allow that to happen again.

"Come on," she said briskly.

"Wait!" Luther said sharply, seizing her once more. "Melissa."

Melissa had gone completely still, her eyes were distant, her face blank and pale. Cassie sighed impatiently; it was a hell of a time to receive a premonition, especially one of the ones that took complete control of her. Melissa gasped suddenly, bending forward she grasped her stomach as she struggled to breathe. Chris grabbed hold of Melissa's heaving shoulders as she choked and panted for air.

Another scream echoed throughout, but this one was far weaker than before. Whoever was out there was losing the battle, and Cassie was not about to let that happen. Tearing her arm away from Luther again, she spun on her heel and sprinted forward. It did not matter that Chris and Melissa were not with her, she would put a stop to this on her own. It was better if they stayed out of it anyway, she did not want them to be hurt.

Cassie ran as fast as she could, her long legs carrying her swiftly across the ground. She didn't bother dodging the headstones but vaulted herself easily over them. Reaching the woods, she darted into the thick foliage, using her hands to deflect the branches and twigs that slapped at her.

"Cassie *noooo!*" Melissa's shrill, terror filled scream followed her into the forest, but did not slow her down.

CHAPTER 21

Devon burst into the clearing. His heightened senses, and the adrenaline pulsing through him, allowed him to take in all of the details at once. The first thing he recognized was the young woman in the arms of the monster.

The second was the monster.

He skidded to a halt, dirt and leaves kicked up beneath him. Shock slammed into him as he gazed into the familiar red eyes of his prey, but it was quickly buried beneath the fury that surged rapidly forth. Stiffening slowly, his hands fisted at his sides as he met those eyes across the clearing from him. This was a fight that he was more than prepared for, and one that was well over a hundred years in the making. "Let her go!" he snarled.

Julian had lifted his head from Marcy's neck when Devon emerged, but he had not released her. Julian broke into a small smile, a dark eyebrow quirked with amusement. "Well, if it isn't the prodigal sire," he purred. "I was hoping we would finally run into each other again."

Devon took a step closer to him, tension thrummed through him as he braced himself for the fight. "I didn't create you Julian," he growled.

Julian's blood smeared mouth twisted into a sneer. "You may not have created me, but you did help to mold me into the best vampire that I could possibly be. You taught me the thrill of the hunt, the pleasure of the kill."

Devon's teeth ground together as he glared fiercely at the man across from him. Julian had once been his best friend, and greatest companion. He was a monster that still wreaked havoc upon unsuspecting innocents with the same joy and pleasure that Devon had once taken in it. Though they had been nearly inseparable for over three hundred years, Julian had become one of his greatest enemies. "What are you doing here Julian?" Devon spat.

Julian leisurely licked the blood from his lips, savoring the taste of it. Devon's eyes latched onto the blood, for a moment he could clearly recall how wonderful and fulfilling human blood was. How powerful and thrilling it was. How much he wanted it! It had been so long since he had tasted human blood, and he struggled daily to keep his murderous urges under wraps. But faced with it so temptingly close, he could feel his restraint starting to unravel.

He struggled to maintain control, the blood was a distraction that would get him killed; Julian was fierce, powerful, and deadly. Devon would be a fine trophy, and a lot of power to add to Julian's collection of victims. Not to mention the fact that most of the vampire race considered Devon a traitor to their kind, and would far prefer him dead.

Julian's eyes slowly turned back to the ice blue color that Devon was painfully familiar with. Around the black pupils of his eyes was a strange band of lighter, vivid, almost white blue color. "Same thing as you I assume, I was drawn by the power. Except, unlike you, I will make use of that power, take advantage of it; savor it."

Devon scowled fiercely at him, taking another step closer as they slowly began to circle one another. Marcy was still held loosely in Julian's arms as he negligently dragged her body along with him. Devon could just barely make out the faint beat of Marcy's fluttering heart. She did not have much time left. "There is no power here."

Julian's face twisted into a leering grin, his sharp canines gleamed in the dim light of the moon. "Oh you silly *silly* fool. Have you been that blinded?"

Devon was growing more aggravated by the second. He did not like being toyed with, especially not by Julian. He was the one that had taught Julian, the one that had molded him; he was not going to be played with by him. "Don't mess with me Julian," he growled.

Julian quirked a black eyebrow, his mouth twisted into a wry smile. "I would never," he replied, his voice light and lilting as they continued to circle. "I am simply pointing out what you have missed."

"And what would that be?"

Julian's eyes gleamed, flashing momentarily red. "The delectable treats in this town. Three little treats to be exact, just so plump and ripe for the taking. Especially the blond, that sweet, *delicious* blond that you have been cozying up to at night. She is so young, so innocent and pure, so full of powerful blood just begging to be savored. I give you credit, to be that close to such a wonderful temptation, and not taste it, not take it. I could never be so restrained."

Fury tore through Devon, shaking him to the core of his being. For a brief moment a red haze clouded his vision, his protective urges drowned out the rest of Julian's words. He didn't understand what the hell Julian was talking about, but he didn't want him anywhere near Cassie, or even *remotely* thinking about her.

"You stay away from her, or I'll rip your damn throat out!" he snarled, his fangs elongating at the mere thought of Julian getting close to her.

Julian grinned back at him; his white blond hair fell into one of his ice cold eyes. "Temper temper," he taunted lightly. "We've shared before, we can share again."

"I'd kill you first!"

Anger blazed from Julian, his lip curled in a contemptuous sneer. His ice eyes raked Devon with a hate filled glare. "You truly have changed Devon; you're such a disappointment, turning against your nature, your own *kind*!"

Devon met his gaze, trying hard to keep the fury boiling through him under control. He couldn't let Julian bait him into losing his temper. Julian was too deadly for that. "You will die before you ever touch her."

"And if she kills you first?" Devon blinked in surprise, unsure what Julian meant by that statement. "You truly do not get it, you *stupid* fool! She has you completely blinded. Could it be that Devon, the master of death, destruction, and torture has been blinded by love?"

"I have not been any of those things in a very long time Julian!" Devon hissed. "You need to leave this town, you are not welcome here."

Julian laughed coldly and shook back his tussled hair. "I am not leaving until I get a taste of that treat Devon. It will be delicious," he purred. "Maybe I'll even keep her for myself, she is a beauty."

Rage tore through Devon, shredding the thin control he had managed to keep. The very thought of anyone touching Cassie, of turning her, of taking her for themselves was enough to bring the bloodlust surging forth. With a roar of fury, the beast burst free of him, clamoring for death and destruction.

He sprang forth as Julian tossed Marcy aside, his eyes lighting with red fire as he braced for Devon's attack. They collided brutally, slamming into each other with the force of two Mac trucks. The sound of their attack rumbled through the forest, their snarls echoed through the air. Devon swung hard into him, slamming his fist into the underside of Julian's jaw, and snapping his head forcefully back. Julian spit and hissed; his face twisted in pure fury as he swung out wildly, his claws raking deep across Devon's chest. He didn't feel the pain as Julian flayed his shirt and skin open, spilling his blood. Seizing hold of Julian's shoulders, Devon picked him easily off the ground. Spinning around, he used his full strength to heave him into the air.

Julian flew backward, his face mutated and furious as he sailed across the clearing. Slamming into the top of an ancient oak, the force of his impact shattered the top of it. Julian fell over the back of the tree, momentarily disappearing into the darkness of the woods. Satisfaction spurted through Devon as he braced himself, waiting for Julian to renew his attack.

His satisfaction was quickly doused with horror, and shock, as his eyes landed upon Cassie. She was standing at the edge of the clearing, her hands fisted at her sides, her shoulders thrust proudly back. Her hair cascaded around her, a golden ray of light against the dark night. She looked beautiful and furious as her startling eyes smoldered with barely contained rage.

He blinked in surprise, unable to fully believe that she was here. Confusion tore through him as he met her fierce gaze. What was she doing here? And why she was standing there glaring at him instead of running away screaming in terror?

He knew what he looked like now, knew that he was ugly and twisted into something she would barely recognize. At the sight of the monster inside him she should have been fleeing in horror, running for her life. Bolting like any sane person would do. Instead, a small tremor was wracking through her; however it was not a tremor of fear, but one of pure anger.

His gaze darted to her fisted hands, widening as he took note of the stake clenched tight in her right hand. He stood for a moment, trying to deny what was before him, trying not to recognize the truth that was slapping him in the face. But it was impossible. Understanding and shock tore through him, rocking him with the awful realization of what Julian had meant about her, and what had drawn Julian here. What had more than likely drawn *him* here, though he had been to blinded by his feelings for her to realize the truth.

Now everything made sense. Now he knew why he had so many questions about her, and her friends. Why they had seemed so odd and different to him. He knew exactly who and what she was now.

His enemy.

***

Cassie ducked, covering her head as shards of bark and branches rained down upon her. It seemed like forever, but was probably only moments before the debris stopped falling about her. She uncurled slowly, rising swiftly to her full height. Pain and hurt twisted through her, anger blazed hotly forth as her gaze found Devon across the clearing. His teeth were extended, so long and sharp that they cut into his full bottom lip. The same lip that had kissed her so gently and reverently now had blood seeping from it. The magnificent face she had come to love so dearly was now twisted into that of a monster, and a murderer. Twisted into the face of the one thing she hated most, and had been born to destroy.

Though she had already expected this betrayal, had already known what she would find here, to see it so closely was a knife to the chest that pierced her heart, tearing it wide, and bleeding her dry. The red in his eyes vanished, shock filled them as they widened upon her, the beautiful green of them blazing to fierce life once more. She saw the confusion in his gaze, but also the realization, the dawning knowledge of what she had come here to do.

"Cassie."

He breathed her name; the wonder in it briefly disarmed her. He sounded so surprised; he *looked* so surprised. But if he had known who she was all along, and had been toying with them, then shouldn't he be expecting her to show up to stop him eventually? Wouldn't he already know exactly what she was, and why she was here? But he seemed completely baffled and astounded to see her in the clearing with him right now. Confusion filled her, for a moment she was disarmed by the wonder in his eyes.

Then her gaze flickered to the body just feet away from him. Marcy lay curled on her side, her coffee hair gleaming in the moonlight. Fury tore through her again as her eyes flew wildly back to his. "You bastard!" she spat. "You murdering bastard!"

She took a step toward him, determined to ignore the guilt and agony slithering through her like a poisonous snake. It was a snake that would only make her slower, only hinder her movements if she acknowledged it for too long. His gaze darted briefly, uncaringly, to Marcy. The negligent look only served to infuriate her more.

"I can explain this. Look out!" he shouted at her.

The terror in his voice rattled and unsettled her; she didn't understand why it was there. She caught a brief glimpse of Devon lurching forward as she swung toward where he was looking. Her eyes widened in surprise and horror as someone, no some*thing*, moved swiftly from behind the ruined tree. She had been so hurt and infuriated with Devon, that she had not taken the time to think about what had caused the shattering of the giant oak. It was now coming at her like a bat out of hell. She had only a brief glimpse of ice cold eyes and white blond hair before it was upon her.

"Delectable."

The word was hissed softly at her, the pleasure and malevolence behind it caused nausea to twist in her stomach. She was enveloped by evil. The same evil she had felt before at the beach, and then again at B's and S's, and the cemetery. The same evil that had been stalking them, toying with them, and hunting their community. With an awful, crushing sensation descending upon her, she realized only too late that she had been completely wrong. Devon may be a vampire, but this was the *real* monster.

This was the creature that wanted nothing more than to destroy her and her loved ones.

Instinct surged forth, all of her training blazed to life as his face twisted into a vicious snarl. His teeth tore into his bottom lip as they sharpened to deadly, eager points. He would kill her, if he got his hands on her, he would kill her. She was no match for this thing. Not by herself, and not being caught off guard.

She turned at the last second, ducking as he lashed out at her, trying to grasp her. A sharp cry escaped as his fingers snagged hold of her hair, tangling tight as he pulled her backward. Cassie flung herself at him, swinging her head forcefully back. A spurt of satisfaction surged through her as she heard the rewarding crunch of his nose beneath the force of her skull.

Stars blazed momentarily before her eyes, the sharp pain in her head blurred her vision, but his grip loosened. Throwing herself forward, she tore free of his grasp, not caring that she lost a handful of hair in the process. Relief filled her as she fell away from him, tumbling toward the ground in what felt like slow motion. She had a brief glimpse of Devon, charging across the clearing, the look of fury on his face caused her blood to run cold. She could see every detail of the ground; tell almost every color of the leaves beneath her. Her heart pounded, adrenaline pumped through her in mighty, heaving bursts.

It seemed as if she was falling forever, tumbling into an abyss that didn't seem to have a bottom. She was just inches from the ground, inches from safety, when she felt it.

Horror boiled through her, shock caused her heart to skip a beat. Her entire body stiffened against the pain that exploded through her. The monster had grabbed for her again; he had tried to seize her once more. But this time he missed her hair, as his fingers had swung further down. His nails tore into her, opening her flesh, spilling her blood as they sliced deep into her neck.

She hit the ground, landing painfully upon her hip as she rolled away. Disbelief and terror filled her as she fumbled numbly at the vicious wound in her throat. Blood pooled over her fingers, it coursed swiftly down her arm to fall soundlessly upon the ground. Devon stopped in his charge at the monster, his eyes widened as he skidded to a halt near her. Astonishment filled his eyes as they met hers. He gazed at her for a long moment, dismay and fear blazing from him.

And then, to her complete horror, the beautiful emerald of his eyes became a violent shade of red as hunger blazed to fierce life within their bright depths.

CHAPTER 22

Devon froze, terror filling him as Cassie fell to the ground in a tumbled heap. Her hand shot up in a vain attempt to staunch the flow of blood that poured freely from the horrendous wound in her neck. It was a mortal wound, he knew that at once. If she didn't get help, she would die.

Then, the scent of her blood hit him, slamming into him with the force of a sledgehammer. It knocked his reason from him, shoving aside all worry and panic over her safety as hunger and bloodlust burst through him. The scent of her blood in the open air was the most enticing thing he had ever come across. He could almost taste the power oozing from her as blood spilled uselessly, and wastefully, onto the forest floor. It was a temptation and treasure unlike any he had ever come across.

And there was so very much power in her; it permeated the air as it ran in tantalizing rivulets across her creamy skin.

Saliva rushed into his mouth, his teeth grew heavier and sharper as the driving urge to bite deep, draining her of all of that wonderful blood, seized hold of him. He took a step toward her, the bloodlust becoming a pounding frenzy inside of him. He knew exactly what she was now, knew the pleasure that her blood would give him, knew the *strength* that she would give to him. He had not drunk from a human in so very long, and she was more than human.

She was so wonderfully much more than human. There was nothing more delicious and powerful tasting than a Hunter.

He did not pause to think about the fact that the Hunter line was supposed to be extinct. Nor did he pause to wonder how he had not picked up on what she was before. All he could think about was savoring every last drop as he drained her dry. All he wanted was to ease the firestorm of thirst that burned through his veins leaving them pain filled, arid, and throbbing.

Her eyes widened in terror as he took another step toward her, his body thrummed in eager anticipation of the kill, and the fulfillment she would give to his long denied body. He could feel the weakening of her body overtaking her; feel the life force draining from her. There was no way that he could allow such a waste of power to occur.

"Devon," she whispered, anguish and a sad acceptance filled her gaze. She closed her eyes, her hand pressed tighter to the gash as she desperately tried to stop the mortality pouring from her open vein.

"Scrumptious," Julian whispered.

Devon turned as Julian came forward. He rushed past Devon, the frenzying scent of her blood taking control of him. Reality slammed back over Devon, crashing down with fierce brutality. This was Cassie, *his* Cassie. He had sworn to protect her from this evil, sworn to keep her safe no matter what the cost, and here he was about to rip her precious life away from her.

Bursting back into motion, he grasped hold of Julian's shirt, ripping him backward. Julian bellowed with fury as he was flung across the clearing. The thick canopy of a tree shook as Julian bounced off of it. Julian rebounded quickly as he launched back to his feet, a fierce snarl escaped him.

Rage blasted from Julian in thick waves. He tore back across the clearing, heedless of the fact that he would have to get through Devon to get to her. Julian slammed into him, throwing them both back ten feet. The small pine they hit snapped in half, the jagged piece of it scraped down Devon's back and ripped into his skin.

Julian beat and tore at him, frenzied to get at her. Devon seized hold of his throat, holding Julian away from him as he squeezed tight. Julian was lost to the throes of bloodlust, animalistic, wild and savage. His eyes were as red as laser beams, his face twisted into a murderous snarl. It was a state that a seasoned vampire rarely let take them over, as it meant giving up all control. And loss of control could be dangerous. When control was lost, a vampire could do anything, and often that was when the human population became aware of the demons lurking amongst them.

A vampire could be lost to the bloodlust for good, if they were not strong enough to pull out of it. At one point a vampire that was lost would have been destroyed by The Elder's, but now except for Devon and Julian, The Elder's had little to do with the rest of the world, and remained locked away. But the powerful scent of Cassie's blood had been too much for Julian to handle. Hell, it had almost been too much for *him* to handle.

They scrambled upon the ground, pummeling each other as Julian tried to get back to Cassie, and Devon fought to keep him far away. Julian was crazed with his hunger, frantic, and deadly because of it. But Devon was determined to keep her safe, determined that she would survive this night. He would not lose her, if he did, he would not be able to endure it. With every cell in his body he knew that he would not survive her death, just as he knew that he would destroy everything, and every*one* that ever tried to hurt her.

Julian drew his legs up under him, somehow getting them between their bodies. Using all of his vast strength, he shoved Devon forcefully off. Devon was thrown into the center of the clearing. Pain jarred through his body as he bounced across the hard ground. Cassie's frightened cry echoed loudly in his over sensitized ears.

Ignoring every ache and pain, he launched himself back to his feet as Julian reached her. Cassie swung at him, but Devon could sense the weakness in her body, the life and strength draining swiftly from her. Terror and rage tore through him as Julian seized hold of her arm, ripping her toward him, a loud hiss of desire escaping him.

Devon sprang forward, seizing hold of Julian, and ripping
him away from her seconds before his teeth sank into her
delicate neck. Turning in midair, he twisted their bodies
away from her, trying to keep her safe from the impact of
their weight. They fell to the ground, bouncing across its
surface mere inches from her. Julian seized hold of
Devon's neck, his hand wrapped tight around it. Using the
palm of his hand, Devon slammed it into the bottom of
Julian's already broken nose. Fresh blood spilled forth
causing Julian to howl in pain as he fell back.

Devon leapt to his feet, grabbing Julian by the shirt.
Lifting him like a rag doll, he shook him fiercely. "Stay
away from her!" he snarled viciously.

Julian's fist connected with his cheek, staggering him
back a few feet with the force of the blow. Bellowing with
fury, determined to destroy the monster he had helped to
create, Devon slammed his fist into Julian's cheek. The
sickening crunch of his cheekbone echoed loudly in the
clearing. Julian's half collapsed face twisted with fury and
pain, his eyes burned with red fire.

He lashed out, panic and agony making him reckless and
dangerous. His claws connected with Devon's chin, the
force of the blow staggered him slightly as blood spilled
free. Grabbing hold of Julian, he picked him up and heaved
him across the clearing once more. The large maple Julian
collided with shook from the force of the blow, a large
crack lanced up its thick trunk.

Julian landed head first on the ground, his legs above his
head against the tree. He lay for a moment before falling
away from the trunk. Staggering to his feet, he shook his
head in disorientation. Shifting his stance, Devon kept his
body protectively in front of Cassie as he waited for
another charge. Julian took a step forward; his gaze darted
briefly to Cassie, hunger and longing burned within the
ruby red depths of his eyes. Then his gaze came back to
Devon, anger, fear, and disgust flashed briefly across his

distorted, beaten features. Though Julian still wanted her, the beating he had received seemed to have shaken him free of the bloodlust. He was back in control of his actions and thoughts.

Weighing the odds, Julian stood for a moment, his gaze darting between them. This fight would go to the death, and Julian would not win. They both knew that. Julian wanted Cassie fiercely, but he wanted to live even more. Julian had always been number one in his own book, always highest on himself. His own life and his love of himself were his two biggest motivators. Devon was relieved to realize that things had not changed. Though Devon was winning this fight, if it continued Cassie would probably bleed to death before Julian's life was forfeit.

"Till next time."

Julian turned and fled into the woods, becoming a blurring shimmer that disappeared swiftly within the trees. Not trusting Julian to stay away, Devon kept all of his senses honed for his presence as he turned back to Cassie. Julian was wounded and overpowered, but he was also reckless and hungry.

Taking a deep breath, Devon braced himself to get close to her again. He braced himself to withstand the enticing lure of her deliciously scented blood, and the power that it possessed. He tried hard to keep control of the fierce, hungry monster inside of him as he approached her slowly. She was scared enough, and confused enough, without seeing him turn back into the demon that he was.

She stared up at him, her eyes wide with horror, hurt, and terror. He continued to move slowly toward her, but to his surprise she did not shrink from him. She did not try to scream, did not even try to scramble away, as he was fairly certain she would be too weak to run. She simply stared up at him with a sad acceptance in her mesmerizing eyes.

Blood stuck to her fingers, coated her arm, and clung to her shirt and jeans. A puddle had formed beneath her; the beat of her heart had slowed dangerously. Fear tore through Devon. Forgetting his need to go slow, he hurried to her side as he dropped beside her. He was surprised to realize that his concern for her life momentarily outweighed his desire for her blood. He did not know how long that would last, but for now all that mattered was her, and her safety.

Gently, he eased her slender body into his arms. She moaned softly, her head dropped limply against his chest as he lifted her swiftly. She felt as light as a feather in his arms, and just as weak.

The fragileness of her life hit him hard as he cradled her, holding her tight against him. He had forgotten how weak and frightening it was to be human, how vulnerable and tenuous. Even if she wasn't entirely human, she still had to face the reality of death. And her life consisted of even more death than most humans, and it was far shorter. It was a fact that he did not want to acknowledge, or recognize, in Cassie.

Though the bloodlust had been crushed beneath his fear, he felt a different kind of urge overtaking him now. This urge was new, and something that he had never experienced before. He was suddenly swamped with the desire to keep her safe from her own mortality, to keep her safe from the fragility of her life. He was consumed with the need to change her, to make her as immortal as he was. To keep her protected from her life and the certain death that accompanied it.

Though he had changed people before, he had never been consumed with the fierce *need* to do so. Never felt the fierce craving to make sure that she never had to face her own mortality again. He closed his eyes, shaking with his urge to change her, shaking with the desire to keep her forever safe, and with him. He could take her away from here, keep her safe, sheltered, and loved. She would never have to worry about fighting again; never have to worry about the brutality of her life. And he knew that her life was brutal. He had known some Hunter's during his long lifetime, seen what they had gone through, and had even killed a few of them. He did not want her to have to experience that. She deserved far better than what her lot in life had handed her.

"Devon." He shook his head, trying to clear himself of his urges as he met her tired gaze. There was a sad acceptance about her; the knowledge of death within her stare rattled him completely. The normal light in her eyes was dimmer; the spark of life that radiated from her was already beginning to flicker. "I'm sorry," she whispered. "I… I…"

"Shh baby, it'll be ok." Her wide eyes met his; tears filled the bright depths of them. "Don't leave me Cassie, just hold on. Don't you leave me," he whispered fervently.

Tears slid down her face. Resting his hand over top of hers, he pushed hard against the wound, hoping to help stem the life pouring from her. There was one way that he knew he could completely stop the bleeding. He was just afraid that it would take more self control than he possessed at the moment.

Her heart fluttered slightly. It was a flutter he knew well, he had caused it in many heartbeats moments before he had taken someone's life from them. It was the sound of that flutter that drove him into action. Bending over her, he pressed her close to him, nuzzling her gently as he inhaled her wonderfully delicious scent. She did not stiffen against him, did not try to push him away. She did not even remotely flinch away as she turned slightly toward him, her warm breath caressing his cheek.

He wished that he could believe it was because she wanted him to change her, but he knew that she simply did not possess the strength to turn away from him, or fight against him. She would not want to be a part of his world, would not want to belong to the darkness, and he was crazy for even thinking about condemning her to such a life. She deserved far better than anything he had to offer her.

Bracing himself, he pulled her hand gently away from the large wound. Blood pulsed out of the jagged cuts with every beat of her heart. His chest clenched at the sight of that blood, his teeth elongated instantly as hunger swamped him. It took him a few seconds to gather himself enough not to sink deep into her throat and taste the delicious blood pouring from her.

When he was in control enough, he bent his mouth to her neck. The sweet scent of her assailed him as he nuzzled her briefly, savoring in the feel of her. Her heartbeat picked up slightly, but he sensed no fear in her, only an excitement that confused him as well as aroused his hunger and desire even higher. Fighting against every one of his murderous instincts, he slowly licked the three vicious gashes in her delicate neck, sealing them with the healing agent in his saliva.

The taste of her blood slammed into him. It was the sweetest nectar he had ever savored, so full of strength and vigor. It pounded through him, hammering throughout his veins. His teeth throbbed with their desire to be sated, he was desperate for the ultimate pleasure her blood would bring him. Never had he tasted anything so sweet, so tempting and delicious. Never had he experienced so much power within one person. He had never even imagined one person could possess so much lure. He had tasted his fair share of Hunters before, but their blood had been nothing compared to this. Their blood had been as powerful as a goldfish's compared to this. Her blood was ambrosia and he wanted more than just a little taste.

Then, her hand stroked over his face, the touch as light as a butterflies caress. It helped to soothe the shaking, thirsty beast trapped inside of him. She helped to keep him from draining her dry in order to satisfy the raging monster inside. Using every ounce of self restraint and control he had, he pulled slightly back; his eyes clashed with her tear filled, curious ones. She smoothed her hand over his cheek, cradling him gently in her grasp. Devon could not move; he was pinned within her gaze, guilt and horror tearing through him.

She was comforting him, and he was thinking about draining every last drop of life from her. She was comforting *him*, and he was on the verge of destroying her. Struggling to regain control, he unfolded himself from above her. Though the wounds were sealed, she was still a long way from safe. A fair amount of her precious life had been spilled. He needed to get her somewhere that would help her.

"Hold on Cassie," he pleaded fervently. "Don't leave me."

Tears slid slowly down her cheeks, leaving a trail in the dirt and blood that marred her delicate features. He wanted to brush them away, wanted to kiss away her pain, but he was afraid to get to close to her again. He didn't know how much torture and temptation he could take before snapping.

And if he snapped, he would keep her as his. A fate he was certain that Cassie wanted no part of.

He quaked with the reserve it took not to finish it, not to turn her. He would not do it; he could not take her youth, her innocence, and her *life* from her. She deserved far better than that. Far better than him.

Devon drew on every ounce of self restraint he had. Slowly, he was able to regain enough control to think straight once more. If he did not get her help, *human* help soon, she was going to die.

A branch snapped loudly. Devon spun, curling her protectively against him. He shouldn't have let down his guard, should not have let his attention wander from Julian, but she had that affect upon him. He lost all his reason, all sanity, and all thought when she was around.

Now, Julian was back. Devon should have known that Julian would not quit, not when he had smelled her blood also, not when he had been in the throes of bloodlust. Devon used all of his powers and senses to hunt him down, but he could not find him within the woods. He did however pick up on three new minds within the forest.

He tensed in preparation as Chris, Melissa, and Luther burst out of the woods, skidding to a halt on the other side of the clearing. Their eyes widened in horror, their mouths parted slightly as they took in the limp, bloody form of Cassie in his arms. He knew what the three of them were, but he had no fear for his own safety around them. They were nothing compared to him, no threat to his survival.

"Cassie!" Melissa cried, rushing toward them.

Luther moved swiftly, grabbing hold of her arm he ripped her back as Devon cradled Cassie tighter, an involuntary snarl tearing from him. He did not know what had possessed him, he knew that they would not hurt her, but the idea of them even touching her made him want to rip their throats out. It made him want to destroy them all.

"No!" Melissa's hand flew to her mouth in shock; horror filled her black eyes as she took in Devon's twisted features, and deadly teeth.

Devon turned away from the pain, disgust, and condemnation burning from all of their gazes. He did not know them well, but he had grown to like them over the past few weeks, and he hated the revulsion in their eyes. Holding Cassie protectively against him, he turned away from their disgust, disappearing into the woods in a blur of motion. Feeling wildly unstable again, he plummeted through the forest, uncertain of where he was going. He just knew that he needed to get away from them, and he needed to get her out of there. He needed to get her somewhere safe.

Moving faster than he had ever moved in his long existence, Devon plummeted through the woods; keeping

Cassie shielded from the branches and twigs that slapped at him. He knew that fear for her life was a big motivator for his faster than average speed, but it was also more than that.

The few drops of her blood he had tasted had already begun to change him. They had already made him stronger, far more powerful and faster. He didn't know how it was possible that she possessed so much power, and he had not picked up on it. He did not know *how* she could even possess so much power. The amount of it was far from normal, even for a Hunter.

He did not know the answers to any of the questions swirling through him, and he didn't really care. The only thing he cared about right now was saving her life. The only thing he cared about was keeping her with him for as long as possible.

He could only hope that she did not hate him for what he was. He could not stop to think about that. If he did, he would lose it. Devon sped through the woods, uncertain of where he was going, or what he was going to do with her. All he could hope was that she survived until he could get her help. Cassie curled tighter against him, her head rested trustingly against the hollow curve of his neck. He did not understand her trust in him, not after everything she had discovered tonight, but it was a trust that he was going to try and live up to. He could only hope that he did not snap and change her before he finally reached his destination.